# TAMAR MYERS

# STATUE OF LIMITATIONS

**A DEN OF ANTIQUITY MYSTERY**

## AVON BOOKS

*An Imprint of* HarperCollins*Publishers*

This is a work of fiction. Names, characters, places, and incidents are products of the author's imagination or are used fictitiously and are not to be construed as real. Any resemblance to actual events, locales, organizations, or persons, living or dead, is entirely coincidental.

AVON BOOKS
*An Imprint of* HarperCollins*Publishers*
10 East 53rd Street
New York, New York 10022-5299

Copyright © 2004 by Tamar Myers
ISBN: 0-06-053514-8
www.avonmystery.com

First Avon Books paperback printing: June 2004

Avon Trademark Reg. U.S. Pat. Off. and in Other Countries, Marca Registrada, Hecho en U.S.A.
HarperCollins® is a registered trademark of HarperCollins Publishers Inc.

Printed in the U.S.A.

10  9  8  7  6  5  4  3  2  1

For the Charleston Authors Society,
particularly my dear friends
Mary Alice Monroe and Nina Bruhns.

# STATUE OF LIMITATIONS

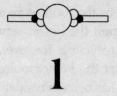

# 1

It is no secret that I am an S.O.B. I love living South of Broad, in the historic district of Charleston, South Carolina. Mine is one of the most coveted addresses in the nation, and it is rumored that God Himself lives here—although I have yet to run into Him on my daily walks. I have, however, met several people who think they fit the bill.

My best friend, Wynnell Crawford, is not as lucky. She's merely a W.O.T.A.—West of the Ashley. The Ashley, of course, is one of Charleston's two principal rivers. The other important river is the Cooper. They meet at Charleston's famous Battery, where together they form the Atlantic Ocean. Please don't misunderstand me. There is nothing wrong with living west of the Ashley, but unless one lives on an honest-to-goodness plantation, being a W.O.T.A. is just not as good as being an S.O.B.

But in Charleston even geography takes second place to genetics. The really old families have bloodlines as tangled as the roots of an azalea in need of repotting. Through the bluest veins courses blood that has been recycling for over three hundred years. The redder the hemoglobin, the shorter the time the family has been in residence.

A growing number of folks are so inconsiderate that they weren't even born in Charleston County. These unfortunates occupy the bottom rung of the social ladder and are referred to as being "from off." The term has variously been interpreted to meaning "from off the peninsula" or "from off someplace far away." It doesn't really matter. If one is "from off," there is simply no getting on.

Although one can always hope. Does not hope spring eternal? Even in the smallest of breasts? And anyway, I had just come from lunch at Chopsticks Chinese restaurant on King Street, where I'd received a wonderful fortune in my cookie: "Big things are coming your way." I immediately thought of my husband, Greg, but when the phone rang at my shop a half hour later, minutes before closing time, and I heard the dulcet tones of one of the city's homegrown S.O.B.'s, my tiny heart began to pound.

"Yes, this is Abigail Timberlake," I said.

"Mrs. Timberlake, I was in your antique store the other day, and I must say, I really admire your taste."

"Thank you." I was so grateful for the compliment, I didn't even consider correcting her. *Ms.* Timberlake is my business name. My married name is *Mrs.* Washburn.

"And how clever of you to call it the Den of Antiquity. However did you think that one up?" She didn't wait for an answer. "Mrs. Timberlake, I was wondering if you did more than just sell your antiques."

Again I thought of Greg. "Uh—well, what did you have in mind?"

"Fisher and I have a little project we're working on. A bed and breakfast is what I'd guess you'd call it. Anyway, I was wondering if you'd been interested in decorating for us."

Would I? Would Bill Clinton like an invitation to a sorority sleepover? I tried to play it cool.

"Where is this bed and breakfast, Miss, uh—"

"Webbfingers. I'm Marina, and Fisher is my husband."

"I'm sorry, Marina, but I'm not sure where Webbfingers is."

I heard the soft, muffled laugh of gentility. "Darling, Webbfingers is our name, not our address. We live at double 0 Legare."

Of course she pronounced the street Legare to rhyme with "Brie." Only rubes, or recently arrived yokels "from off," pronounce the word as it is spelled. But double 0? Oh, why not! This is

Charleston, after all, where many addresses begin with 0, and sometimes it seems as if there are more half than whole numbers.

"Double 0 Legare," I said, and jotted the address down on a notepad on my desk. As if I would forget. I could barely control my excitement. It was all I could do to keep from hanging up, calling the *Post and Courier*, and taking out a full page ad saying that I, little old Abigail from the Upstate, was now officially a decorator to one of Charleston's finest.

"If it's convenient for you," she purred, "I thought you might stop by this evening, and I'll show you around. Let you get a feel for the place."

"What time?"

"Say seven. Fisher and I have theater tickets, but we don't need to leave until almost eight."

"I'll be there with bells on," I said, and then immediately regretted both my excessive enthusiasm and my choice of words. A strap of sleigh bells hangs from a nail on the back of the door, and the bells had begun to jingle as if Santa himself was driving the sleigh.

"My, you are a clever woman," Marina said, but this time she didn't mean it as a compliment.

"A customer just walked in," I said. "The door does that."

"Yes, of course. See you this evening, then." She

hung up first, a not so subtle reminder that she was a real S.O.B. and I merely a Johnny-come-lately.

I glared at the woman who'd just walked in the door. She wasn't a customer, but my buddy, Wynnell. What are best friends for, if not to occasionally serve as whipping boys? And anyway, the woman has only one eyebrow, a tangled hedge of black and gray. I point that out to illustrate that not only is she oblivious to expressions, she's oblivious to faces. My glare meant nothing to her.

"Abby, why aren't you closed?"

"But it's just now five-thirty."

"Abby, it's girls' night out, remember? You and I and C.J. are going out for dinner and then a movie over in Mount Pleasant, remember?"

I sighed. "Yes, I remember."

"But C.J. can't go. She forgot that she has a shag lesson tonight."

"So then maybe we should reschedule." I wasn't wild about this girls' night out anyway. Greg is a studmuffin, and if it wasn't for the fact that my mama lives with us, I'd be happy to do the nesting thing practically every night—or at least until high society came calling.

"We can't reschedule, Abby. I got Ed's dinner ready for him this morning. All he has to do is zap it in the microwave." Wynnell's plaintive tone reminded me that she had moved here even more recently than I and had yet to make friends. Her marriage to Ed, while a long one, was as rocky as a shrimp boat during a tropical depression. In other words, she was dying to get out of the house.

"Okay, dinner and a movie. But I need to run an errand before the movie."

The hedgerow shot up. "What kind of errand?"

I was torn between blurting out my good news and treading carefully. Wynnell has her own antique shop, Wooden Wonders, but she can't afford lower King Street. Her business, like her residence, is West of the Ashley. It seems that she regards everything I have, as well as everything I do, with a mixture of envy and admiration.

"This woman and her husband are creating a bed and breakfast. They want me to decorate. I'm supposed to stop by and look the place over at seven."

The admiring side of her nodded. "Well, there's no question you have good taste. What's the woman's name?"

"Marina Webbfingers."

Wynnell's mouth hung open while her brain switched over to its envious side. "*The* Marina Webbfingers?"

It was my turn to exercise a jaw. "Do you know her?"

"Of course not personally. But her picture was

in the paper last weekend—on the society page. Didn't you see it?"

"No." I have given up looking at the society page. Greg and I attended a number of charity functions, even given freely, but never found our grinning mugs on that page. There is no use in torturing myself.

"Abby, she's in there practically every week."

"That's nice. So, I take it you don't object to popping by her house on our way to the movies?"

"Are you kidding? Abby, I don't suppose you'd let me—uh, you know."

"Choose the movie? By all means. Go for it."

"No, Abby. What I mean is that business is a little slow at Wooden Wonders. Nobody seems to know that I'm there. I was wondering if—well, if you'll let me help you decorate this woman's bed and breakfast . . ." Her voice trailed while her eyes pleaded. She took a deep breath. "Abby, this could make all the difference. To my business, to me, and to Ed."

"To Ed?"

"Abby, you know my husband didn't want to move down here. Too hot, he's says. Too many mosquitoes. Up in North Carolina he could afford to be retired. What I brought in was just gravy. Now he has to go back to work."

"How's the job search coming?"

"Well, of course he can't find work in a textile mill down here. He's got applications in at Lowe's and Wal-Mart—but even if he gets a job, it won't be what he's used to."

"I'm sorry." I wasn't apologizing, merely expressing sympathy. It was Wynnell's idea to follow me to Charleston, not mine. At the time, I'd tried to warn her that starting all over at her age was not just a walk in the park. Of course she didn't listen. I probably wouldn't have, either, if all my friends had pulled up stakes and moved to where, at least according to DeBose Heyward, "the living is easy."

"Abby, it's not all your fault," Wynnell said generously. "But if you really want to help, give me this chance. I'll do whatever you say. I just want to be your assistant on this project. Please, Abby. Pretty please with sugar on top?"

It was embarrassing to hear a strong woman like Wynnell beg. Besides, there was bound to be some task I could assign to her that wasn't crucial to the overall success of this project. But I had to be careful. The woman has atrocious taste in furniture, and knows nothing about color coordination, which helps to explain her lack of success—even West of the Ashley. Maybe she could act as my gofer, or I could set her to work stripping wallpaper. She would share in my earnings, to be sure. Possibly even some of my forthcoming fame.

"All right, you can help me this once, but if—"

"Oh, Abby, you won't regret it!" She flung herself into my arms. Given that she is five-foot-eight and I am four-foot-nine, and she weighs at least sixty pounds more, I felt like a very small gazelle being hugged by a lioness.

I gasped for air. "I mean it, Wynnell. You have to follow my instructions to the letter. And they may not be jobs that you like. Is that clear?"

"Baccarat crystal clear," Wynnell said, and took the liberty of laughing at her little joke.

My best buddy is not known for her sense of humor, so I took advantage of the rare opportunity and laughed with her. Meanwhile my inner voice was shouting an alarm. Nothing good was going to come of this partnership. If I was a true friend, I'd renege on our agreement.

Sometimes, however, it is easier to be kind than to be wise.

# 2

I'd driven by double 0 Legare hundreds of times, always admiring its architecture, but never dreaming that someday I would be privy to the secrets that lay behind its wrought-iron gates. The mansion is a superb example of the Greek Revival style, with two-story columns topped by Corinthian capitals. In Charleston, porches are called piazzas, and this magnificent structure had ground and second floor piazzas across the front. In the side garden, which was to the left, a fountain splashed in the center of a box-wood parterre. A main path led past a massive Canary Island date palm to a second, more informal garden—well, to be honest, it was more of a jungle of overgrown azaleas. Peeking above them were several brick structures clad in creeping fig vines. I guessed these outbuildings to be a carriage house and servants' quarters.

Wynnell and I were five minutes early, and so as not to be too obvious, we parked along the seawall on Murray Avenue and strolled along South Battery Street. It was obvious, at least to us, that we were not tourists. We both wore dresses, unlike most of the milling throng. Tight shorts and either T-shirts or tank tops seemed to be the preferred uniform. I do believe that one can view more wedgies per capita in the historical district of Charleston than anywhere else in the country.

"Yankees," Wynnell hissed.

"You don't know that," I said. My friend is not a racist, and harbors no prejudice against gays, but anyone from north of the Mason-Dixon line gets her knickers in a knot. Never mind that—and I know this for a fact—she has a Yankee in her woodpile.

"Abby, look at that woman. She's spilling out of her clothes in every direction. A Southerner would never disgrace herself like that."

"Want to bet?"

"I'll bet tonight's movie. I'll even buy the snacks."

"You're on." As short as I am, I had to run to catch up with the woman, who was walking rapidly the other way. "Excuse me," I called after her.

She stopped and turned. "Ma'am?"

"Do you know how to get to the Gibbes Museum?"

"No ma'am, I'm sorry. I'm just a tourist myself."

"Oh, I'm not a tourist. I live here. I'm only—"

"Directionally challenged," Wynnell said. She had had no trouble keeping up.

I smiled at the stranger. "If you don't mind me asking, where are you from?"

"Nawlins."

"Nawlins, Louisiana?" I presumed she meant New Orleans.

She smiled back at me. "Is there another?"

"Not in my book, at any rate. So what do you think of Charleston?"

"It's so interesting. I had no idea."

Now that I had established that she was indeed a Southerner, I had to decide if it was worth it to me to decipher what she'd said. We Southerners— especially we women—have been brought up to always be polite, even if that requires telling a white lie or two. By saying that she found my adopted city "interesting" and that she had "no idea," the lady from Louisiana could have been saying one of a dozen things. Perhaps she found it interesting that sections of King Street smell like garbage on Sunday mornings, and that she had no idea there would be a dearth of public rest rooms along the Battery. On the other hand, she could have meant that it was interesting that a local person would not know her way around, and that she had no idea that Charleston was the most beautiful—not to mention the friendliest—city in the nation. In the end I decided it wasn't worth it. Not if we were going to get to Marina Webbfingers's house on time.

But I couldn't resist rubbing it in to Wynnell when we were alone. "I told you."

My friend frowned, the hedgerow all but obscuring her eyes. "She could be a Yankee spy."

"A what?"

"You heard me, Abby. I read that there is a special training school—up in Michigan, someplace—where they teach Yankees how to speak correctly. Make them insert the proper number of vowels, soften the R's, that kind of thing. If we should ever decide to secede again—"

"Which we won't!"

"But if it should happen, they'd have their people in place."

"Then what about her clothes? Wouldn't she have been trained to dress properly?"

"Maybe that was just to throw us off track."

Perhaps it was Charleston's heat and humidity that had gotten to her. At any rate, I was beginning to think Wynnell's trolley had leaped its tracks. Thank heavens Marina Webbfingers was not a Yankee, or the Late Unpleasantness might indeed have begun all over again. And only yards from its original birthplace.

* * *

Marina may not have hailed from up the road a piece, but her behavior was definitely atypical. We were only fashionably late, yet there she was on her lower-level piazza, waiting for us. She even waved when she saw us, and practically ran down the steps to open the metal gate.

"Mrs. Timberlake, how nice of you to come."

"Well, actually my name is—"

Wynnell thrust out her hand. "I'm her assistant, Mrs. Crawford."

Marina smiled. "How nice. I'm sure the work will progress a lot faster with two of you."

I gazed up at the towering house. "How many rooms will we be decorating?"

"Oh my, I hope I didn't give you the wrong impression. The bed and breakfast will not be part of the main house." She pointed to the outbuildings. "Two above the carriage house, and three in what used to be the servants' quarters. We made a nice little apartment on the third floor for Harriet— that's our maid."

The third floor was the attic, for crying out loud. What kind of people would stuff a maid under the eaves when a perfectly good quarters already existed? People who were strapped for cash and didn't want strangers invading their home, that's who. I'd seen it happen before. The best bed and breakfasts in Charleston can charge as much as three hundred dollars per night, and the demand is constant. Even if the Webbfingerses averaged only three guest rentals on a daily basis and charged just two hundred dollars a night, their gross income for the year would be over two hundred thousand clams—which is not such a gross figure. Not if poor Harriet was going to do all the work.

I confess to being very disappointed as Marina led us around the side of her mansion. One of the perks of my job is the peeks I get into other people's homes. While it is true that for some folks possessions are just things, in many cases home furnishings tell fascinating tales about their owners' lives.

"Will we be using any of your pieces from the main house?" I asked hopefully.

"No," she said. Her one word answer made it clear that my question had somehow been inappropriate.

"What a lovely garden," Wynnell said, obviously trying to curry favor.

Marina shrugged. "The front garden is. Some of my husband's ancestors were French. They have a thing for formal gardens. He does all the work on the parterre himself." She waved a manicured hand. "But the back garden is going to need a lot of work. Would either of you happen to be knowledgeable about landscape design?"

"Not me," I said. "If I just look at a plant, it dies. I've even thought about hiring myself out as a weed killer."

No one even chuckled at my little joke. But Wynnell, who has farther to climb on the social ladder than I, was quick to jump at the opportunity.

"I don't have professional experience," she said, "but I had a prize-winning garden back in Charlotte. Didn't I, Abby?"

"I do recall that you won some sort of prize."

"Not just any prize, but the blue ribbon for the prettiest yard in my subdivision. There was even an article about it in the paper." What she neglected to say is that it was her neighborhood rag, and not the *Charlotte Observer*, that covered the story.

Marina may have been desperate for cheap help, because she stopped dead in her tracks. "Mrs. Crawford, isn't it?"

"Yes, ma'am. You may call me Wynnell."

"Mrs. Crawford, would you be willing to handle the garden aspect if Mrs. Timberlake does the rooms?"

Wynnell sneaked a glowering glance at me. "I could do both."

"Oh, I couldn't ask that."

"But I don't mind at all."

Perhaps because I am a very small woman, my

wicked streak is small, but it does exist. "Come to think of it," I said, "that was a first-class garden you created up in Charlotte, Wynnell. But didn't it take you awhile?"

"I took my time because it was for a contest," Wynnell said. I gathered from her tone that she would no longer be buying the snacks at the movie. In fact, we might even be attending separate features.

Like my mama, Marina had selective hearing. "Well, then we're in agreement. You'll do the garden, and Mrs. Timberlake will do the guest rooms."

Wynnell's withering look took a few precious millimeters off my already compromised height.

To say that Wynnell and I didn't speak to each other for a spell would be only partly true. Although we no longer exchanged pleasantries, there were harsh words on more than a few occasions. My best friend likened me to Attila the Hun, Judas Iscariot, and Martha Stewart all rolled into one. I chose to take the Martha part as a compliment.

I tried not to react to her vehement verbiage, but it was tough. Still, I like to think of myself as a fair-minded woman, and I couldn't help but admire the job she did on that garden. She whipped those azalea bushes into shape, installed a brick walkway all by herself, and even built a raised planting bed as a focal point. In this circle, she planted colorful annuals, which I must admit were a nice touch, especially now that azalea season was over. But I could no longer hold my tongue when she placed a really tacky statue in the middle of a bed.

It was David. You know, *the* David by Michelangelo? Of course this wasn't the original, which is over fourteen feet tall and is housed in the Accademia museum in Florence, Italy. This replica—and it wasn't a very good one—was only about three feet tall. At least it appeared to be made of marble, and not plaster or concrete, like the ones you can buy at garden centers.

"What an interesting choice," I said to Wynnell at the earliest opportunity.

"What's that supposed to mean, Abby?"

Even though I was irritated with my buddy, I couldn't very well tell her that this particular statue was the ultimate cliché. "Well, it's just that since you've done such a beautiful job on the plantings, I'd hate to see the statue detract from them."

"What you're saying is that you don't like it."

"No. I merely meant—"

"That my taste isn't as good as yours?"

"Wynnell, I didn't say that!"

"Then give me one good reason why I shouldn't use this statue."

"Feng shui."

"Come again?"

Believe me, I'm no expert on this ancient Chinese philosophy which deals with, among other things, the placement of objects in such a way that they facilitate the positive flow of energy. But it was a safe bet Wynnell knew even less than I.

"You see, Wynnell, the chi will have no problem flowing along that beautiful path you made, but when it reaches the statue—well, I'm afraid it will all puddle up."

"It's a statue, Abby, not a dam."

"It's a damn knockoff statue, Wynnell. That's probably not even real marble. Composite at best. You can buy one at any flea market in the country." That's when I sank to my lowest—so low that any chi present flowed right over me. "Is *that* where you bought it, Wynnell? At a flea market?"

Wynnell stared at me while her face underwent a plethora of changes. The look she finally settled on was one of pure disdain.

"For your information, Miss Know It All Big Shot Antiques Expert, I found this statue under one of those azalea bushes over there. It was buried under dead leaves."

*  *  *

That, I'm ashamed to say, was the last time I spoke to my buddy for well over a month. My husband Greg, Mama, my friends C.J. and the Rob-Bobs—they all tried to get Wynnell and me to kiss and make up. Neither of us would budge, even after our work for Marina Webbfingers was done. And we both stupidly boycotted the Grand Opening reception the Webbfingerses threw, an event that would have supplied the social contacts we both craved.

In retrospect, our stubbornness was a sure sign of our friendship. I had absolutely no doubt that Wynnell would remain my friend no matter what. This afforded me the luxury of waiting for her to apologize. I'm sure the feeling was reciprocal. I am told that friends and family actually began to bet on who would cave in first—my friend with the pedestrian taste, or me, the big shot know-it-all.

Unfortunately, our standoff came to an unnatural conclusion. On day forty the phone rang at the house, just as I leaving for work. I wouldn't have answered it, except for the intriguing fact that my caller ID listed the city of Charleston as the calling party. Perhaps—and I'll be the first to admit that I tend to have an active imagination—Mayor Joseph Riley wanted to invite me to some prestigious shindig. One that would finally get my picture on the society page.

"Hello?"

"Abby, this is Wynnell."

"Where are you?" So it wasn't the mayor, but a contrite friend. Well, at least she'd crumbled first.

"I'm in jail," Wynnell said, clipping her words to near Yankee brevity. "You're my one call. What do I do?"

"Jail?"

"Marina Webbfingers was murdered yesterday afternoon. They think I did it."

# 3

A few of my brain cells must have misfired, no doubt a legacy of sleeping on curlers when I was a girl. That had to be it. For a minute there I thought my best friend had said she was in jail for the murder of Marina Webbfingers.

"Wynnell, please be a doll and repeat what you said."

"I said I've been arrested for murder. Abby, I didn't do it. You and Greg have got to help me. Ed will kill me when he hears about this. Then he'll be in the slammer, and there will be no one to water my flowers—unless you water them for me. Will you do that for me, Abby? And now that you have C.J. as your assistant, would you mind terribly minding my shop? I mean, if worse comes to worst. You've already got a key, and the only thing you might need to know is that the walnut breakfront near the front door has been sold to a Mrs. Thornapple, and she's promised to pick it up on Thursday. I didn't put a sold sticker on it because—"

"Wynnell, stop it! You haven't been convicted yet." Carrying the portable phone, I staggered to the nearest chair and plopped my petite patootie on it. More accurately, because I'm a mere four-foot-nine, I had to first hoist myself onto the genuine Louis XV. "Besides, maybe Greg and I can post bail."

"The arraignment is this afternoon at three. Can you keep Ed busy until it's over?"

"Where is he now?"

"Fishing off Folly Beach pier."

"Wynnell, he's going to find out about this. The police will be asking him questions."

"Abby, he'll be furious."

"I don't think that should be your main concern, dear. Do you have an attorney?"

"You know we don't have any money, Abby. Not since our stock portfolio dwindled away to nothing."

"What about Ed's pension?"

"It's barely enough to cover the cost of living here in Charleston. Oh Abby, I know we should have stayed up in Charlotte. Sure it's pretty down here, and you've got the ocean, but I miss the hills, and all the dogwood in spring, and—"

There was no time to argue about geography. "Don't worry. The court will appoint an attorney." What was I saying? Wynnell was my dearest friend in the world—outside of my husband, of course. And if you don't count Mama. Besides, while I wasn't exactly rolling in dough, I did have more than enough to meet my needs. "Tell you what," I heard myself say, "I'm going to get you the best lawyer in Charleston."

"Really? You mean that?"

"Absolutely." If Greg objected—and I knew he wouldn't—I'd have to remind him that it was my shop that brought in most of our money, and not his shrimp boat in Mount Pleasant.

"I knew you'd come through. So you'll take care of it, then? You'll call Elias Hammerhead?"

"Who?"

"The best lawyer in Charleston. Abby, don't you watch television?"

"It's no secret that I'm addicted to *All My Children*."

"I mean the commercials. 'So you're in jail? What the hell! Call Hammerhead, White, and Sand.' "

"No, I seem to have missed that little jingle."

"Well, they're the best. Everyone says so."

"Wynnell, are you sure they don't handle just car accidents? Personal injury, that sort of thing."

"Positive. Will you call them?"

I sighed. "If that's what you really want."

"Abby, I couldn't ask for a better friend."

"Think nothing of it."

"I mean it—oh, oh, I have to go, Abby." She hung up.

I stared at the phone in my hand. If I hadn't answered the dang thing, if only I'd left for work five minutes earlier, I wouldn't have to hire one of Charleston's finest and, no doubt, most expensive lawyers. Unable to reach me with her first call, my friend would have settled for a court appointed attorney. And since she wasn't guilty, a public defender would do just fine with the case.

Shame on me for thinking that. I'd made the offer, and I'd given my word. It was as simple as that.

Finding the offices of Hammerhead, White, and Sand was anything but simple. The phone book listed them as being located on King Street, and I assumed that meant somewhere south of Calhoun. *Au contraire.* The address I jotted down was halfway between Calhoun and the Crosstown, and there wasn't even a number on the building. I had to stop and ask for help three times. The first two times, the folks queried had less of a clue then I did. I got lucky the third time, but only because the woman I accosted for directions lived in an apartment directly beneath the law firm.

The white frame building sagged, bulging outward toward the sidewalk. The stairwell was the perfect temperature for roasting a turkey, although it smelled of urine and bacon. Had it not been for the tarnished brass plate on the upstairs door, I would have assumed that I'd been tricked.

"Come in," someone called when I rang the buzzer.

I opened the door to a room that looked like the remains of an exploded library. Books, papers, and folders were scattered everywhere. One document appeared to be tacked to the ceiling. It took me a few seconds to realize that in the center of this mess, behind a small desk, sat a heavyset woman with a round, pleasant face. It took me a couple more seconds to stop staring at her hair. Or rather, her lack of it. The receptionist had obviously been shorn with an electric razor and was sporting what I've sometimes heard referred to as the Parris Island cut.

"How may we help you?" she asked, in a voice as soothing as that of a kindergarten teacher.

"My name is Abigail Washburn. I'm here to see Mr. Hammerhead. I have a ten o'clock appointment."

She whispered something into a small box on her desk and smiled. "He'll just be a minute. Won't you please have a seat?"

I looked around in desperation. It was the first time I regretted not taking archeology in college. I finally located a folding chair, but it was buried under a stack of heavy law books.

"I don't mind standing," I said.

"Just put the stuff on the floor, darling," she said. "It really doesn't matter where. We're in the process of getting new furniture. I'll be sorting through everything anyway."

"That's all right, I really don't mind standing."

She covered the intercom with the palm of a plump hand. "I'm supposed to keep you waiting ten minutes," she whispered to me.

I moved closer. "Excuse me?"

"Makes it seem like we're busy."

"But you're not?"

"Confidentially, you're our first new client this week."

"What about White and Sand? They get a lot of clients, right?"

"I'm afraid there are no White and Sand."

"Come again?"

"Mr. White moved to Atlanta three years ago, and there hasn't been a Mr. Sand as long as I've worked here, which was five years in May."

I took a step back. "I'm terribly sorry, ma'am, but I just remembered that I have a doctor's appointment."

She smiled. "Most new clients say something along those lines. But those who stay are glad they did. He really is the best."

"Then why doesn't he have more clients?" I

clapped a petite paw over my maw. Sometimes my upbringing as a Southern lady is overridden by my curiosity.

Her eyes widened. "You haven't heard the rumors?"

I shook my head. "He's not the one who killed his parents, is he? I remember reading something about that in the paper once. Managed to acquit himself by playing on the jury's sympathy for orphans."

She laughed softly. "No, he didn't kill his parents. He cut his wife's hair."

"Say what?"

She leaned across the desk and used her ample bosoms to cover the intercom. "He has a hair fetish."

"He does?" Okay, so maybe a smart Abby would have backed out of the room and taken the bacon-and-bathroom-scented stairs at breakneck speed.

She nodded vigorously. "He gets his jollies from cutting women's hair. His wife finally divorced him, but by the time she did, she looked just like me."

"You don't say!" Actually, there was a good deal more I wanted her to say.

A good secretary knows how to read minds, and this woman proved the rule. "Yes, he cut mine as well. Paid me a thousand dollars each time I let him do it."

"Indeed. So everyone in Charleston knows about Mr. Hammerhead's fetish?"

"Oh, not everyone. You didn't. Mostly just people of a certain—how should I put this?"

"Social standing?"

"Your words, darling, not mine."

Before I had the chance to protest being lumped with the hoi polloi, the door to Mr. Hammerhead's office opened. The man framed by the sill was surprisingly handsome. Tall with dark hair and green eyes, he looked entirely normal to me— not that I am qualified to judge. Even his clothes— blue and white seersucker suit and white buckskin shoes—were everyday Charleston attire. At least among the gentry.

"Ah, Mrs. Washburn, I presume."

"Yes, sir."

He moved quickly to shake my hand. "Please, come into my office. I think I can find you a chair. Mrs. Dillsworth," he added, "please hold all my calls."

I thought I saw the receptionist wink just before I was ushered into the inner sanctum. She could have been winking at either of us. It didn't matter; I've had experience dealing with smarmy men. That's why I carry pepper spray in my purse.

* * *

But Mr. Hammerhead proved to be a perfect gentleman. He listened attentively to everything I said, and even jotted down notes. I haven't been taken that seriously by a man since my courtship days with Greg.

"That about covers it," I said, reluctantly ending my spiel.

"Yes, I'll handle her case," he said, without a moment's hesitation.

"That's wonderful. Forgive me for being blunt, but what do you charge? Per hour, I mean."

He glanced at a wall calendar of Charleston. Perhaps he had seasonal rates.

"Three hundred."

I couldn't help but gasp. "An *hour*?"

He looked at the opposing wall. "Well, that's my usual rate. Is Mrs. Crawford indigent?"

"Not exactly, but she is indignant. Anyway, I plan to cover her expenses."

"I see. And where are you employed, Mrs. Washburn?"

"I own the Den of Antiquity on King Street. It's an antique store."

"Tell you what, I'll give you my special new customer discount, which is one-third off."

"Two hundred?"

He looked at me. "On top of that you'll get another fifty percent off if you'll agree to do some of the legwork. You see, I'm a little short on staff at the moment."

"What sort of legwork?" I hoped that wasn't a come-on.

"I seem to remember reading in the paper recently that this inn is now open for business. Am I correct?"

"Yes. La Parterre—that's French for little garden—has already received a rave review in the *Post and Courier*." There was no need to remind him that it was the landscaping for which the reviewer couldn't seem to find enough praise. My rooms, on the other hand, were merely referred to as pleasant.

"Well then, perhaps you could speak with some of the current guests. See what, if anything, they might have seen or heard. But"—he raised a recently manicured hand, which was surely an extravagance, given his apparent lack of business—"if you encounter the police, leave as discreetly as possible. This is all on the QT."

"I understand."

"Now, if you'll excuse, I'm going straight over to interview Mrs. Crawford."

I stood. "Thank you so much, Mr. Hammerhead."

He stood as well. "Thank *you*, Mrs. Washburn."

I turned to go just as he was clearing his throat.

"Mrs. Washburn?"

"Yes?"

"I hope you don't find this too forward of me, but you have very nice hair."

My hair is short, and until recent years a deep chestnut brown. It's nothing too special by any means, but it is mine, and I plan to keep it that way. I was out of that office quicker than double-geared lightning.

I drove straight to my shop, which, although on King Street, is in another rent district altogether. Before I did any snooping, I needed to touch base in person with C.J., my assistant. The girl has a 160 IQ and is a crackerjack businesswoman, but some-how still manages to be one variety short of a three-bean salad. Born and raised in Shelby, North Carolina (trust me, I have nothing against that fair city), she spins stories that make the Paul Bunyan tales seem like unassuming collections of facts.

"Abby," she practically shouted when she saw me enter, "the most incredible thing just hap-pened."

"Here, or in Shelby?"

"Here, of course."

Experience has taught me that humoring the big gal can pay off in spades. Or not.

"Do tell," I said cautiously.

"See that William and Mary walnut highboy over there?"

"What about it?"

"I made it move—by telekinesis."

"That's nice, dear."

"Abby, you don't believe me, do you?"

"I didn't say that. It's just that something else very important happened—"

"Watch!" C.J. is over a foot taller than me, and built like a linebacker with hips. She squared her shoulders, thrust her head forward, and screwed her face into what quite possibly resembled a constipated bulldog. For a minute I thought her eyes might pop out. Of course nothing happened.

"Maybe if you don't concentrate so hard," I suggested.

"Ooh, Abby, but that's the key. Granny Ledbetter back in Shelby was able to move a mountain just by staring at it."

"Perhaps metaphorically."

"No, I mean for real. Abby, you remember Crowders Mountain?" She was referring to an isolated peak just west of Charlotte, North Carolina, near the South Carolina border, that offers hardy hikers spectacular views of both Gaston and York counties.

"Yes," I said warily.

"Well, it used to be even further west, on the other side of Shelby. But Granny wanted the afternoon sun to shine on her tomatoes, so she moved it. Took her two tries, though. The first time, she accidentally dumped part of it into Lake Norman. That's how come Crowders Mountain isn't quite as high as it used to be, and why the lake has so many islands."

I tried not to roll my eyes. This was her most ridiculous yarn yet. If I didn't put a stop to things, she might well scare away customers.

"C.J., darling, imagination is a good thing, but—"

"Abby, you don't believe me, do you?" The hurt in her large gray eyes made me instantly regret my words.

"I believe you." Being a little too much on the perky side, I could always use a longer nose.

"No, you don't."

"Yes, I—"

I was saved by the bell. The sleigh bells, that is. The person I least wanted to see at that moment had just entered the shop.

# 4

"**M**ama!"

Please don't misunderstand. I love my mother dearly, but she makes Ozzy Osbourne and his family seem like boring, middle-class, everyday people. That's because Mama's eccentricities take her in the opposite direction. Stuck in a mid-fifties time warp, she wears dresses with snug waists, and full-circle skirts puffed out by piles of starched crinolines. Even while vacuuming, my minimadre wears heels and pearls, and she never leaves the house without first donning gloves and hat. According to her, the second saddest day of her life—the day my daddy died was the saddest—was the day she, while on vacation to California, spotted the real-life June Cleaver, Barbara Billingsly, sporting a pair of slacks. If that wasn't bad enough, the pants were purportedly white, and it was already two weeks after Labor Day.

"Abigail Louise," Mama breezed, as she sailed

into my shop on wind-filled skirts. "Why didn't you tell me you were in trouble again."

I got to her as fast as I could and pulled her between two facing armoires. C.J. tried to join us, but I waved her away.

"I'm not in trouble, Mama. Wynnell is."

"That's the same thing, dear. You two are practically joined at the hip—well, at least you used to be. Before your silly little tiff. Besides, you know I can smell trouble, and that's exactly what I smell right now."

Mama was serious. She claims she can detect danger with her nostrils, and if the wind is just right, even minor impediments to my happiness will show up on her nose radar. I respectfully dismiss the notion that she has this ability, and suggest that this delusion is a result of all the hair spray she uses.

"All I did," I said, "was speak to a lawyer on her behalf."

"But that's not all you're going to do, dear."

I avoided her eyes. "Mama, how do you know about Mrs. Webbfingers's death?"

"Mrs. who?"

"Don't play games with me, Mama. I want the name of your source."

My petite progenitress—she is only three inches taller than I—lives with Greg and me. She hadn't been in the room when I received Wynnell's call, but that didn't mean she hadn't over-heard my half of the conversation. It is even possi-ble—and it pains me to say this—that she was listening in on the phone extension in her room. After all, this is the same woman who picked open my diary when I was a teenager, and then blamed it on the cat.

Mama sighed. "I slept in late this morning, dear—but that phone call just before eight woke me up."

"Aha, so you did listen in!"

"Gracious, no. I wouldn't do anything so rude. Besides, the phone in my room makes a terrible buzz when a third party is on the line. You really should replace it, dear."

"Mama!"

"All right. You hadn't been gone a minute when the doorbell rang. Of course I wasn't dressed yet, but I had to answer it, didn't I? I mean, what if it was you, and you needed to get back in for some reason, but you'd left your key? Anyway, it was a reporter from *Post and Courier*—don't ask me to remember her name—and since she was a she, I invited her in and made her some coffee. Real cof-fee, by the way—not that instant stuff Greg has to make for himself in the morning, because you won't get up and make it for him. Abby, if you don't mind me saying so, I never sent your father out into the world without a proper breakfast."

"I do mind you saying so. Greg leaves the house at four-thirty, and he is every bit as capable as I am of making coffee. He prefers the instant, because that's what he's used to on the boat. Now back to the reporter. What did she want?"

Mama patted her pearls, which is the first indication that she is annoyed. "The reporter," she said, curling her upper lip, "didn't want to talk to me at first. Just you. But I made her real coffee and served her some nice warm cinnamon buns—"

"Which were Sarah Lee."

"But I warmed them first, which is more than you do for Greg. Now where was I?"

"About to tell me what she wanted."

"Ah, yes. Well, she asked if you'd ever worked for Marina Webbfingers. And I said that of course you knew the woman very well, but you'd never worked for her."

"But I have!"

"Darling, decorating her bed and breakfast is hardly the same as working for her. I didn't want her to think you were the maid."

"Not that there would be anything wrong with that, but please, continue."

"So anyway, after her second cinnamon bun she let it drop that Marina Webbfingers had just been found dead, and word on the street was that your friend Wynnell Crawford was the killer."

"Word on the street? Mama, you've been watching too much television."

Mama gasped. "Abby, you know I don't watch TV. Since *Green Acres* left the air there hasn't been a thing worth watching."

I couldn't have agreed less, but there was no point in arguing. "Word sure gets around fast in Charleston," I said, shaking my head.

"Not as fast as in Shelby."

"C.J.!" I whipped around the corner of the nearest armoire. Sure enough, there stood the big galoot, a hand the size of Connecticut cupped behind her left ear.

"Abby, please don't be mad. There aren't any customers in the shop right now, and I couldn't help overhearing."

"Just like I won't be able to help docking your pay if you don't find something useful to do—*out* of earshot."

"Abigail!" Mama started to frown, but remembered in the nick of time that it causes wrinkles. Besides, Donna Reed never frowned.

"Sorry, C.J.," I mumbled.

"Oh that's all right, Abby. I know you mean well. And you can't be expected to know everything."

"What is that supposed to mean?"

"Well, like you never met Evangeline Graff from Shelby. Of course I never did either, on account she died before I was born, but Granny Ledbetter sure did. In fact, they were best friends growing up. But Evangeline never could keep a secret—and Granny had a lot of those. Anyway, everything that Granny told her friend, the whole town ended up knowing. Took just a few minutes, too. 'Tell a Graff,' the people started to say, 'and you might as well tell everybody.' So when Cousin Ebeneezer Ledbetter invented a machine that could send messages over a wire, that's what they named it. Did you know that, Abby?"

I bit my tongue, but just for a second. "And I suppose your cousin invented the telephone and named it after someone named Phony?"

"Oh no, Abby. Alexander Graham Bell invented that—although I'm sure he got a little help from Cousin Ebeneezer."

"That does it, ladies. I'm out of here. You can reach me on my cell phone, but only if it's an emergency."

Mama tried to follow me, but one of her heels got caught in the sidewalk. She didn't fall, thank heavens, but as she struggled to maintain her balance she reminded me of the thirty-four hours of excruciatingly painful labor she had endured in order to bring me into this world.

"It was thirty-six, Mama," I said. "And it has absolutely nothing to do with where I'm going now."

"I know where you're going, dear. You're going to try and find whoever it was who murdered that Webbfoot woman."

"That's Webb*fingers*, Mama. And I don't want you following me."

"But I could help. You know I'm good at getting people to talk about themselves."

"Sorry, Mama. I have to do this alone."

"Alone! That's what I am." She stepped out of her shoe and yanked it loose with both hands. "Honestly, dear, sometimes I think I should have stayed up in Rock Hill."

"Don't be silly, Mama. You love it here. And you have your friends at Grace Church. Not to mention all your buddies in that club you belong to—the Heavenly Hopefuls, isn't it?"

"It's Heavenly Hustlers, dear, and it hasn't been the same since one of them almost killed you."

"Have you thought of getting a job?"

"Of course I've thought of that, but what would I do? You know I haven't worked outside the home since marrying your daddy."

"Well, you were a secretary—" I choked back the rest of my sentence. Secretaries these days need computer skills. All Mama knows about computers is that if you take one apart to dust it, you better know how to put it together again. Otherwise your daughter could get very irritated.

Mama held her gloved hands in the air, as if surrendering. In reality, she was preparing to deliver her famous victory speech.

"Don't worry about me, dear. Just go on and do whatever it is you need to do. I'll be fine." She blinked away a bogus tear. "I can sit at home and cut coupons. Who needs friends when you get to be my age? They're liable to die soon, anyway."

"Cutting coupons is a wonderful idea," I said malevolently. I didn't think for a minute she would. When Mama gives her victory speech, it isn't just to make me feel guilty; it's a sure sign she has something up her shirred sleeve.

I had no doubt that Mozella Wiggins was going to be just fine.

Although Marina Webbfingers's murder had presumably happened only hours prior, there was no telltale sign announcing the fact. No yellow tape, no stone-faced detective barring access to the property. Either the police had already done their job or discretion had won over detection. This was, after all, double 0 Legare Street.

Mama hadn't succeeded in making me feel guilty, but the pangs were certainly there when I pushed open the wrought-iron gate, wound my way through the parterre, and entered the garden

Wynnell had reclaimed. The friend who I had imagined had no taste had turned out to be rather talented—if you discounted the hideous knockoff statue of David which, incidentally, was no longer in evidence. In the weeks since I'd last seen the garden, the annuals had come into their own; masses of flowers bloomed everywhere. It was a scene deserving of its own month on a Charleston calendar. Thank heavens someone—no doubt the deceased—had removed the silly sculpture.

"Well done, Wynnell," I said softly to myself.

"It is kinda pretty, ain't it?"

I whirled. It was Harriet Spanky, the Webbfingerses' overworked maid. I'd gotten to know her quite well during the decorating process, because the elderly servant had seen to it that Wynnell and I were well-supplied with sweet tea—the Southern elixir of life.

Judging by her perpetually tired eyes and the deep creases on her face, Harriet had played with God when He was a child. Perhaps she'd even baby-sat for Him. I knew she was a widow whose husband had died in a war, but which war was anybody's guess. It would have come as only a mild surprise to learn that he had perished in *the* war, sometimes referred to hereabouts as the War of Northern Aggression.

If Harriet needed to work, for whatever reason, that was her business. It was, however, my right to think it shameful of the Webbfingerses to require such an elderly woman to wear a uniform. Except for the length of the skirt—which mercifully came down to her knees—it resembled the classic French maid's uniform. How degrading this must be to a woman who should have been at home baking cookies for her great-grandchildren, not scrubbing the toilets of the aristocracy.

"Hi Harriet," I said warmly. "How's the arthritis today?"

"Could be worse. I could be dead like the missus."

"You have a point there."

"So you heard? Ain't that awful?"

"Were you here?"

"No ma'am. It happened sometime last night—after I got off work."

"But you're still living on the third floor of the main house, right?"

"Yeah, but it was my birthday. My son Nolan took me out to dinner."

This was my golden opportunity, so I can't be blamed for what I said next, can I? "Harriet, if you don't mind me asking, what's the magic number?"

"Excuse me?"

"How many years did you celebrate?"

"Sixty-three."

"Not your son, dear . . ." I realized just in time that she wasn't referring to her son. "I mean, happy birthday." I paused an appropriate length of time before switching back to the somber purpose of my visit. "Your employer's murder must have come as quite a shock."

"Yes, ma'am, it sure did."

"Do you know how it happened?"

Her tired eyes gave me the once-over. "So then you haven't heard."

"Just that she was dead, and it was murder."

"It was your friend who done it," Harriet said in a tone that was remarkably unaccusatory.

"Maybe that's what the police think, but it isn't true. And even if she did, how did she do it? Wynnell hates guns."

"Oh, it weren't no gun, ma'am. The missus was blood-joined with a statue."

It took me a second. "Bludgeoned. With a statue?"

"The police won't say for sure with what, but I know that's what it was. Look there"—she pointed to the center flower bed—"it's gone."

"I saw that, but I thought maybe Mrs. Webbfingers had ordered it removed."

"Why would she do that? It was such a pretty thing. Told my son I wanted one just like that for my birthday—I seen them at the flea market, you know, and they ain't all that expensive. But," she sighed, "I guess he done right by taking his old mama out to dinner."

"Yes, that was thoughtful, but Harriet—or do you prefer Mrs. Spanky?" The strictures of our working relationship had required we use last names.

"Harriet. I don't stand on no formality, Mrs. Tomberlake. Now that I ain't serving you no tea."

"That's *Timber*lake—and really Washburn now. So just call me Abby. Anyway, Harriet, I just wanted you to know that Mrs. Crawford would never have done anything like that."

"Folks is capable of anything, ma'am, if you don't mind me saying so."

"That may be. But Wynnell is my best friend. I've known her for years. She isn't capable of murder. Besides, what would be her motive?"

# 5

Harriet snorted. "They didn't get along, them two," she said, "she and the missus."

"That's news to me."

"Yes, ma'am, they sure didn't. Had themselves an awful row during them weeks your friend was working here."

"What was it about?"

"Mrs. Crawford wanted to use the bathroom in the main house, on account the water was turned off in the outbuildings the day you was having them tubs changed. But the missus said she weren't going to have no help coming inside—except for me, and I have to use the third floor bathroom—but your friend said she weren't no help, but a professional. Then the missus said she was acting pushy like a Yankee, and that's when all hell broke loose—pardon my French."

To Wynnell, those would certainly have been

fighting words, but she'd never kill over them. Not unless they'd been uttered by a Yankee, and even then she was only likely to maim.

"Harriet, where was I when this happened?"

"You was with them shower installers. Took them forever, if you ask me. The missus was all upset about them blocking up Legare Street like that. She was sure she was going to get a situation."

Ah, a citation. "Harriet, I assure you, no matter what you heard, my friend would never kill anybody."

She tucked a wisp of gray hair under her white maid's cap. "Ma'am, you ever look closely at your friend?"

"Of course."

"Don't it bother you that she has just one eyebrow?"

"But it stretches all the way across her face. Besides, you can't judge a book by its cover."

"I ain't judging no books, ma'am."

"What I meant was—"

"Excuse me for interrupting, ma'am, but if the mister sees me standing here talking, he ain't gonna be too happy. I need this job."

"Yes, of course. Although I must say, I'm surprised he made you come in today. You'd think he would have things on his mind other than housecleaning—not that it isn't necessary," I added quickly.

"It's them tourists, ma'am. The ones renting them rooms you fixed up. The police are making them stay until they're done investigating. Don't none of them want to stay someplace where someone's been killed, so they ain't at all happy. Just wish they wouldn't take it out on me."

"I understand. Maybe I can help."

"Yeah?"

"I could talk with them—maybe calm them down a bit."

Her laugh was like marbles being shaken in a jar. "You gonna make them lunch, too? 'Cause I ain't seen a bunch of pickier eaters."

Unfortunately I cook about as well as I can sing. The last time Greg cajoled me into trying karaoke, the manager of the establishment refunded our admission charges and bought us drinks, *after* I promised never to sing in his establishment again.

"Well, I guess I could *take* them to lunch—somewhere not too expensive. But I'm sure they're not allowed to leave the premises."

"No, ma'am, they're allowed to leave—they just ain't allowed to leave town. In fact, they're all off to the Market to buy souvenirs—just like nothing had happened—except for them Greeks."

"Fraternity kids? Here?"

The marbles got another good workout. "These ain't kids. These is real Greeks. Papa-something is their name. Wanted me to cook them some lamb. You ever eat lamb, Mrs. Timbersnake?"

It was my turn to laugh—a ladylike chuckle, of course. "That's Timber*lake*. Timbersnake was my first husband. But yes, I've eaten lamb many times."

"It stinks, don't it?"

"Not if it's fresh and prepared properly." I sucked in deeply but was unable to retrieve my words. "A nice tender leg of lamb with mint jelly—but it's definitely not for everyone."

To my relief, she nodded in apparent agreement. "Well, I got to get them rooms cleaned while the folks is out. But you can talk to them Greeks if you want to. They're in the King George room above the carriage house. But you might want to stomp on the stairs or something, and let them know you're coming before you knock. You know how it is with them foreigners."

I couldn't resist. "No, how is it?"

"Always having sex, that's what."

"Is that so?"

"That's why there's so many of them."

"I'll definitely have to put a stop to that," I said, "or the next thing we know there'll be big fat Greek weddings popping up all over the place. The smell of lamb will permeate the city. Vegetarians will have to flee for the sake of their nostrils. Beef prices will plummet and—"

"You making fun of me, Mrs. Timbershake?"

"Absolutely—not. Well, I'd better get to it."

She gave me a cynical look, straightened sagging shoulders, and marched off to strip linens and scrub toilets.

I didn't bother to stomp on the stairs. I weigh less than a hundred pounds, and with my tiny feet, I'd sound more like a palmetto bug than anything else. These bugs are merely a variety of roach, and are essentially harmless, but they are the SUVs of the insect world. Although not quite the size of cats, I have been known to trip over them. Tourists invariably freak when they see them. If frightened badly enough, the guests in the King George suite might greet me at the door with a can of Raid. Maybe even a baseball bat.

The only thing that appeared to be imminently dangerous about the man who opened the door was his brilliant white smile. I am a sucker for tall, dark, handsome men, and although I am happily married to one, that doesn't always stop me from lusting in my heart. Sometimes, even, the feeling extends to my loins—although that's as far as it gets. How fortunate I am to be a somewhat lapsed Episcopalian and don't flog myself with chains of guilt. Besides, I'm sure Greg has similar thoughts when he sees a pretty woman.

This dude in particular was worthy of a little

drool. His nearly black hair was nicely accented by silver sideburns, and he had a cleft in his chin that rivaled that of Kirk Douglas. His brown eyes were alert and intelligent. And not that it really mattered, but he appeared to have his financial ducks in a row as well. That is, if the heavy gold chains and Italian suit were already paid for.

"Ah, you must be the masseuse," he said.

"I beg your pardon?"

"Pay no attention to Nick," a female voice behind him said.

A second later a tall woman pushed the gorgeous man aside. Thanks to Botox, beauty is no longer just skin deep, but even then it is wrong to judge folks on their natural physical attributes. Perhaps I may be given leeway, in light of that fact there appeared to be very little that was natural about this woman.

Her pinched face hinted at more than one facelift, and her deep, even color spoke of days spent supine on a tanning bed. And why is it that some bottle blondes let their dark roots grow out to the point that they look as if they're wearing dead skunks on their heads? This woman's short hairdo even included a flip that resembled a tail.

"Hi, I'm Abigail Timberlake Washburn," I said. "I'd like to welcome you to Charleston."

"Are you with the *Post and Courier*?" She referred to our local newspaper, which is an excellent publication, by the way. It was, however, an odd assumption, and raised some interesting questions.

"I'm afraid not. I'm just a private individual—a friend of the family. I heard that you are stranded in town, so speak, and I want to offer you hospitality." Strictly speaking, it wasn't a lie. I was a friend to many families—just not the Webbfingers family.

"Oh, I thought you might be here to do a story on my husband. You know, him being a Wall Street mover and shaker. You probably don't get too many of those in Charleston."

"Actually, we get a surprising number of celebrities. Why just last week I thought I saw Brad Pitt walking up Pitt Street." I couldn't help but laugh when I realized the connection.

"Is that supposed to be a joke?"

"No. Honestly. A lot of movies are shot here because of the mild climate, and because there is so much historical architecture."

She nodded. "Well, Miss—uh, I'm afraid I've forgotten your name."

"That's Mrs. Washburn."

"Yes, of course. At any rate, I'm afraid my husband and I have a few things to do, so if you'll excuse us—" She started to close the door.

"Not so fast, Irena." Tall, dark, and handsome was turning into a blabbermouth.

"I came to invite you to lunch," I said, while I still had the chance.

"To lunch?" the woman with the roadkill hairdo asked.

"Yes, ma'am."

"Why would you do that?"

"It's just our way of showing hospitality, ma'am." I doubt if knocking on hotel doors and inviting the occupants to lunch is customary anywhere. In fact, one would think a normal person would consider it rather strange. But when a well-dressed middle-age woman with a strong Southern accent offers a free lunch, it is apparently a hard thing to pass up.

Irena, however, was obviously still wary of Charlestonians bearing Greeks gifts. "Lunch with you and who else?"

"Just me."

"Are you part of some kind of organization? Because if you're trying to convert us to your religion, I'm telling you now, it isn't going to work. Nick and I already belong to one, and I assure you, we're not going to change."

They may be tiny tootsies, but sometimes I can think fast on them. "Yes, ma'am, it is an organization, but it isn't religious. It's called People Interested in Treating Yankees. We're just a group of citizens who are proud of our town and love to show it off to those not fortunate enough to live here."

"Hmm. We're from New York City. You can't beat that."

"Yes, but do you have a chapter of P.I.T.Y.?"

She looked like a cat that had been asked a calculus question. "Uh—we have thousands of organizations. I'm sure we have one of those."

"There you go. P.I.T.Y. must be nationwide. So then, how about it? Lunch at Slightly North of Broad? That's the name of the restaurant, by the way, as well as its location."

She glanced at a watch which, if genuine, cost as much as a year's tuition at the College of Charleston. "Isn't it a little early for lunch?"

"Yes, of course. My reservation is for twelve. Would you like me to pick you up?"

"Hey, that would be nice," Nick said. He flashed me a smile that, had it reflected off a tin roof, could have put someone's eyes out. "We're the Papadopouluses, by the way."

"We'll meet you there," Irena snapped.

I got my petite patootie out of there before she changed her mind.


I had parked along the seawall, so I took the opportunity to enjoy the view while I called for backup. I may act foolishly from time to time, but I wasn't about to dine unchaperoned with two strangers from the Big Apple, especially since one of them was so hostile. With my luck, they'd slip me a Mickey, then pretend I was drunk so they could carry me out, and then the next thing I'd know, I'd find myself in the harem of a third-world potentate.

My friend and colleague, Bob Steuben, picked up on the first ring. "The Finer Things," he said, referring to the name of the antique store he co-owns with his partner Rob.

"Bob, darling, what are you doing about lunch today?"

"Hi Abby. Well, I brought in some smoked emu salad sandwiches, two dozen deviled quail eggs, and a rhubarb tort." He was serious.

"Sounds yummy." I was not serious. "How about I treat you to lunch at Slightly North of Broad?"

I must have been speaking louder than usual, or Rob has exceptional hearing. There was a brief scuffle while he managed to get the phone away from Bob.

"Does that invitation include me?"

"Definitely."

"Then we're on."

"But what about the lunch I made?" I heard Bob whine in the background.

"We can give it to C.J., can't we, Abby?"

"Well, she does eat everything," I whispered, so Bob wouldn't hear. The man considers himself a gourmet, and I suppose he is, but neither Rob nor I can stomach some of his concoctions.

"Abby says that's a great idea," Rob said, with more emphasis on my name than was needed.

There was a good deal of conversation that I couldn't decipher, and then Bob got on the phone again. "It's not that I'm unappreciative, Abby, but I wish you'd give me more warning. Do you know how hard it was to peel those quail eggs?"

"I'm sure it was a pain. So, are we on?"

He sighed. "All right. What time?"

"Noon. But there is a condition I haven't yet explained."

"Which is?"

"You two are not going to sit with me."

"I don't understand."

"It's a long story, dear, which I'll tell you some other time. But basically I want you two to just keep an eye on me."

"And who else?"

"Always the perceptive one, aren't you? It's this couple from New York."

"Abby, I smell a rat."

The phone on the other end of the line changed

hands again. "I smell Bob's lunch. Abby, out with it. Are you working on another case?"

"What makes you say that?"

"We heard about the murder. Wynnell's lawyer called us. He wanted to know if we were willing to be character witnesses. I said of course, but that I thought the whole thing silly, because she isn't capable of killing anyone."

"You said it."

"Abby, I thought you promised Greg you weren't going to do any more sleuthing. The last time, you almost got yourself killed."

"Wynnell's my best friend, Rob—well, except for you two. Besides, what he doesn't know won't hurt him."

"Yeah, right." If Rob wasn't careful, his sarcasm was going to drip all over his Ferragamo shoes

"I wouldn't be calling the kettle black, dear. How many times have you pretended to eat Bob's cooking, but somehow managed to dispose of the food by other means?"

"Touché. But promise me you aren't going to take any unnecessary risks—oh what the heck, there's no stopping you. Do what you have to. Just remember that we're both here for you. You've got my cell phone number, right?"

"Right. Hey, I've got to go. Love you guys," I said, and pushed the Off button before he had a chance to give me the third degree about my plans.

But before I could drop the cell phone back into my shoulder bag, I was grabbed from behind. The phone flew out of my hand, and I literally crumpled to my knees in sheer terror. Fortunately I don't have very far to fall.

# 6

"**M**iss Timberlake, are you all right?"
It took me a second or two to realize that the man was trying to help me to my feet. Another few seconds passed before I realized who he was.

"Mr. Webbfingers!"

"Sorry, I didn't mean to scare you like that."

I steadied myself and then glanced around. "Where's my phone?"

"I'm afraid it landed in the water."

I staggered to the edge of the seawall. We happened to be standing at the exact spot where the Ashley and the Cooper rivers meet to form the Atlantic Ocean. Even though it was low tide in the harbor, that cell phone had sailed permanently. It is possible I cussed like a sailor.

"Don't worry, I'll replace it," Fisher Webbfingers said.

I stared at the man. I hadn't liked him from the moment I met him. It's hard to pinpoint why, and I certainly hope I'm not so shallow that I subconsciously based my opinion on his looks. And anyway, he's not bad-looking, just sort of creepy.

He was originally a carrot top, whose hair is now fading to grayish beige, and like Irena Papadopoulus, he is deeply tanned. But Fisher's tan comes from the real thing—hours spent in the sun golfing and fishing—and thanks to a zillion and one freckles, has an orange cast. It's the eyes, however, that set him apart from anybody else I know. His irises all but lack color. So pale is the blue, that the blood vessels behind them show through, like tangled clusters of red spiders.

"I had so many numbers programmed into it," I said with remarkable composure, which, hopefully, made up for at least some of my foul language earlier.

"Mrs. Timberlake, do you have a minute?"

"Well, now that I can't call anyone—" I forced a smile. He was, after all, a grieving widower. *And* on my list to interrogate. "What can I do for you, Mr. Webbfingers?"

"Take my wife's place."

"I beg your pardon?"

"I saw you talking to Harriet, and then you went around to one of the guest cottages. You know your way around the place, Mrs. Timberlake. You know the setup. You know Harriet."

"I still don't understand." So help me if the man

was hitting on me. With Marina barely cold, and my cell phone in the marina—I wasn't in the mood for sexual shenanigans. Not that I normally engage in extramarital pursuits.

"You see, Mrs. Timberlake, the police won't let my guests leave town, and the stress—plus all the work—is too much for Harriet."

"I'm not surprised, given her age. Maybe you should get her some help."

"Those are my thoughts exactly, Mrs. Timberlake. That's why I've come to you."

"I'm afraid I don't know much about the domestic scene in Charleston, Mr. Webbfingers. But I believe you can find the numbers of cleaning agencies in the yellow pages."

"Thank you for the suggestion. However, in addition to hiring an additional maid, I was thinking—well, I was thinking of hiring you."

I saw red, and it wasn't just in his eyes. "Mr. Webbfingers, I am a professional antiques dealer. I do not clean other people's houses—not that there is anything wrong with that. And frankly, sir—and I mean no disrespect—I doubt if your wife did much housework."

Pale, almost invisible eyelashes flickered. "Oh no, I wasn't asking you to clean. I want you to be more like a hostess."

"Mr. Webbfingers, this conversation is over." I must admit, however, that I briefly entertained the thought of being a hostess—well, a geisha, really. Those platform shoes they wear would add several useful inches to my height, and I'm extraordinarily fond of sushi.

"Mrs. Timberlake, you misunderstand."

"I understand enough, Mr. Webbfingers." I turned and walked away in the direction of the Cooper River. A group of tourists was in need of someone to snap their photo. They kept taking turns, which meant one of them was always out of the shot. They were young and loud and appeared to be having a great deal of fun. Judging by their accents—and the fact two of them were wearing Cleveland Browns T-shirts—they hailed from someplace north of the line. At any rate, by volunteering to play photographer, I could give them a dose of Southern hospitality, as well ensure my safety. Fisher Webbfingers wouldn't dare mess with a bunch of boisterous Buckeyes.

"I only want you to take them out for meals and show them around," he shouted to my back.

I whirled. "I beg your pardon?"

"You know, act like a tour director. Keep their minds off of what happened."

*What happened?* He made it sound like palmetto bugs had invaded the guest cottages. This was his wife he was talking about. Someone had bludgeoned her with a knockoff statue, for crying out loud.

"I know what you must be thinking," he said, as if reading my mind. "That I didn't love my wife. That I'm not showing enough emotion. You'd be right on both counts."

Nothing can be quite as startling as the truth. "Please, continue."

"We've been married for thirty-three years. That's a long time to remain faithful to one person."

Having been the wronged party, I had no sympathy for him. "Half the world's problems could be solved if men kept their peckers in their pants," I said peevishly.

"I quite agree. It wasn't mine that got out."

"Oops. I apologize. It's just—well, never mind. The relationship you had with your wife is none of my business."

The washed-out eyes insisted on locking on mine. "She's had three affairs—that I know of. The last one was with this college kid down here on spring break. Happened two years ago. A spindly little guy—not at all her type. Still, he must have had something she wanted."

"TMI!"

"No, MIT. He was an engineering student from the Massachusetts Institute of Technology. I'm an engineer, you know. Retired from Nucor Steel just this year. Early retirement, of course, because I'm only fifty-five. Anyway, could be Marina thought bedding an engineering student would be especially hurtful. I don't know. She always refused to talk about any of this. Wouldn't go to therapy or marriage counseling. Over the years our love just plain eroded. I only agreed to the bed and breakfast because I thought it would make her happy. Sort of a last chance." He paused just long enough to catch his breath. "Well, apparently, it didn't make her happy. My guess, Mrs. Timberlake, is that my wife was killed by her newest lover."

"Mr. Webbfingers," I said, wagging one of my fingers in his face, "Wynnell Crawford may be many things, but she is not a lesbian—not that there's anything wrong with that."

"Oh no, not Mrs. Crawford. My wife didn't swing that way, either."

This was worth having to buy and reprogram a new cell phone. "So you don't think my friend is guilty?"

"Of bad taste, yes. That statue was really ugly—but Marina liked it. Insisted on keeping it there. But of murder?" He shook his head. "Nah, I don't think so."

My heart started to pound. "Have you met this new lover? Do the police know about him?"

"No, and yes. I can't prove that she had a new lover, but I told the police that I thought she might. And that something went terribly wrong. It's the only reason I can think of for what happened."

My hopes were dashed like waves against the seawall. "Mr. Webbfingers, I'm sure you know that ordinarily the police would consider you the prime suspect."

"I'm aware of that."

"But they made an exception in your case." I raised my voice slightly, but not enough to turn it into a question.

"I'm sure I would be their prime suspect if it hadn't been for that catfight between my wife and Mrs. Crawford—"

"Catfight?"

"You haven't heard?"

"Enlighten me. Please."

"Yesterday afternoon Marina called Mrs. Crawford. Asked her to stop by and check on some of the flowers. They were looking pretty droopy, I guess."

"They looked fine to me a few minutes ago."

He stared at me through his transparent irises. "They didn't yesterday. Anyway, one thing must have led to another, because pretty soon the whole neighborhood could hear them."

"What did they say?"

"I wasn't there. I was playing golf. Heard about it when I got back—after I found Marina. Dead."

"It was a hundred degrees yesterday. You play golf when it's that hot?"

He turned a deeper shade of orange. "We play in the mornings, and refresh ourselves in the afternoons. But I don't do the hard stuff anymore—just beer, and the occasional glass of wine. Anyway, Mrs. Timberlake, would you consider helping me with the guests? At least until after the funeral? Which, by the way, I'm not even allowed to schedule until Forensics is through with—uh, Marina's body. I know this must sound like a strange request. Let them fend for themselves, is probably what you're thinking. But Mrs. Timberlake, if I don't keep them distracted somehow—even show them a good time—they might get it in their heads to sue me."

"Sue you? On what grounds?"

"Emotional distress. Mental agony. I forget the exact phrase my attorney used. The point is, we're living in a litigious society, and appeasement seems to be the best form of prevention."

Unfortunately he was right. But how lucky for me! Now, not only did I have an excuse to visit double 0 Legare, I practically *had* to hang out there. If the police didn't shoo me away, this case was just about closed. Sure, I had only just begun my sleuthing, but I was a veteran at this. Heck, someday I might even consider private detective school, or whatever it was I had to do in order to hang out a shingle.

**DEN OF ANTIQUITY/DEN OF INIQUITY**
*Fine antiques and murder investigations our specialties*

There was one condition, however. After all, Mama didn't raise any fools—if you discount my younger brother, Toy. By helping Fisher out, I could, perhaps, spring Wynnell from the clinker, but it would also mean less coins for my coffer. While C.J. is competent enough to do the work of two people, she can't do the of two people *plus* me.

"Of course you'll be compensated," he said, reading my mind again.

"Well, uh—"

"I'll pay twice what Marina paid you to decorate."

"And expenses?"

"Absolutely."

"Then it's a deal," I said, and proffered a petite paw, which he was glad to accept.

The boisterous Buckeyes had been replaced by jovial Japanese. Not only were they eager to accept my offer to photograph them, but they insisted I be in the picture as well. On each and every camera. Although there were only eleven tourists, there were twenty-some cameras, and by the time my likeness had been properly captured on each, my hospitality streak was wearing thin.

Finally, I was able to make a break for it during a film change. A young girl named Teruko, wearing a T-shirt that bore an early likeness of Michael Jackson, had become especially attached to me. She tried to follow me, but I dodged deftly behind a throng of morose visitors from Finland. Their Scandinavian solemnity was too much for the teen from Tokyo, and I was once again on my own.

I needed to think. Something was rotten in Denmark, maybe in Helsinki as well. Why had Fisher Webbfingers selected me as his social hostess? Didn't he have friends or relatives who could perform the task? If not, why hadn't he hired a professional tour guide, or even a party planner? Or perhaps he had tried to—and none of them were willing to take the job. Perhaps they all knew something I didn't know about the man.

Just because the police hadn't put Fisher Webbfingers at the top of their list didn't mean he was innocent. A cheating wife is not only a common motive for murder, but in some cultures these killings are even sanctioned. Of course the folks in Charleston wouldn't condone such behavior, but given Fisher Webbfingers's high social standing, it wouldn't be unreasonable to expect the police to begin their investigation with someone else. Someone who didn't always keep her lips buttoned when circumstances called for discretion, and who, reportedly, had engaged in a catfight with the deceased.

It could also be that the surviving owner of the bed and breakfast was on to me. He'd seen me snooping around, and since he seemed to be adept at reading minds (mine is small and doesn't take very long), he'd rightfully concluded that I was on a mission to free Wynnell. Having me get involved with his guests was a great way to keep tabs on me. It might even afford him the opportunity to whack me over the head with a heavy object.

Unless . . . maybe I had it all wrong. Maybe Fisher Webbfingers believed that I had a part in his wife's murder. He had to know that Wynnell and I were buddies, and that I was responsible for getting her the job. Perhaps he thought we were in cahoots, and he was conducting an investigation of his own. Why the nerve of that man!

I felt like marching right back to double 0 Legare Street, but then remembered Wynnell's request that I stall her husband. That was going to take some doing, considering the fact he was out on Folly Beach pier, and I had a noon lunch engagement downtown at Slightly North of Broad. Besides which, I had no idea how to stall a depressed man in his sixties. Were we both not married, and if Ed had a little more zip in him, a game of beach blanket bingo might have done the trick.

As it was, a sandy game of Scrabble was the best I could offer.

It's often said that we're better off not knowing what the future will bring. If I had known about the can of worms waiting for me to open at beach, I would have gone straight home. There's not a lot of trouble one can get into under the covers. At least not alone.

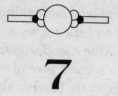

# 7

South Carolina coastal islands are not what typically springs to mind when one hears the word island. Forget Tahiti and Bora Bora. Forget even the Bahamas. Yes, our islands have plenty of palm trees, but they are as flat as a putting green and are not set apart from the mainland by large expanses of water. Tidal creeks and salt marshes help define many of our islands, so that it is possible to drive from one island to another and not be aware that one is actually island-hopping.

The town of Folly Beach is on Folly Island, although the two are virtually synonymous. This gem of a community has managed to maintain much of its charm, and here, very simple cottages, some barely more than a shack, somehow mix harmoniously with much grander residences. The main axis is Ashley Avenue, which runs parallel to the coast and is, at most, just one block from the ocean's fury. One might surmise that it was folly to build a settlement on a mere spit of sand, and that this is the origin of the name. For indeed, hurricanes do reshape the island, and from time to time the owners of a second row of homes suddenly find themselves with beachfront property. The name, however, derives from an Old English word meaning "heavily wooded."

When I got to Folly Creek, I lowered my window in order to smell the tidal flats. Pluff mud is what we call the dark, odoriferous muck. It's one of those love it or hate it scents, but to most Carolinians with early child beach experiences, it is definitely a love affair, a symbol of homecoming. The smell was particularly strong that morning, and I felt blessed to catch glimpses of crabs scuttling over the soft surface. Here and there, where rivulets of water remained, stately white egrets and blue herons were busily fishing.

I raised my window again after crossing over to the island so I could savor a few more minutes of air-conditioning. I needn't have bothered. A strong breeze was blowing off the ocean, and its salty fingers caressed my face as soon as I stepped out of my car.

Folly Beach Edwin S. Taylor Fishing Pier, as it is officially called, extends over a thousand feet into the Atlantic. One gets the impression that if the pier was just double in length, it would be possible to walk all the way to Africa. A look back at the shoreline certainly offers one of the most impressive views in the country.

And while it is a great place to fish, it is also a popular spot to people-watch. Although tame by West Coast standards, the waves here are among the highest in the state, and it is a common sight to see surfers trying their luck on colorful boards. Even more common are the tourists, many of unsinkable proportions, who need only roll out of their hotel beds and onto the beach. One sees them even in the winter, when the locals are huddled around their fireplaces. In the summer, when the water temperature is eighty-five degrees, it gets harder to tell the natives from the visitors.

There are fishing stations at regular intervals along the pier, but I found Ed Crawford at the very end of the pier. He was leaning forward, half over the rail, as if he wanted to get as far away from land as possible.

"Hey Ed," I said, trying to sound cheerful.

He turned slowly. "Wynnell send you?"

"So you know?"

"How could I not? Every day that woman makes it clear what a big disappointment I am."

Thank heavens I hadn't yet spilled the beans. "Ed, I really doubt that's true. She loves you very much."

He glanced at his line, then turned back to me. "I worked hard all my life, but I never made the kind of money Wynnell wants. She doesn't just want to keep up with the Joneses, she wants to keep up with you."

"Me?"

"Living south of Broad, that's all she talks about, Abby. We had a perfectly good house back in Charlotte which was already paid for. Unless we win the lottery, there's no way we could ever afford one of those S.O.B. places."

"Well, they're not all they're cracked up to be. A centuries-old-plus house can be a nightmare when it comes to upkeep. And most of the really old ones have to be shared with Apparition Americans."

"What was that?"

"Ghosts. Apparition American is the p.c. term."

He couldn't even spare a chuckle. "Abby, back in Charlotte I had friends. Not just buddies, but guys I'd known my whole life. Guys I could trust like brothers. It's hard for a man my age to make new friends, especially when your wife's working all the time. Heck, I'll just come out and say it—I'm lonely."

I wouldn't trust my brother with bringing in my junk mail. Even though Toy is now on course to become an Episcopal priest, and Mama worships the ground he walks on, his track record speaks for itself. When he left Rock Hill originally, to seek

fame and fortune in Hollywood, he not only borrowed money from me, which he has yet to repay,
but he borrowed my car—without permission.
The congregation that eventually hires him better
keep a close eye on the offering plate. But I digress.

As I was standing there, pretending to look at
Ed's face, but actually looking past him to the sea,
I had an epiphany. My best friend needed help in
her shop—especially now that she faced the threat
of imprisonment—and her lonely husband
needed human contact. The solution to both problems was as obvious as the eyebrow on Wynnell's
face.

"Guess what?" I said excitedly.

He pivoted. "Something on my line?"

"No, it's about a job."

"Abby, don't go there. I didn't work my butt off
for forty years to take orders from some kid at
Burger King."

"That wasn't going to be my suggestion. Ed, I
think you should work in Wooden Wonders
alongside Wynnell."

That finally brought a laugh. "Good one."

"I'm serious."

He cocked his head, like a puppy hearing a particular sound for the first time. "Abby, selling antiques is ladies' work."

"The Rob-Bobs are great at it."

"My point exactly."

"Now that's just mean. They're every bit as manly as you are. You don't see them roll over and whine when the going gets tough."

He glared at me. "Wynnell can't even make a go of it as it is. What the heck am I supposed to do at the store, stand around and twiddle my thumbs?'

"How about charm the customers?"

"Are you being sarcastic?"

"You bet. But you could, you know. Turn on that Southern charm of yours—you'd have ladies offering to pay twice the asking price just to hang around you."

"Shoot. You sure know how to spin one." A twinkle had appeared in his eyes.

"I'm serious. A husband and wife team—you'd have all the bases covered."

"Just one thing, Abby."

"What's that?"

"I don't mean to badmouth my wife, but most of the stuff she's got for sale is pure crap. At least compared to what you and the boys handle."

"That can be fixed. We can take you to auctions and point out the bargains—only quality stuff, of course."

He sighed heavily. "Yeah, but that takes money. Serious money we don't have."

"I could spot you the money."

"What does that mean?"

"I could loan you the money—I'd even charge interest if you prefer."

He cogitated on my offer for moment. "What if we can't pay it back?"

"Oh but you will. I'll only let you buy merchandise that has a high probability of resale at a profit. Of course it can't be all heavy wooden pieces, like Wynnell sells now. You need a little glitz in that shop. Some crystal chandeliers, original oil paintings, objects d'art—you know, a little pizzazz. My customers like to feel that they're about to make an important discovery every time they walk through the door."

Ed nodded. "Yeah, I can see that. Like maybe they could take your stuff to the *Antiques Roadshow* and find out it was worth a mint."

"Exactly. So how about it, Ed? You want to give it a shot?"

He nodded more vigorously. "Yeah, I think I do. It could be fun at that. How do you think Wynnell will react to this idea, or have you already run it past her?"

"You're the first. Say Ed, what are your plans for the rest of the day?"

"I was going to fish for another hour or two—what the heck, I'll quit now and run by her shop." He started to reel in his line.

"No, don't!"

Ed turned immediately. "Abby, what's wrong? Is Wynnell in trouble?"

I knew he could read my face as well as my tone. The dang cat was already out of the bag. The only sensible thing to do was let him help. Besides, he had every right to know.

"She's in jail, sweetie."

"Not street-walking again!"

Who knew Ed could joke? "Murder," I said quietly.

He made me repeat it. I did, then he asked, "Who is she accused of killing?"

"Marina Webbfingers. The woman for whom she did that landscaping job."

"Where's she being held?"

"City jail, I guess. I've already gotten her a lawyer—a Mr. Hammerhead on King Street."

When he reeled his line in without saying another word, I knew I'd done the right thing. Edwin Crawford now had two projects to work on, of course one much more urgent than the other. But with Wynnell's husband fully on board, I felt better about throwing myself into the investigation.

Even though he had his gear to pack, Ed made it out of the parking lot before I did. Although it was the middle of summer vacation, it was a late Tuesday morning, which meant it was the slowest time of the week for traffic. Mine was the only car I could see in my lane when I crossed the bridge over Folly River. Ahead of me lay Oak Island, with its tidal flats, and then Folly Creek. I lowered my window again to savor the smell of the pluff mud, but in the second or two it took to do so, a pickup truck appeared in my rearview mirror.

"What the heck?" Perhaps I used a stronger word, since one need not worry about being a lady while alone.

There was simply no reason why the truck couldn't pass me. Didn't the fool ever take driver's education? Although there are only three people in the entire state of South Carolina who don't tailgate—all three of them are nearsighted nuns—there is a limit to how close we follow cars. Less than one car length is just too close.

I stepped on the gas. So did the driver of the truck. Pushing the pedal further, I strained to get a better look in the rearview mirror. Faded blue overalls, no shirt, and a head the size of Crowders Mountain—*before* Granny Ledbetter dumped half of it into Lake Norman. Then he grinned, and I saw more spaces than teeth.

"I can ID you, you S.O.B.," I screamed. I was not, by the way, referring to Charleston's choicest neighborhood.

He appeared to laugh. I am ashamed to say that I responded by flipping him the bird. In fact, I pumped my middle finger up and down several times for emphasis. For your information, this is not how I raised my children, Susan and Charlie. My excuse, feeble though it may be, is that I was pretty sure he would understand the gesture. And I was right, because he flipped the bird right back at me.

But what he did next came as a total surprise.

# 8

At first I thought I'd hit a pothole. Although uncommon this far south, where freezes are infrequent, they do occur. At any rate, that's when I decided it was more important to keep my eyes on the road then it was to vent. Besides, who knew what jerks like him were capable of if they got angry?

It didn't take long to find out. The next time he hit the car, the jolt made my head snap forward. I couldn't believe what was happening.

"You idiot!" I screamed. "Stop it, stop it!"

Of course he couldn't hear me. Not that it would have made a difference. He backed off just enough to accelerate, then he rammed me again. If this kept up, my air bag would deploy, and it would probably smother me when it did. I had to get away. I literally pressed the pedal to the floor, and my car shot ahead. But it remained ahead for only a few seconds. Whatever make of pickup he was driving, it had a lot more pick-me-up than I would have thought.

What was I to do? I couldn't very well pull over, because there was virtually no shoulder to the road. Neither could I call the police on the spare cell phone I kept in the car, because I needed both hands to steer. It's not easy to handle a car hurtling down a rough asphalt road at ninety-plus miles.

"Use your head, dummy," I shouted aloud. "Don't freak out, dear. Use your head." Incidentally, I often call myself "dear" when talking to myself. If I don't consider myself precious, who will?

Fortunately, I often take my own advice as well. This time I took it literally. I had to stand on the gas pedal and crane my neck in order to get my brow to make contact with the center of the steering wheel, but when I did, I found the horn immediately. If I hadn't expected the blast—and there was just one short one—I would have veered off the road for sure. Lord knows I came dangerously close while honking with my head.

I looked in the rearview mirror as soon as I felt back in control. My intention had not been to startle my tormentor, but to draw attention to us. Although we still had not encountered traffic, there were some homes ahead, scattered along the edge of the marsh, and hopefully some kind soul, looking out his or her picture window, would summon help. Unless two vehicles mate—a rare occurrence even in car-crazy South Carolina—such close proximity would be a certain indicator of foul play. The same thought must have occurred to the tailgater. After a few seconds he dropped back a dozen yards, and then in a cloud of smoke he roared past me and into the horizon.

"But you pulled over and called the police the instant you could, right?" The concern on Bob's face was touching, but his tone reminded me of my high school algebra teacher, Mr. Sawyers, when he asked the class to turn in their homework.

"Of course not. I have my lunch date, and you know how time-consuming filling out a police report can be."

We were standing on the sidewalk in front of Slightly North of Broad. Both the Rob-Bobs and I had shown up five minutes early, but unless both of the Papadopouluses had popped in to use the potty, they had yet to arrive.

Rob laid a protective arm around my shoulders. He is the younger brother I wish I had.

"Abby, darling, Bob and I don't fill out a great deal of police reports. Yet when we do, you're always somehow involved."

I was about to protest when I spotted the well-dressed couple strolling up East Bay. Apparently they had elected to walk to the restaurant.

"Okay, you guys, go on and get yourselves seated. They're coming."

Rob slid his arm down my back. "Where? Not that pair of giant marshmallows wearing identical shorts and tank tops! Slime green and purple spandex—that was so 1990s."

Bob shuddered. "There should be a law against men who dine in tank tops. Underarm hair does not mix with food." He shuddered again. "Surely a restaurant this nice has a dress code."

"Relax guys, that's not them. It's the couple behind them. Tall, good-looking man—"

"You mean the stud?" Rob asked.

"Hey!" Bob is the less physically blessed half of the Rob-Bobs, and therefore a mite insecure.

"Guys, hurry up. I don't want them to know you're with me." I gave Rob a gentle push.

"All right, darling. Just make sure you seat him facing me." Of course he was only teasing his partner. They have been together eleven years and are as faithful as any heterosexual couple—hmm, perhaps I shouldn't take Rob's fidelity for granted.

At any rate, my friends slipped inside the restaurant while I straightened my clothes and pasted a cheery Charleston smile on my face. Every Southern girl of good breeding is skilled in the art of faux friendliness, so I had no doubts that mine was convincing.

The New Yorkers were quick to respond with

porcelain smiles of their own, and when Nick shook my hand, I felt a jolt of electricity that traveled well beyond the length of my arm. If Irena noticed the spark between us, she didn't let on.

"Is it always this humid?" she demanded.

I slipped out of Nick's grasp and opened the door for them. "Not always, dear. If a low front stalls along the coast, it can get a great deal more humid."

She didn't say anything else until we were seated and it was time to give our drink orders. "A dirty martini," she snapped to the waitress. "Vodka. Three olives. And it better be cold."

Even Nick blushed with embarrassment. Yet when he ordered his beer, he insisted that the foam head be no less than a quarter inch thick, and no more than an inch.

I ordered a sweet tea (ice tea with tons of sugar, for those of you who live north of the Line). This, not coffee, is the liquid that keeps the South running. There are folks who firmly believe that in the absence of the right blood type, sweet tea may be used for transfusions.

The Papadopouluses were a little less sure of themselves when it came to ordering from the lunch menu. After driving our waitress, a sweet young girl from Savannah, to the brink of madness, they both decided to begin their meal with chilled gazpacho soup, to be followed by poached mussels in white wine and garlic sauce. Irena selected the sautéed grouper glazed with whole mustard as her entrée, and Nick finally decided on the sautéed duck breast with plum glaze and mashed sweet potatoes. Much to my surprise, neither of them ordered the roast rack of lamb.

Yours truly had only the jumbo lump crab cakes, served over a sauté of corn, okra, and roasted yellow squash. I intended to save some room in my tiny tummy for the establishment's to-die-for crème brûlée.

As a matter of course we were all served a delightful sourdough bread, in which Nick seemed to take a special interest. He broke off a bite-size piece and smelled it, before rolling it into a little ball, which he popped in his mouth. His smile was a pretty good indication that he approved of the selection. That, and the fact that he hogged most of the loaf.

"So, tell me about yourselves," I said casually when the meal was well under way.

Irena, who was gorging on her grouper, dropped her fork. "Like what?"

"Well, what do you do for a living?" It is, I believe, the most frequently asked question in America, and therefore entirely safe.

"You already know that my husband is a stock market phenomenon." The fork was not only back in Irena's hand, but on the way to her mouth. It was soon apparent that the woman had no compunctions about chewing and chatting at the same time.

"But what about you, dear? Are you employed outside the home?"

Irena stabbed at her fish. "I'm a gem buyer."

"Diamonds?"

"Yes, of course."

I glanced at my engagement ring. Medieval theologians used to argue about how many angels could fit on the head of a pin. Well, only half of a very small angel could fit on the only diamond Greg could afford on his policeman's salary. And now that he was a shrimper—well, if I wanted to upgrade my stone, I'd have to pay for it myself.

"What does a good diamond go for these days? I know one has to take into account the four C's, but I just want a ballpark figure."

The skunk on her head came alive as she recoiled in horror. "I don't handle CZ. My gems are the real thing."

"I meant cut, clarity, carat, and color. Those are the four C's, aren't they?"

"Uh—certainly. But lately I've been dealing mostly with secondary gems. You know, emeralds, rubies, sapphires. That sort of thing."

"How interesting. I've never met a gem buyer

before. Does this mean you have to do a lot of traveling?"

She nodded. "Constantly. It's getting to the point where I'm going to have to soon get extra pages glued into my passport—what with all the stamps I've accumulated."

"Do you go with her?" I asked Nick.

"Every chance I get," he said. They were the first words he'd spoken all meal, discounting instructions to the waitress.

"But isn't that difficult, given your job on Wall Street?"

The dead skunk lurched forward. "Mrs. Washburn, did you invite us here to give us the third degree?"

"No, I'm only trying to be friendly. Down here the first three questions you ask new folks are: who are your people, where do you go to church, and where do you work. You'd already made it clear you didn't want to discuss religion, and I didn't feel comfortable leading with the 'who are your people' question, on account I always lose out when it's put to me."

"Oh? Why is that?"

"Because although my family has been in the South for generations, I'm the first to live in Charleston."

"I hear you," she said with surprising sympathy. "Manhattan has its pecking order, too. Fortunately my Nicky is so successful that we don't have that problem—not that we would anyway." She took a sip of her third dirty martini. "You see, my ancestors came over on the Mayflower."

"All the way from Greece?"

The dead skunk scowled, but I swear Nick snickered. "Mrs. Washburn," Irena said, "do you make it a habit of insulting your guests?"

"No, ma'am. I'm sorry. Say, did either of you happen to witness the argument yesterday between Mrs. Webbfingers and her garden designer? I hear it was quite something."

Irena gave Nick what I could only construe as a warning glare. "I'm afraid we were out," she said. "Went to some plantation. Boone Farm, I think it was."

"That would be Boone Hall, the most photographed plantation in America—well, that's what they claim. Did you enjoy it?"

"Actually we did. They have a cotton patch where you can pick your own cotton—although they said it was too early in the season. Still, who knew cotton grew on plants?"

Hadn't the woman ever cracked open a history book? Had she never read about slaves toiling in the broiling sun as they picked cotton? Had she not been forced to memorize the name of Eli Whitney, inventor of the cotton gin? Or did she think that was the name of a cocktail?

"There's another plantation nearby that has polyester bushes," I said wickedly. "They also have special plots where they hybridize cotton and polyester bushes to produce a cotton-poly blend. It's really quite interesting."

"Maybe we could see that tomorrow."

"Oh—and I forgot, there's a rayon farm just south of here on James Island. Rayon grows on trees, you know. The leaves are smooth and shiny, and the color is spectacular, but they tend to wrinkle when it rains."

Irena pushed her now empty plate aside. "Mrs. Washburn, I realize you're a businesswoman, and probably have a full schedule, but would you consider showing us around the area—for a fee of course?"

I pretended to ponder her question. "Yes," I said after a long pause, "I suppose I might be able to rearrange my schedule."

"Excellent."

Feeling that I had made a little progress, I quite enjoyed my crème brûlée. Irena made no comment about her Key Lime Tart, although she wolfed it down in exactly four bites. Nick, on the other hand, carefully dissected his triple chocolate cake before eating it crumb by crumb.

I assumed that since the Rob-Bobs left the restaurant during our dessert, they had concluded that I was in no kind of danger. But when I called them the minute I was free of my guests, I learned just how wrong my assumption was.

# 9

"**I** don't like them, Abby," Rob said, before I had a chance to even say hello. The inventor of caller ID is not going to get a Christmas card from me.

"*Why* don't you like them? It's her hair, isn't it?"

"No, but come to think of it, she could get a job hosting late night horror flicks on TV. But they're fakes, Abby."

"What do you mean?"

"Well, they're not married, for one thing."

I sighed. "Here we go again. I suppose you're going to tell me that Nick Papadopoulus is gay. For your information, Rob, not every handsome man is gay. And neither is every celebrity. And don't you start in again on Santa Claus."

"Abby, darling, how many straight men do you know who wear bright red suits with white fur trim?"

I was unconvinced. "How many gay men wear red suits with white fur trim?"

97

"Touché. But it was as plain as the nose on Bob's face that this couple had no chemistry between them. Zip, zero, nada."

I could hear Bob protesting loudly in the background. His nose is remarkable, but his deep bass voice is his most distinguishing attribute.

"Leave my schnoz out of this," he boomed.

"That's right," I said, "leave Bob alone. Besides, I know plenty of married couples who lack chemistry."

"Then how about his chains?"

"What about them?"

"Ten carat gold, Abby. And the longest one is just plate."

"You can tell that from across a room?"

"Seen enough cheap stuff to spot the difference. What is this guy, anyway? A pimp?"

"He's a Wall Street broker."

"Just like my grandmother was a grand champion on *Fear Factor*."

"She was? I mean, so what's this guy's game?"

"It's your job to find out, Abby. Looks like you've got your work cut out for you. By the way, thanks for a really good lunch. Bob thanks you, too."

"But we still have the lunch I made, and the emu salad sandwiches are soggy now," Bob blared in the background. "And what the heck am I supposed to do with all those quail eggs?"

Mercifully, Rob hung up.

* * *

Bob should have given his peculiar lunch to C.J. The big gal will eat anything. Her Granny Ledbetter back in Shelby believed that every living creature was a potential meal. She used real amphibians when she made toad-in-the-hole. When she couldn't find toads, she used frogs. Kiss one of Granny's casseroles and you might well find yourself face-to-face with a prince—albeit a dead one.

C.J. had just closed a sale on a Hepplewhite dining room set when I entered my shop. She greeted me with her usual goofy grin.

"Hey Abby, you're not here to check up on me, are you?"

"Of course not, dear. But how are things going?"

She told me about the sale.

"Did you give them the standard discount?" I asked. Many customers don't realize that we in the trade often build a discount into our asking price. Since this particular dining room set cost an arm and a leg (very nice legs I might add, barely scarred by centuries of use), ten percent was a hefty hunk of cash.

"They didn't ask, Abby."

"Well, in that case, you and I will split the difference. And no need to thank me, C.J., because you deserve it."

"Actually, Abby, they paid me more than the listed price."

"Get out of town!"

"You see, some other couple was looking at it first, and I started going on and on about what a great deal this was, so then this second couple jumps into the conversation, and the next thing I know they're bidding."

"C.J., you're a genius, you know that?"

"Don't be silly, Abby. I've known that since I was one."

I smiled patiently. "C.J., one-year-olds don't know anything about intelligence quotients. They can barely speak."

She looked me straight in the eye—of course she had to look down, while I looked up. "I could talk at three months, Abby. I began to read at four months."

There was no point in arguing, especially since she was probably telling the truth. The woman could speak seventeen languages, including Mandarin Chinese. I, on the hand, sometimes have trouble with English—especially the hard words like "subliminal."

"C.J., darling, as long as everything is fine here at the shop—and you're obviously doing a great job—I'm going to leave everything in your hands for the next few days. If that's all right with you."

"Sure, Abby. And if you need any ideas about how to track down the killer, just holler."

I turned my head so that rolling my eyes wouldn't offend her. Having raised a teenage girl, I know firsthand just how irritating ocular rotation can be—at least for the observer. For the roller, it does help to relieve stress.

"Thanks, C.J., but I'll manage just fine."

"I'm sure you will, Abby. But if it was me, I'd start by inviting some of those bed and breakfast guests to tea. Tourists love having tea in historic Charleston homes. And that way, you could kill two birds with one stone."

"Excuse me?"

"You know, give your mama some business. Mozella is going to hang out a sign, but I'm sure she'll appreciate any customers you bring over."

"Hold it right there! Mama's in business? What kind of business?"

"Serving tea. Abby, are you a little bit slow? Not that there is anything wrong with that. Cousin Arbuckle was the slow one in our family. Couldn't even tie his shoes until he was six months old. Granny says she thought he would never amount to anything, until he and Al Gore invented the Internet together."

"Mama can't run a business out of our—make that *my*—home!"

"Why not, Abby? You told her to get a job."

"Yes, but—oh, never mind. Where is Mama now?"

"Baking scones, I think."

I ran for my car.

I was too late. In the space of a few short hours Mama had turned my beautiful eighteenth century home into a tea shop. She'd even hung her shingle: MAMA'S TEA PARLOR. It was a only a temporary sign, Magic Marker on cardboard, but she had done a good job of drawing a cup and saucer, and I must admit that the overall affect was cute. Mama was cute as well in her pink and white gingham apron with the extra long ruffles.

"So, Abby, what do you think?"

"I think you should have asked me first, because I would have said no."

"That's why I didn't." The oven timer buzzed. "Just a minute, dear, while I check on the scones."

I followed her into the kitchen. "It's not just that I don't want a parade of strangers in my house, Mama, but this is illegal. You need a business permit, and a certificate from the board of health."

She pivoted on her pumps. "But what will I do with all this food? Besides the scones, I made gingerbread with lemon sauce, some yummy macaroons, the cutest miniature quiches, and these little sandwiches with the crusts cut off. Let's see, there's cucumber, watercress, tuna salad—"

"I'll have some friends over for tea."

Mama frowned. "Abby, I already know your friends. I want to meet new people."

"These are new people, Mama."

She yanked the scones out of the oven at just the right moment. They were golden brown, without being overdone, and smelled heavenly. There appeared to be two kinds: cheese and raisin.

"Will you have to be here when they come, Abby?"

"Of course. In fact, I was just about to ask you if you wouldn't mind hanging out in the kitchen."

"Why Abigail Wiggins Timberlake Washburn! Shame on you for trying to banish your poor old mama from her own living room."

"Technically it's my living room, Mama, and I need to speak to these people alone."

"Abby, are you ashamed of me? Because if you are—well, I've never been so hurt in all my born days."

My sigh helped cool the scones. "I'm not ashamed of you, Mama. Honest. It's just that—well, these aren't really friends. They're just people I need to interview."

Mama put her hands on hips, a gesture that emphasized her cinched waist even more. "This has to do with Wynnell, doesn't it?"

"Maybe—okay, yes."

"So what do you want me to do? Leave *your* house?"

"No."

"Oh I see, you're going to banish me to the kitchen. Well, in that case, there's one thing you should know."

My next sigh rustled Mama's ruffles. "Make it fast, because I'm really pressed for time."

Mama had a strange, triumphant look in her eyes.

# 10

"Abby, darling," Mama said, "I've already invited guests to tea."

I wish I could say that I couldn't believe how much nerve she had. Unfortunately, I could. The examples were legion. Perhaps the example that stood out the most in my memory, and which I still chafed at, if I allowed myself to think about it, was my high school prom. The *senior* prom. Mama canceled my date with Brad Belk, a college freshman she didn't like, and "substituted" Howard Craighead, a high school *sophomore*. I would have spent the entire night on my bed crying, but since Howard had yet to get his driver's license, and had a daddy richer than Howard Hughes, I got to ride to the prom in a real, chauffeured limousine, one that was privately owned. Not the kind that smells vaguely like puke, and into which promgoers pack themselves like circus clowns.

"Then you'll have to uninvite them, Mama."

"You don't want me to, dear."

"Yes, I do."

The smallest of smirks played at corners of her perfectly rouged mouth. "I invited the Zimmermans and the Thomases."

"I don't care if these are your church friends—"

"They're not, dear. They're guests at double 0 Legare St."

When I was a little girl and stared with my mouth wide open, Mama used to say that my eyes would pop out. Not that it would matter, she'd tell me, because I would choke to death on a fly at the same time. It's a good thing there weren't any flies in the house at the moment, and although my peepers didn't pop, they must have presented quite a sight.

"Abby, that look—you're doing it again. Just don't be mad, dear, because I'm only trying to help. Wynnell is my friend, too, remember?"

Never look a gift horse in the mouth, even if it's just a tiny pony named Mozella. Besides, there would be plenty of time to yell at her—respectfully, of course—when my friend was cleared of wrongdoing and out of the clinker.

"Why not the Papadopouluses as well?" I asked.

"They said you were meeting them for lunch. Lordy, Abby, it was hard enough trying to find these two couples. I had to get descriptions from the maid, and then hunt for them in the Market. You know what that's like."

Indeed I did. The Market, which runs the length of Market Street, between Concord and Meeting, was built in 1788, and is at times referred to as the Slave Market, although slaves were never sold there. House slaves were, however, sent to shop for produce and dry goods at the many stalls on the lower level. Today it is thronged by tourists in search of a good deal on souvenirs, which range from elegant sweetgrass baskets woven by the Gullah descendants of slaves to general flea market knickknacks manufactured in China. At times the narrow aisles of the market can get so crowded that a small woman like myself—or Mama—can get literally carried along with the masses. I once visited all the buildings *twice* without ever intending to do so.

"Yes, I know what the place is like. It's a wonder you found them. Did you have any trouble convincing complete strangers to come over for tea?"

Mama has a strong Upstate accent, the kind folks up there used to have before Yankee transplants, relocating to Charlotte, spilled over the border into South Carolina and modified our speech. Although I suppose television is partly to blame for homogenizing our speech. At any rate, Mama's Rock Hill accent differs from a Charleston one. The latter pronounces "house" a bit like they do in Tidewater, Virginia, which, to my ear, sounds a bit like the way many Canadians say it. Fortunately, most tourists from north of the Line can't tell the difference between Upstate and Lowcountry accents.

"Now, sugar," she said, "you know I can be just as charming as Miss Scarlet herself."

"Frankly, Mama, I'm surprised you don't wear wooden hoops instead of petticoats. Think of the all money you'd save on starch." I smiled sweetly. "So, what time is this tea?"

"Four o'clock. That gives you plenty of time to change into something decent."

"You mean a dress, right?"

"Of course, not dear. I'm not as old-fashioned as you think. A Sunday skirt and blouse combination will do just fine."

"Whatever, Mama. Just as long as you agree not to bother us during tea."

"Don't be silly, dear. It was my idea."

"I know, but this is a murder investigation, and I'm the one with the expertise. Relatively, at least." I already knew that Mama was going to be as hard to shake loose as a tick, but it was worth a try.

"Abigail, darling, what if I serve you the tea, and then retire to the kitchen?"

"Promise you won't interfere in any way?"

"You have my word."

"And you won't stick your head out the door every five seconds with questions of your own?"

"Why Abby, I'm offended."

"Mama!"

"All right, dear. There is no need to get your knickers in a knot. I'll behave."

And I'll never eat another piece of chocolate.

The two couples arrived separately. Like most tourists, they'd elected to stroll through our charming streets and absorb the ambiance. The route from number 7 Squiggle Lane to double 0 Legare is flanked by the some of the city's most historic architecture, and certainly its finest gardens. I often wish I could see my new hometown through the eyes of a tourist again.

At any rate, Herman and Estelle Zimmerman arrived first. Herman is a beefy man with a farmer's tan and a ruff of graying hair sticking up from underneath his collar. He is one of those rare people whose lips don't part when smiling, but the huge grin stretches practically from ear to ear. His wife Estelle is a slender woman whose body looks much younger than her head. I'm sure she cannot help the suitcase-size bags under her eyes (no doubt quite handy for short trips), but it is immediately obvious that her hair is not only an improbable color, but too dark for a woman her age. As for her thin penciled brows, she would be better not having any. She looks perpetually surprised, although perhaps she is— every time she sees her blue-black coiffure in the mirror.

"Howdy, little lady," Herman said, and thrust out a hand the size of Switzerland.

I shook hands reluctantly. I value my fingers and the ability to write and eat unaided. Although I was not permanently maimed by this senseless ritual, I would like to refute the adage that one cannot squeeze blood from a stone.

Estelle's handshake was quite the opposite. It felt like someone had placed a boneless, skinless fillet of fish on my palm. Mahi mahi, I think. I dropped it as soon as I could do so without appearing rude.

"Welcome to Charleston," I said, and ushered them inside.

Herman and Estelle glanced around my living room with the same apparent reverence and awe one might experience at a special exhibit at the New York Metropolitan Museum of Art.

"Are those sconces Venetian?" Estelle asked. "If you don't mind me asking."

"Yes. Aren't they lovely?"

"I thought so. Eighteenth century?"

"Right again. Are you an antiques collector?"

"Me?" She giggled behind a damp hand.

"My wife was a history major," Herman said. "But she knows everything. Ask her a question. Any question. Doesn't have to be about history."

I attempted a gracious smile. "Maybe later. Won't you two please be seated?"

They appeared not to hear me. "Go ahead, ask her," Herman insisted.

"Okay," I said, grasping the first thought that flitted through my mind. "Why was Napoleon defeated at Waterloo?"

She giggled again. "Because he had hemorrhoids."

"I beg your pardon?"

"Well, most history books will tell you that he made a tactical blunder by waiting until midday for the ground to dry out before moving his troops. But they don't usually print why such a brilliant mind made a mistake of this magnitude. The answer is that he suffered from hemorrhoids and was sleep-deprived that day."

It sounded like one of C.J.'s infamous Shelby stories, but who was I to argue? I had, at best, a precious few minutes to grill this couple before the Thomases arrived, or before a crafty Clouseau clad in crinolines cavorted in, carrying coconut cookies.

"Please," I begged, "have a seat."

One of the perks of owning your own antique store is that you get to redecorate with whatever pieces of merchandise catch your eye. One month I'm in a Victorian mood, the next month I'm in a rococo frame of mind. This month it was Italian. Although Herman wasn't the largest man I'd seen lately, I must confess I was nervous about him sitting on my eighteenth-century chairs, which, although quite sturdy when they were built, were not intended for twenty-first-century bottoms. To be sure, I breathed a small sigh of relief when the gilt and needlepoint chair held its own.

But no sooner had his bottom connected to the chair than Dmitri came prancing in from one of the rear rooms of the house and jumped into Herman's lap. My beloved pussy must have landed on a fairly sensitive area because Herman gasped loudly.

"Dmitri off!" I commanded.

My ten pound bundle of joy ignored me as usual. In fact, his reaction was to knead Herman's thigh while swatting the poor man in the face with his tail.

"It's all right," Herman said, between swats. "I love cats."

I smiled, much relieved. The world is sharply

divided between cat lovers and cat haters. There doesn't seem to be much middle ground with this species. Incidentally, I love both cats and dogs, but lost custody of our dog when Buford and I divorced.

Dmitri appeared to love the Zimmermans, because after finally settling in Herman's lap, he left abruptly to explore Estelle. However, it didn't take him too long to decide that Herman's lap was more comfortable, and after settling in a second time, he fell right to sleep.

"Mr. Zimmerman," I said, over the sound of Dmitri's snores, "where is home, and what do you do there?"

"Call me Herman, little lady. And we're from Wisconsin. We own a dairy farm—mostly Holsteins. Of course we've got ourselves some help now that we're getting older. Used to sell our milk to the big cheese outfits—" He slapped his knee. "That one always makes me laugh. Anyway, still do, but ice cream's the moneymaker now. You ever count the number of flavors at your local supermarket?"

"I can't say that I have. So, what brings you to Charleston?"

He looked confused. "We're on vacation."

Estelle leaned forward. She seemed uncomfortable on her chair. Perhaps she was worried that she might perspire and stain the needlepoint with unabsorbed hair dye.

"We've heard so much about South Carolina," she said. "Charleston in particular. It certainly lives up to its reputation."

"Thank you." I could only hope that was a compliment. "Herman, Estelle—if I may—"

"Please, call me Estee."

"Estee, it is. And you may call me Abby. I hope the two of you don't judge Charleston by what happened last night. It's really a very safe city."

Herman forgot to grin. "I had no idea I would be putting Estee in so much danger. This kind of thing doesn't go on in Wisconsin."

Estelle reached over and patted her husband's knee. "It does in Milwaukee, just not where we live."

Herman looked at me. "Tell me, little lady, why a maniac like that was running loose in the first place."

"We heard the fight," Estee said, before I could defend my friend. "It was horrible. At first I thought it was someone's TV. All that screeching, and those ugly threats."

Herman nodded. "Sounded like crazed banshees—not that we hear a lot of them up in Wisconsin, mind you."

Fortunately for all three of us, the doorbell rang before I could formulate a careful reply. I skipped gratefully from the room to answer it. But man, was I ever in for a big surprise.

# 11

"**C**an I help you?" I asked the man on the front porch. He was wearing a clerical collar, but I'm not up on my denominations. All I know is that he wasn't from Mama's church. She's drags me to Grace Episcopal on Wentworth Street whenever she can (which isn't frequently by a long shot). I don't think she's interested in saving my soul as much as she is shoring up my social standing. In Charleston the big three are St. Michaels, St. Philips, and Grace. Since our pedigree isn't quite as long as a roll of toilet tissue, she finds Grace to be the best fit. Their motto is: "There are no strangers at Grace; only friends you haven't met."

"Abby?" the strange priest asked.

"I gave at the office," I blurted. "I mean, I wrote a check and put it in the offering plate."

"Abby, I'm your brother. Toy."

I pulled the door shut behind me. *Toy?* That simply wasn't possible. Sure, I'd heard that my ne'er-do-well sibling had decided to quit drifting through life and attend an Episcopal seminary. But that took years, didn't it? Besides, he only chose that vocation to curry Mama's favor. He never intended to stick it out. And anyway, my brother inherited all his genes from Daddy's side of the family. Toy was tall and lean, with movie star good looks. His thick hair was naturally blond and the envy of every girl who knew him. This man, although tall, was fleshy, like an ex-football player gone to seed. He did, however, have a fine head of golden hair.

"Abby, remember when I poured a jar of honey into the back of our piano and blamed it on you? It took you two weeks to clean the strings."

My knees went week and I grabbed the lion's head door knocker for support. "What was the name of the gerbil I had in the third grade?"

"You mean the one I flushed down the toilet? To be fair, Abby, I was only five. And by the way, its name was Jolie. You just thought it was a girl, but it really was a boy."

How should one act when a prodigal brother— uh, make that a Father—returns home? Toy had been the golden boy, the apple of both my parents' hearts. No doubt he would have remained a luminous fruit had not Daddy died prematurely. For the next thirty years my perfect little brother dedicated himself to proving that he wasn't so perfect.

He was quite successful in that endeavor. He seldom called home, never visited, and, by his own admission in the only letter he ever wrote, liked to "get high and have a good time with the ladies." Most of what we knew about Toy we heard through the grapevine.

Mama's heart, which hadn't had a chance to heal after Daddy's demise, remained broken. Still, she managed to keep a stiff upper lip—perhaps she used her crinoline starch—whenever discussing her son. She didn't fool me, however. I knew she mourned her beloved son, and if I allowed myself, I could a dredge up a great deal of resentment—both toward Mama and Toy. For the sake of my sanity, I rarely visited that basement room in my soul.

"Are you all right?" Toy asked. He seemed genuinely concerned.

I tried to smile. "I'm fine as frogs' hair—heck no, I'm not! Why are you here, Toy? To make amends now that you've apparently found religion? So help me, if you hurt Mama, I'll—I'll—"

Toy started to reach for me, so I flattened myself against the door, like a Carolina chameleon trying to avoid detection. I still have all my own teeth and I don't bite my nails. If he didn't respect my need for distance, he might require a little first aid.

"Abby, I came here to say I'm sorry."

"You should have called first. We're very busy."

I saw the look of hurt in his eyes, and I am ashamed to say that I was glad. If Toy had the slightest idea of how much pain he'd caused us, he would never have just shown up out of the blue like that.

"Abby," Mama called from behind the door, "who is it? Is it the Thomases?"

I froze. Mama couldn't find out like this. She hated surprises, changes of any kind. If she saw Toy without first being prepared, she might suffer a heart attack.

"Shhh!" I glared at my brother. "Don't you say a word."

Toy never did obey me. "Mama!" he called out in a voice loud enough to wake the dead over in Berkeley County. "Mama, it's me—Toy!"

I heard the door behind me open and then a soft "mew" like a kitten might emit. Before I spun around, she'd collapsed in a pile of crinolines.

There was nothing I could do to stop Toy. He carried Mama into the house, and since my fancy-schmancy living room doesn't have a sofa, he laid her on her own bed. Meanwhile the Zimmermans trotted after us, all the while staring wide-eyed at what they probably considered to be typical Charleston tea entertainment. After all, just the evening before, a woman had been bashed over the head in the garden outside their bed and breakfast.

Mama—thank heavens—had not suffered a heart attack, but had merely fainted. Her voluminous skirt and petticoats had saved her from any physical injuries. They had not, of course, saved her from her prodigal son. When she came to on the bed, she clutched at her pearls, meowed like a kitten again, and fainted. Just in case we didn't understand just how upset she was, she repeated the procedure twice.

"I told you," I snarled. "Now leave."

Neither the Zimmermans, nor my brother, budged.

"I'm not going anywhere," Toy said. "She's my mother, too."

Mama came around the third time. Her eyes were as wide as magnolia blossoms, and her cheeks were just as white. It took her a few tries to speak, but when she did, her voice was calm, almost dispassionate.

"Would everyone please leave the room—except for you, Toy."

"Mama," I wailed. "Don't listen to him. He's a snake in a priest's collar."

Herman had the nerve to step even closer to Mama's bed. "If you can't trust a priest, little lady," he said, "then who can you trust?" Never mind that Herman was holding Dmitri, who was trying to rake Toy with his claws. When an animal hates you, there is usually a good reason.

Toy cleared his throat. "I'm actually still a deacon; I have a year left of seminary. I don't get ordained to Holy Orders until next spring."

"So, he's a snake in a deacon's collar, Mama. He'll only let you down."

Mama sat bolt upright. "Abigail Louise Wiggins Timberlake Washburn. I've had quite enough of that. I wish to speak with your brother alone, and that's that."

Or what? She'd send me to my room in a house that I owned? She'd ground me from going out with my husband? She'd withold the allowance from herself that I gave her every month? Toy's sudden appearance was bound to twist our family dynamic into an unrecognizable shape.

"The 'or,'" Mama said, unfairly reading my mind, "is that I'll be disappointed in you."

"In *me*? Mama, I'm the one who's always been there for you."

She looked me straight in the eye. "Exactly. Please be there for me now."

Although I was the shortest adult I knew, Mama had still managed to hit me below the belt. I had no choice but to follow her wishes.

The Thomases were a full half hour late, and they didn't have the courtesy to apologize. They did, however, bring a bottle of wine. It was a good California wine, but with a Piggly Wiggly sticker, which probably meant it was purchased right here in Charleston.

It may be unfair, but beautiful people can get away with murder. The Thomases were disgustingly good-looking. John Thomas was tall, with a wasp waist and muscles that bulged beneath his crisp, baby blue shirt. His wife Belinda was also tall and with a tiny waist, but instead of muscles, she bulged with silicone. Between her improbable bosoms, and lips the size of a taco, she never need fear drowning. Both of them were blond and blue-eyed. But remarkably, it appeared as if John was the one who had to apply the bottle on a regular basis.

To determine if one is a natural blonde, besides the matching cup and saucer test, closely scrutinizing the eyebrows usually suffices. True blondes have to *add* color. And speaking of color, Belinda sported a deep tan, but despite the claims of sunless tanning manufacturers, you can tell the difference. Especially when several days have elapsed since the last application and the product starts to wear off. Belinda, it appeared, had missed a couple of days.

At any rate, by the time the Thomases had arrived, the Zimmermans were back in their chairs, and I had begun to lay out Mama's spread of goodies. The two couples had already met, so ostensibly I could get right down to business. But first I had to concentrate, a near impossible task with Mama and Toy holed up in a bedroom whispering. I know, I could have just acted the part of an interested hostess—Lord knows I'd done plenty of acting during my first marriage, to Buford, but that was only five minutes at a stretch.

"Would you like some milk with your lemon?" I asked my guests. "Or would you prefer tea?"

The Zimmermans chose milk—no surprise— and the Thomases, who confessed to being vegans, elected for lemon. I had a feeling they would all have gone with beer, if given the opportunity.

Since I'd already chatted with the farmer and his wife, it was time to concentrate on the younger couple. And frankly, it was not hard to look at either of them.

"Where are you from?" I asked, trying to sound casual. What I really wanted to be doing was holding a glass against Mama's bedroom wall.

"California."

"That's nice. L.A.?"

"Cambria."

"That's near San Simeon—where the Hearst Castle is, right?"

"Right," John said. "Have you been there?"

"Yes. I love that part of the country. Cambria is so charming, and as for the Hearst Castle, I've never lusted in my heart so much—except for maybe when I visit the Biltmore. We stayed in this very reasonable motel where they served us breakfast in bed. Now what was the name of it? It was right on the ocean, and we had a spectacular view of waves crashing on rocks."

The Thomases exchanged glances. "We just recently moved there," John said.

"Oh, from where?"

"Santa Calamari," Belinda said. "Have you been there?"

"I'm afraid not. What do you do?"

"We're travel agents," John said quickly.

"Estee and I plan to do a lot of traveling when we retire," Herman said. He looked at his wife as if for confirmation.

But Estee's mind was elsewhere. She poked her blue-black do with a finger, perhaps to stimulate the brain cells. Not that they needed any.

"I've never heard of Santa Calamari," she said. "Calamari is squid. I don't think the Church would name a saint after squid."

"My Estee knows everything," Herman said, with unmistakable pride in his voice.

John squirmed. "The founding fathers did it as a joke. All the streets are named after seafood. There's, uh—Octopus Alley, Roe Row, Pompano Place, Lumpfish Lane—"

"Herring Heights," Belinda said. John gave her what my children used to call "the evil eye."

Something was rotten in California, and it

wasn't just the seafood. Something was rotten in New York and Wisconsin as well. No matter. That's why I had agreed to entertain these folks, even before Mama interfered with her tea. Fortunately, I knew just the right question to ask next.

# 12

"How did y'all learn about the Webbfingerses' bed and breakfast?"

"You mean La Parterre?" Estelle asked.

"Do they own another?"

"I'm afraid I don't know the answer to that. But Herman and I read about this one in the back of a magazine."

"Oh? Which one?"

She shrugged and looked at her husband.

"A dairy magazine," he said, after the slightest of pauses. "*Udder Perfection*, it's called. They have ads in the back for vacation rentals, hotels, and such. Most of the stuff is up in Myrtle Beach, but there were some Charleston listings."

I turned to the Thomases. "How about y'all?"

John's smile revealed that either life was very unfair or else he had a very good dentist. "We travel agents get tons of brochures. But if we really want to recommend a place, we have to check it out ourselves. La Parterre sounded particularly appealing, and neither of us had ever seen Charleston."

"Did any of you keep the ads?"

They all shook their heads.

I turned back to the Thomases. "Did y'all witness the incident last evening?"

Belinda blinked. "Which one?"

"I beg your pardon?"

"Well, there were two incantations that I know of."

"She means 'altercations,' " John said quickly.

"There were?"

Belinda nodded vigorously. I was absolutely right; there were no dark roots.

"There was that fight between that crabby old maid and the woman with only one eyebrow, and then there was that couple from New York."

"Oh yeah," Herman said. "I nearly got involved in that one. A man shouldn't ever talk to his wife that way."

For a second or two I forgot all about Toy. "Tell me about both fights," I said to Belinda. "Which took place first?"

"The two women. At first it was kind of hard to understand them because of their accents—no offense, Mrs. Washburn—"

"Abby."

"Mrs. Abby. But then I sort of got used to the way they talked—well, screamed really. People don't usually get that mad in California."

"I'm sure Calamari is a very calm place, dear. Please continue. What were they fighting about?"

"Dead flowers. Can you believe that?"

I couldn't. Wynnell has been under a lot of stress, and she does possess a wee bit of a temper, but she is a mature woman with experience in solving conflicts—never mind that the last time she and Ed had a major tiff, she ran off to Japan to become the world's oldest geisha-in-training. Besides, Marina Webbfingers was a blue-blooded society dame. I couldn't imagine her getting all bent out of shape over wilted wax-leaf begonias. The dryness of her martini might be a serious issue, but not her flower beds.

"There had to be more to it than that," I said.

"Money," John said.

Belinda's blond locks opened and shut like a stage curtain when she nodded. "The truth of all evil, isn't that what they say?"

"That must be a Calamariism," I said, suppressing a smile. I turned to John. "Money?"

"Mrs. Webbfingers shouted that she wasn't going to pay the landscaper for a bunch of dead plants. She said if she had wanted a desert garden, she would have asked for cactus. Then the landscaper said that she was going to sue for her wages, and Mrs. Webbfingers said that would be a big laugh because she knew all the judges and they would decide in her favor. Then they started trading insults, until finally they were just cursing. Frankly, Abby, I was rather surprised by their language. Well, the landscaper's didn't surprise me as much as Mrs. Webbfingers's did. I'd pegged her for a real Southern lady."

"She called the landscaper a 'hankie,' " Belinda said. "What's so bad about that? Anyway, that's when she really blew her pop."

"Her top," John said gently.

"Whatever."

"Could Mrs. Webbfingers have said 'Yankee'?" I asked.

John winked his answer. It is a good man who doesn't want to embarrass his wife.

"Well," I said, "calling someone a Yankee, when they're not, can be fighting words around here. But no one would kill over them," I added hastily. That was sort of true. The War of Northern Aggression is not over for a few folks, but they tend to come from the fringes of our society, and most of them feel cheated by life in general. Wynnell Crawford, however, is not one of them.

"Southerners are strange," Belinda had the nerve to say.

I counted silently to ten before responding.

Then I counted backward to one. In Spanish. Since I nearly failed that course in college, it took me longer than you might think.

"What about the New Yorkers?" I said, addressing John.

"Mostly she was yelling at him for talking too much—said he'd blow things if he kept flapping his gums. Then he started in swearing. Said some really ugly things—things I shouldn't repeat here."

"I see."

The Zimmermans had remained strangely quiet during my exchange with the Thomases. Perhaps they had nothing to share. Just because they heard the ruckus didn't mean they'd been able to catch what was being said, except for the cuss words. On the other hand, they'd seemed quite willing to talk before the Thomases showed up. And, if body language meant anything, the two couples did not appear to be on the best of terms. Of course people can lie with their bodies, just like they can lie with their tongues.

It was my intention to put the Zimmermans back on the spit for a more thorough grilling, when Dmitri leaped off Herman's lap and bounded for the front door. The poor dairy farmer shrieked in a falsetto voice that was, fortunately, only temporary.

My cat's behavior could mean only one thing.

Greg, my husband, the love of my life, was home. Although Greg is a shrimper, and not a fisherman, a good many fish find their way into his nets, and by the end of the day he smells like the bottom two inches of an aquarium—one that hasn't been cleaned in days. Oddly enough, this aroma doesn't do much for me, but Dmitri goes gaga over it. He can smell his pungent "papa" from a hundred feet away.

Sure enough, seconds later the door opened and in stepped Greg, all six feet of him. A well-bred man, he tried hard not to appear startled by the assemblage in his living room.

"If y'all will just give me a moment," he said, "I'll wash up and be back to introduce myself."

I grabbed one of my hubby's slimy sleeves. "No need, darling, I'll make the introductions for you. You see, my guests were just about to leave."

John Thomas was the first to take the hint. He sprang to his feet and announced his name. But instead of extending his hand, he waved. Everyone laughed, and soon the others were up and doing the same thing. For the record, the affable Herman Zimmerman was the last to get up—although that may simply have been because he had more to hoist. Nonetheless, it took a good five minutes for everyone to leave.

They were halfway down the walk before I remembered to make plans for the following day. "Anyone up for a private tour tomorrow? I promise to show you sights most tourists don't see."

"I'm a happily married man," Herman said without missing a beat.

Everyone laughed, but all agreed that a private tour would be just the ticket. We settled on ten o'clock as the perfect time to embark on our adventure. And in a rare moment of mental clarity, Belinda Thomas not only remembered the Papadopouluses, but volunteered to pass the news on to "that cute man and his wife."

When we were finally alone—except for Dmitri—I threw myself into Greg's redolent arms. "Darling, you wouldn't believe what happened today!"

"Can't wait to hear. You're always a trip, hon. You want to tell me now, or after I shower?"

In the meantime Dmitri was trying to climb Greg's pant leg. No doubt my normally fastidious feline thought he would find fish if he only climbed high enough.

"After you shower is probably best—but I need to fill you in on one thing first."

"Let me see . . . your brother Toy has decided to grow up, and to prove it, he just married a widow with thirteen children. Of course now he has to give up watching cartoons all day and get a job.

Hey, I could always use somebody to scrape the barnacles off the bottom of my boat—especially when there are sharks around."

I pushed myself from his embrace. "How did you know?"

"Know what?"

"That Toy decided to grow up?"

"I was just kidding, Abby. Sorry, if I went too far. It's just that I feel like I know him, even though I've never met him. Well, at least I know his type."

"You know the old Toy's type. The new Toy is in Mama's bedroom."

"What?"

"He just showed up at the door this afternoon. He's almost a priest now—already been ordained a deacon or something. Remember I told you he was tall, blond, sort of an Adonis type? You've seen pictures, you know what I mean."

"Are you trying to say he's gotten shorter?" Greg's sapphire blue eyes twinkled.

"No! But he's gained a lot of weight and looks a whole lot older. I didn't recognize him at all."

"Maybe he's an impostor." Greg was only half kidding.

"No, he's the real thing. He admitted to flushing my gerbil, Jolie, down the john."

"Holy smoke, hon. This has got to be a shock for Mozella."

"What about me?" I wailed.

Greg folded me back into his arms. "Maybe it's an opportunity, hon."

"For what? To be hurt again?"

"To get to know the real Toy better."

"The real Toy parks cars in Hollywood because he can't get a job as an actor. The rest of the time he spends drinking and smoking Acapulco Gold—or whatever the latest preferred marijuana variety is." Dang it. It was much easier when my little brother could be pigeonholed as a dropout and a loser. A penitent prodigal potential priest was a whole different ball game.

"Give him a chance, Abby. Someday you'll be glad you did."

I grunted agreement. Anything to get Greg into the shower and off my case.

Mama is a miracle worker. Despite all the work she'd done on the tea, not to mention the shock of having her baby boy back home again, she whipped up a proper dinner for the four of us. But the biggest miracle was seeing Toy help her in the kitchen.

When they walked out of Mama's bedroom—seconds after Greg got in the shower—Mama had her arm around her son's waist. From that moment on the two were inseparable. When Toy started peeling potatoes, I'm the one who nearly had a heart attack.

The last time I saw Toy do anything to help around the kitchen was when he was seventeen. He'd been given the simple job of loading the dishwasher. How hard can that be? It's not like he had to chop down a tree, saw a cord of wood, boil water, butcher a hog and render its fat to make soap, etc. But instead of performing his straightforward task—except for having to first unload the dishwasher—my lazy brother rinsed off the dishes and then spray-painted them white. Even the pots and pans. Of course the paint didn't stick. Toy then loaded the dishes in a cardboard carton and put them in the back of a friend's pickup and drove them through a car wash. While trying to unload said carton, the soggy box split open, and every single one of the dishes broke. Mama's favorite skillet was dented as well.

Do you think Toy got in trouble for that? Think again. Mama's baby boy . . .

"Abby, wake up!" Mama's voice was unusually sharp, so I started. Somehow I'd managed to fume my way into a fog that lasted until we were all seated for dinner. Greg and I were in our rightful places as host and hostess, while Mama and Toy sat across from each other, beaming like a pair of headlights. "Toy," Mama continued, "is going to say grace for us, now that he's almost a priest. My son the Father. Toy, sugar, do you think I should call you Father Wiggins, Father Toy, or Father Son?"

"Oh brother," I groaned.

"Shame on you, Abby." Mama said, but Toy smiled.

His grace, however, was nothing special. It was the same short blessing Mama taught us as children—one that I've come to think of as an Episcopal prayer, although it probably isn't.

Judging by our mother's expression, my errant sibling had just recited half the Bible from memory. "So you still remembered it, sugar."

I started the pot roast on its circuit. "Mama, the wallpaper in your old Rock Hill house remembers it."

"Very funny, dear. You should be nice to your little brother. After all, he's going to help you."

My heart sank into my stomach, pressing down my bladder. I had a sudden urge to use the bathroom.

"Help me with what, Mama?"

# 13

"**G**reg, darling," I cooed, "will you be a doll and fetch the saltshaker from the kitchen."

"It's right here on the table, hon. Next to the pepper."

"Those are both peppers, dear. You'll find the saltshaker on the top shelf above the refrigerator. The step stool is getting kinda shaky, so you'll probably want to get the aluminum stepladder from the garage."

At least I can be thankful that I did not marry a fool. Greg's eyes locked on mine, holding me in my seat just as securely as if he'd grabbed my shoulders.

"Somebody please tell me what I've missed."

"Nothing, dear. Just a little problem with Wynnell." I tried in vain to force my gaze away from Greg so I could glower at Mama.

"Horse dooky," Greg said, out of deference to his mother-in-law.

My sigh flickered the flames on the candles Mama had set out as a centerpiece. "It's just that Marina Webbfingers—you know, the woman whose bed and breakfast I was decorating—was bashed over the head with a heavy object—"

"You don't need to be so graphic," Mama objected.

"Anyway, she's dead, and the police think Wynnell did it, on account of she was last seen and heard having a screaming fight with the deceased. Now darling, you know I wouldn't normally interfere, but Wynnell's lawyer asked me to gather what information I could. *And*, coincidentally, Mr. Webbfingers himself asked me to entertain his guests until they were free to leave."

"That part sounds suspicious to me," Toy had the nerve to say.

This comment from the peanut gallery irritated me so much that I was able to break free of Greg's hold and glare at my uninvited house guest. It was, however, a very short glare, because clerical collars can be rather intimidating.

"You weren't there. It made perfect sense to me."

"Does it still?" Greg asked softly.

It took awhile for his question to register. I couldn't believe my beloved hadn't blown his stack. As a former Charlotte detective, he is intimately acquainted with just how dangerous a murder investigation can be—especially for the nonprofessional.

"Do you think I'm being set up?" I finally asked.

"It's something to think about. Charleston isn't exactly Podunk, Nowhere. Most visitors find there is too much to do and see, and that they don't have enough time. I've never heard of someone needing to be entertained."

"Well, then think of me as a tour guide. We have plenty of those."

Three pairs of eyes looked pointedly at me.

"Okay," I wailed, "so maybe it is a little odd. But I'm not an idiot. I know how to take care of myself."

Greg cleared his throat. "Like that time you found yourself in a suit of armor about to be dumped into Lake Wylie?"

"Or," Mama said, not without the tiniest bit of glee, "the time you almost became a life-size, glass-encased statue, intended for someone's foyer down in Miami? Abby, you hadn't even shaved that day. You would have had stubble on your legs for years. Maybe even centuries."

I clapped my hands over my ears. "So I've had a few narrow escapes. So what?"

"So," Mama said triumphantly, "that's why your brother Toy will be helping you with this investigation."

"Sounds like a good idea to me," Greg said before I could protest.

"I don't mind, sis," Toy had the temerity to say.

One of the worst things about having such short arms is that I couldn't stab people like Toy with my fork without having to first get up. Not that I would have hurt him, mind you. But he deserved a little prick.

I was clearly outnumbered. For now. But Toy was sure to do something so irresponsible that even Mama would send him packing. And if he didn't, well—perhaps I could get him distracted enough to bolt from the case on his own. I still wasn't sure which team my brother batted for, but either he was gay or he wasn't, and I had single friends of both genders. In fact, the first thing I would do the next morning is try him out on C.J.

"Well then, I guess it's settled," I said.

Greg raised a neatly trimmed eyebrow. "Abby?"

"What?"

Mama didn't believe me, either. "She's got something up her sleeve, Toy darling. Don't let her out of your sight."

Toy winked at me. "Don't worry, Mama. I've got her covered."

"Yeah right," I muttered. Little brother was no match for me.

\* \* \*

I awoke to the competing smells of sizzling bacon and fresh-brewed coffee. The clock face read seven, which meant Greg had been gone two hours, and Mama still had a good hour to go before she began yet another day in the 1950s. This meant that some stranger had broken into my house and was cooking himself, or herself, breakfast. Not a common occurrence, I'm sure, but it does happen. At any rate, I had already dialed nine and one when somebody rapped loudly on my door. Terrified out of my wits, I accidentally dialed the second one. Meanwhile Dmitri, who'd been curled up on Greg's side of the bed, jumped off to hide under it. A guard cat he is not.

"Sis, you up?"

I was only partially relieved to hear my brother's voice through the door. Before I could respond, someone on the other end of the phone line demanded my attention.

"Nine-one-one dispatcher."

"Uh—sorry, but I dialed the wrong number."

The phone rang the second the receiver was back in its cradle. "Mrs. Washburn?"

"Yes?" I tried to sound innocent, but thanks to my caller ID, I knew exactly who it was.

"This is the Charleston police. Is everything all right?"

"Yes, ma'am."

"Do you mind if we send a uniformed officer to your home?"

"There is really no need. Like I said, it was an accident."

"Mrs. Washburn, we have an officer in your area. He will be there in about five minutes."

"But—"

Nine one one hung up on me. In the meantime, Toy was trying to reconfigure my bedroom door with his knuckles.

"Sis! The eggs will be cold if you don't eat them soon."

I flew to the door, but remembered just in time that my sleeping apparel was not intended to be seen by anyone except Greg. Fortunately I keep my robe on a chair by the door, but I was panting when I opened the door.

"Well," he said with a smirk, "maybe breakfast can wait after all."

"Greg has been gone since five. Toy, what's going on? Who's cooking?"

The smirk morphed into a smile. "I am."

I put as much stock in my brother's answer as I do White House press releases. "Toy, so help me, if you've dragged Mama out of bed to make her cook—"

He put his hands up in a mock defensive posture. "Come see for yourself, sis. I hope I remembered correctly—you do like your eggs over easy, right?"

The doorbell rang. I knew exactly who it was.

"Toy, be a doll and get that, will you?"

My little brother loped obediently away, but was back in a few seconds. "Abby, it's the police. They want to speak with you." He put his arm around my shoulder. "Hey sis, whatever trouble you're in—well, I just want you to know that I'm here for you."

"I'm not in any trouble. I called nine one one by mistake, and it's their policy to come in and look around. See if everyone is really all right. Trust me, it's happened before."

Toy hadn't heard a word I'd said. "This may come as a shock to your ears, sis, but I love you."

I cinched my robe tighter before following Toy back to the living room. The world was turning topsy-turvy on me. A loving, protective brother who cooked breakfast without being asked? I never could have even dreamed that up. Not in a million years. Did this mean I was going to have to rethink the last thirty years and forgive the man? The day had gotten off to a rotten start.

The police were there for only a minute, and Toy's eggs were still warm. Delicious, too, I'm loath to say. Mama, who had been unnecessarily roused during the cursory search, was quick to compliment her son on his culinary achievement. But cooking eggs is not brain surgery, or even antique-collecting. A hen and a Charleston sidewalk in the summertime—that's all one really needs.

After Toy loaded the dishwasher and wiped down the counters—again, without being asked—we left for the Den of Antiquity. Mama waved us off with a conspiratorial grin. A stranger might have thought we were newlyweds. Okay, so I'm much older, but that kind of thing happens more and more these days.

At any rate, when we got to my shop, I was almost ready to believe that my baby brother had turned over a new leaf—a great big banana leaf in his case. C.J. wasn't there yet, and when I gave him a quick tour of the place, he actually asked questions.

"So what's your markup on this stuff?"

"That depends on how much I paid for it and what I can expect to get. Three times the acquisition price is what I strive for."

He nodded. "Say, sis, I don't suppose you could float me a loan, could you?"

"I beg your pardon?"

"Not a big loan—just a little cash to hold me over."

"How little?"

"A hundred thousand, that's all. I promise to pay you back—and you name the terms."

"Say what?"

"I wouldn't ask you, sis, but I got in a little deep with some loan sharks, and the word on the street is that they have Mafia connections. You wouldn't want to see me get my legs broken, would you?"

# 14

My petite patootie connected with the nearest chair while I struggled to catch my breath. So the leopard hadn't changed his spots! I knew it! And what really made me sick to my stomach was that if I didn't help Toy out of this jam, he would no doubt hit Mama up for the money. Perhaps he already had. Maybe that's why they'd had their heads together so long the day before.

"You haven't changed a bit," I gasped, "have you?"

"Psyche!"

"What?"

"Isn't that what we used to say as kids when we fooled somebody."

"Maybe you said that—wait a minute. Do you mean you aren't trying to borrow money? That the Mafia doesn't want to break your legs?"

Toy laughed heartily. He'd either picked up the skills of a good actor while in Hollywood—despite never getting an acting job—or he was as sincere as a nun on her deathbed.

"Sis, I may not have a whole lot of money, but I don't have any debts, either. I don't want anything from you—well, except—well, I thought maybe we could be friends."

"Is this another 'psyche'?"

He raised two fingers. "Scouts' honor."

"Toy, how do feel about taking a lie detector test? I have a friend in the police department who could arrange one."

That was actually a bit of a fib. When Greg was a detective up in Charlotte, he might have been able to arrange such a thing. *Might*. Sergeants Scrubb and Bright on the Charleston force knew me, but they weren't likely to do any favors for me. Of course I had yet to sleep with them—and probably never would.

Ever lucky, Toy was saved by the sudden appearance of C.J. The big galoot likes to come in through the delivery entrance, she claims it makes her feel special, on account of the fact that customers aren't allowed through that door. When I remind her that neither do the customers have keys for the front door, she shakes her massive head and sighs.

"Abby," she says, "you don't have a sense of drama, do you?"

C.J. has nothing but. This morning she popped out from behind an armoire like the killer in a horror movie. That's what it must have seemed like to Toy, because he let out a bona fide yelp when he looked over and saw the clumsy gal looming behind me.

"Holy—uh—moly," he said, catching himself just in time.

My friend and employee is without guile. "So who's the hunk, Abby?"

"He's no hunk! He's my brother. Toy."

"Ooh, don't tease me, Abby. You said your brother was a scumbag, not a priest."

I could feel my toes swell as the blood drained from my cheeks. "C.J.!"

Toy chuckled. "That's all right, Abby. You have my dispensation for any unflattering remarks you may have said in the past."

"He's not a real priest yet," I hissed.

I'm not sure either of them heard me. There were so many pheromones wafting back and forth between the two of them that I found it hard to breathe. My summer allergy pills don't cover sexual stimuli. At least I finally knew which direction my brother's pendulum preferred to swing.

I jumped off the chair and grabbed Toy's arm. "We have some serious sleuthing to do, remember?"

"Ooh, Abby can I come, too?"

"Someone needs to mind the shop, dear—and last time I signed a paycheck, it had your name on it."

"But three heads are better than two."

"Two will do just fine."

"That's what cousin Merckle up in Shelby said, but was he ever wrong. When he had that third head removed, he just couldn't make up his mind anymore."

I turned to Toy. "C.J. is originally from Shelby, North Carolina. She has a very—how should I put this—interesting family."

"I'd like to hear more about your cousin Merckle," Toy said. He sounded genuinely interested.

My young friend smiled gratefully. "Well, he was born with three heads, you see. They were normal-size heads, too, but he only had one body. It was a cesarean delivery of course. Anyway, this was the first time in history anything like this had happened in Shelby, and everyone said that cousin Merckle was going to be in all the record books, and that would put Shelby on the map. And cousin Merckle was going to be really famous, too, 'cause the job offers just came pouring in even when he was a baby. You wouldn't believe it, Abby—"

"I'm sure I wouldn't."

Toy glared at me, so I put a sock in it. "Go on," he said kindly.

"This big company in New York wanted him to model hats. Another wanted him to model sunglasses. Ooh ooh, and this shampoo company wanted to do a commercial where they washed each head with a different kind of shampoo to compare the differences." She hung her enormous, but single, head and sighed. "Of course none of that happened after he had the third head removed."

I looked down at the floor so I could discreetly roll my eyes. "C.J., with all these endorsement offers pouring in, why did he have the third head removed?"

"Because he got tired of looking different than the other members of his branch of the family—the Wicky Fork Ledbetters. So he had the doctors take off one head—the middle one, of course—but like I said, it was a huge mistake. You see, that was the head that made compromises between the other two, which clearly had minds of their own. From that day on cousin Merkle was never able to make another decision. And of course all those job offers fell through, now that he looked like everyone else in his clan."

"Toy, darling," I said, trying not to smile, "I keep a saltshaker in my locker in the storage room. How many grains would you like?"

"What I'd like to do," he said, without missing a beat, "is to ask you out, C.J."

"Be careful, C.J. It might be a ruse. He could be after your money." Despite the fact that she works for me, C.J. has done quite well for herself. She had her own shop up in Charlotte.

"Don't worry, Abby. I can't date a priest."

"Episcopal," Toy said quickly. "We're allowed to date—just as long as we're not married. Of course the people we date should be single as well."

I have never seen C.J. look so happy. "Do you like hops and scotch?"

"Never tried them together, but I'm game."

"Then pick me up at seven."

"Excellent."

I couldn't move fast enough to avoid C.J.'s arms. To say she gave me a bear hug would be the understatement of the year. It was more like the embrace of an amorous yeti. Not that I've experienced a whole lot of those, mind you.

"Ooh Abby, I owe you one."

"You'll owe me a new set of ribs if you don't let go."

Toy tried to hug me as well, but I saw that coming, and the second C.J. released me, I dashed for the door. "Toy, if you're coming with me today, you've got to keep up."

He reluctantly followed me out to the street.

\* \* \*

There was something fishy about Fisher Webbfingers, something I couldn't pinpoint, but I aimed to discover what it was. Maybe it was just his weird request that I entertain his guests, although the more I thought about it, it seemed strange that a couple with marital difficulties, but no apparent financial difficulties, would open a bed and breakfast. What was in it for them?

"Toy," I said, continuing my train of thought aloud as we drove from the shop to double 0 Legare, "can you think of any way we can check on somebody's financial history?"

"Abby, you're not Internet savvy, are you?"

"I am so. It's just that I'm too busy to spend a lot of time cruising the Net."

He laughed far too long and hard. "That's surf, sis, not cruise. Unless you want to pick up guys."

"Whatever. Well, can you?"

"No problemo. But it would help if we had his Social Security number."

"Yes, but how do we get that?"

"He's alone in the house now since his wife died, right?"

"Except for the maid. But so what?"

"So you distract him outside, and I'll slip in and have a look-see."

"What about the maid?"

"I'll seduce her." There wasn't a trace of a smile on his face.

"Toy, she played with God as a child. She may even have been His baby-sitter. Besides, you're supposed to be a man of the cloth."

That's when he grinned. "Just kidding, Abby. It's fun to pull your leg, sis, you know that?"

But when we got within spitting distance of double 0 Legare street, it began to look as if seducing anyone was a moot point. There were no cars parked on the street anywhere near the place and, we soon discovered, the two car garage was empty.

"Perfect," Toy said, and rubbed his hands together in anticipation.

"But it's already nine, and we're all supposed to meet here at ten."

"Maybe they didn't like the breakfast that was served. It doesn't matter, does it? We're in luck. Now remember, your mission is to head straight for the office—"

"Excuse me?"

"Every house has an office, Abby. It may not be a special room, but there's always at least a corner with a desk in it, or at the very least, a box of papers stashed somewhere. What you're after is anything with a Social Security number. You know, three digits, dash, two digits, dash, four."

"But I'm not going in, you are!"

"Think about it, sis. They already know you. If

they catch you, they're more likely to accept your story than mine. I mean, how do explain a strange priest in your house? You could at least claim you needed to use the bathroom."

"Which Marina never allowed me to use."

"There you go—that's your cover. You felt insulted by that, and since there was no one home, and you had to go—you decided to take a stand. Or a sit, as the case may be."

"After breaking and entering. Toy, I could be arrested for that."

"Don't worry. Unless someone bothered to put the security system on—and believe me, a lot of people only use theirs after dark—I can get you in without the breaking part. You can say you found the door unlocked."

"And what if the security system is on?"

"Then we run like hell."

By then I was parked along the curb, so I was at liberty to turn and stare at him. "Have the folks who run your seminary ever met you?"

"Good one, sis." He unbuckled his seat belt. "Okay, are we on the same page?"

"We're not even in the same book, Toy. In fact, we're not even in the same library. I'm not going to trespass, and that's that."

His blue eyes didn't waver. "How bad do you want to clear your friend?"

"That's not fair."

"And I thought you were a sleuth, Abby."

"A law-abiding one."

I doubt if he heard me. He'd turned and was scrutinizing the main house like a hawk hovering over a meadow.

"Aha! We're in luck."

"You've come to your senses?"

"That upstairs window is open. Chances are security is off, but we can test it."

"How?"

"I'll throw a stick through the window. It's not as likely as a rock to break something, and the movement will set off the censors."

"Even so, how do you propose that I get up there—assuming I agreed."

"That's a piece of cake. I'll hoist you up to my shoulders, then you can grab that vine—wisteria, right? All you have to do is go in through the window. You can come out through a door."

"For your information, that's not wisteria. It's creeping fig."

A relative of the edible fig tree, the creeping variety (*Ficus pumila*) looks nothing like its cousin. Its juvenile foliage is delicate, and the tracery of the vines adds architectural interest in brick and stucco walls. But as the plant climbs, the foliage triples in size and the vines become woody. The only way to maintain the more desirable form is to keep it heavily pruned.

Wynnell tried to get Mrs. Webbfingers to let her remove the vine altogether, so it wouldn't ruin the brickwork with its roots. But Mrs. Webbfingers said it was too late, that the roots had already dug in too deep, and that removing it would create "an eyesore."

Just thinking about my pal made me ache to help her. But I was a soon-to-be respected member of the community. How could I even contemplate doing something illegal?

Of course Toy didn't care two figs about my angst. "Great," he said. "All those roots should keep you nice and safe."

There must have been a small part of me that wanted to break the law. How else can I explain the phrases that pushed their way into my mind.

*If I am not Wynnell's friend, then who is?*

*If I don't act now, then when?*

I flung open my car door. "Let's get going, then, before they get back. And keep in mind, Toy, that I don't look good in horizontal stripes. Vertical, on the other hand, might add the illusion of an extra inch or two. Oh, and make sure someone remembers to feed Dmitri."

"Will do, sis," he said with a laugh.

But it was soon no laughing matter.

# 15

Harriet did not answer the door when I rang, and the stick that Toy lobbed through the window failed to set off an alarm. But a six-foot, out-of-shape priest trying desperately to hoist a very short woman onto his shoulders should have set off mental alarms in any neighbor glancing that way, or in the throngs of tourists just starting to make their circuits.

Perhaps no one perceived us as doing something illegal precisely because we were so obvious about it. The neighbors were probably used to seeing people climbing in and out of windows, and the tourists, I'm sure, had all been warned about Charleston's eccentric citizenry. We were simply part of their day's entertainment.

At any rate, reaching the open window was not as easy as Toy had made it out to be. He staggered under my weight, light as I am, and for a few perilous seconds I thought we were going to topple over backward. If at all possible I planned to land on top of Toy, who was undoubtedly softer than the ground. When I was finally able to grab some fig vines, the leaves ripped off in my hands.

On my third try I was able to grab a woody stem, but I was totally unprepared when Toy stumbled out from beneath me. I might well have fallen to my death—or at least broken my back—had not a band of tourists started to applaud enthusiastically. Heartened by their support, and the sudden knowledge that a break-in with such encouraging witnesses was not really a crime after all, but merely an unconventional entrance, I grabbed a stem with my other hand and managed to climb inside. Still, my heart was pounding like a madman on a xylophone.

My heart beat even faster when I beheld the glories of Fisher and Marina's boudoir. Or perhaps it was just Marina's boudoir, as couples of their ilk and means often prefer to sleep apart. It was, in any case, a very feminine room, with peach and cream being the dominant colors. Fine silks swirled down from the gilt canopy, and silk damask had been glued to the walls in lieu of paper. The dark, gleaming hardwood floor was covered in part by a French Aubusson rug with an immaculate cream background. A bottle of fine champagne, a Mozart CD, and of course Greg—I shook my head to clear it of this fantasy. I had a job to do. Wine, men, and song would just have to wait.

The bedroom didn't seem like a place in which to find paperwork, so I tiptoed to the door and peeked into the hallway. Somewhere in my youth or childhood I must have been a very good girl, because the open door across from me revealed a spectacular office setup. Who wouldn't want to balance their checkbook while seated at a late eighteenth-century mahogany desk embellished with ivory inlays and polished brass finials? If I owned that desk, I would botch up my accounting just so I had an excuse to sit there longer.

I ran my fingertips over wood as smooth as satin but not entirely dust-free. Oh well, Harriet Spanky was up in her years. Now where in this beautiful desk would important papers be? One thing for sure, the Webbfingers were not clutterbugs. Except for a stack of papers lined up with precision on the left of the inkblot, and an equally precise pile of open envelopes on the right—mostly business correspondence, from the looks of it—the top of the desk was clear. There were eight cubbyholes—four on each side—but they contained only writing implements, a stapler, cellophane tape, and similar items indispensable to the home office.

A pair of heavy drawers on either side of the knee space were more promising. I pulled open the one on the left, and grunted with satisfaction at what I saw. Files. Oodles of files. *American Automobile Association, American Airlines, Artie's Auto-*

*mobile Detailing Service, Azure Skies Window-washers, Babaloo Bakery and Party Rentals, Bank of America, Bell South* . . . hmm. The files were in alphabetical order, all right, but according to company names, not category.

I backed up to Bank of America. There were a zillion statements of deposits and withdrawals, a few attesting to CD ownership, and—aha—an unfinished application for a new debit card. Sure enough, there was Fisher Webbfingers's Social Security number. Marina's, too! But before I could fully appreciate my coup, I heard what sounded like a thud downstairs. Was that a door slamming? Yes, it must have been, because seconds later I could hear the unmistakable sound of footsteps on the stairs.

Toy was going to pay for this! By now he was probably back in my car, hot-wiring it for his getaway. It wouldn't surprise me if he drove all the way back to his seminary in Sewannee, Tennessee, and hid out in his cell. Or did he have a dorm room, plastered with posters of J-Lo and Britney Spears? Well, he belonged in a padded cell, that's for sure, and so did I for listening to him.

The sound of footsteps grew louder. The person approaching was in the hallway now. It was too late to make a dash for the bedroom and its open window. It was too late to do anything but find someplace in the room in which to hide. But where? This room, like many to be found in old houses, relied on armoires and cupboards for storage. Alas, the only furniture, besides the desk, was a Chippendale settee and a pair of matching chairs. Even my shadow couldn't hide behind those graceful legs.

For a split second I thought of emptying out the contents of the drawer and crawling inside. There are actually advantages to being small, but even if I managed to fit, who was there to close the drawer? Besides, a neatnik like Fisher was going to notice a mound of files sprawled across his floor. Now if this was Elias Hammerhead's office, I could hide behind existing piles on the floor. Properly supplied with food, water, and bathroom necessities, I could live the rest of my life undetected by the attorney and his freshly shorn secretary.

*Dang it, Abby, think!* I kicked one slim ankle to jump-start the process.

Alas, I am perfectly capable of hurting myself, and my yelp all but drowned out the sound of the front doorbell. Fortunately it rang twice.

I froze. Doorbells, even more so than phones, are almost impossible to resist. "Opportunity knocks" is not so much an adage as it is a universal hope that good fortune will miraculously appear at our doorsteps—although these days a serial killer is more likely to show up than a great opportunity. At any rate, whoever was approaching the Webbfingerses' office made an abrupt turn and thundered down the steps to answer the door.

"Mr. Webbfingers?" I heard Toy ask loudly. "I'm the Reverend T. J. Wiggins. I'm here to express my heartfelt condolences on the recent passing of your wife. May I come in?"

I couldn't hear Fisher's response.

"That's all right," Toy shouted. "I'm an Episcopalian. We're very inclusive."

A fear-filled moment of silence followed. I realized what Toy was doing, but I didn't know if he'd succeeded. After what seemed an eternity—hopefully baggy shorts had finally gone out of fashion—I heard the door close. Then I heard Toy's voice on the *inside*.

"Mr. Webbfingers, it's all right. Crying is a natural response at a time like this."

I didn't stay put to hear more. In what I considered a brilliant act on my part, especially given the stress, I quickly wrote Fisher Webbfingers's Social Security number on my wrist, using a felt-tip pen I found in one of the cubbyholes. After returning the pen to its proper place and closing the file drawer without making a sound, I removed my shoes and tiptoed back across the hall.

But climbing down a vine from a second story

window is not nearly as easy as climbing up. And what about the ten foot drop at the end? Well, they say there are no atheists in foxholes, to which I will add, neither are there atheists on creeping fig vines.

"Oh Lord," I prayed, "help me get down safely, and I promise to give Toy a second chance." That was, I am ashamed to say, my first prayer in—oh well, does it really matter?

Of course one has to back out when exiting a window that high. Having failed every P.E. test I took, and possessing the upper body strength of a Muppet, I clung desperately to the windowsill with both hands while my bare toes tried to make purchase with the vine. C.J., I've noticed, has toes like fingers; I wouldn't be surprised to learn she types with them. In contrast, my tootsies are so tiny that my toes are like skin tags with nails.

I scraped a good deal of skin off my forearms before I managed to grab a stout vine between my big toe and its sister. From that point my descent got a little easier, until I reached the juvenile foliage. The leaves here grew flat along the face of the wall, and their stems were as thin as toothpicks.

"Holy guacamole," I said. I still hadn't looked down.

"Jump, Mrs. Washburn. I'll catch you."

I gasped and nearly lost my grip. About four feet below my dangling extremities was the handsome head of Nick Papadopoulus. Thank heavens I was wearing white cotton slacks that morning—although my underwear is almost always in good repair.

"This isn't what you think," I whispered.

He smiled. "It's not important what I think, is it? It's more important that you get down in one piece."

"Are you sure you can catch me?"

"Pretty sure."

My fingers were beginning to grow numb. "That's not good enough."

"What other choice do you have?"

"Bonsai!" I yelled, and trusted my fate to the man from New York.

# 16

For what it's worth, the tourist from the Big Apple smelled like limes and salt. Add two ounces of premium vodka, a splash of orange liqueur, and he was a walking margarita.

I may be happily married, but I didn't park my hormones at the door of the church. Alas, my fantasy was short-lived, for almost immediately my right arm became tangled in his web of gold chains. The more I struggled to free myself, the more entangled I became. The fact that I accidentally grabbed a handful of chest hair shows you just how desperate my situation was.

"Ouch!"

"Sorry, but I seem to be trapped."

"Hold still, please, Mrs. Washburn."

"No problemo." I threw back my head and willed myself to go limp, like a Victorian damsel who had fainted. Except that I kept one eye open. I don't know how long Nick held me in that position, but it wasn't long enough.

"What the heck is going on?" Irena Papado-poulus glared at me beneath her two-tone do. I was suddenly glad there had been no recent reports in the *Post and Courier* of rabid skunks.

"Sorry."

"Put her down."

"Sorry." The second apology, which was whispered, was for my ears alone.

Nick set me carefully on the grass in front of the window. It took him a minute to untangle the chains from my arm, which gave me time to think of an excuse for being in his arms. To be absolutely honest, I thought seriously of being wicked and collapsing at his feet, but in the end I was a good girl.

"I started to pass out," I said. "The heat does that to me. Your husband very kindly caught me."

Irena wasn't buying it. "Alcohol makes people pass out, too, Mrs. Washburn."

"I haven't had a margarita—or a drink of any kind—all day."

She approached and actually began to sniff me. You can bet I backed away. Of course I wasn't looking where I stepped, or I wouldn't have trod on a sharp twig.

"Dang!" I hopped up and down on one foot.

Irena's beady eyes widened. "Where are your shoes?"

"My shoes?" *My shoes!* What a dingbat I was. I'd left my sandals behind in the Webbfingerses' bedroom. How else could I have climbed down the vine like a mini-Tarzan, using my toes as well as my fingers? It came back to me in an unpleasant flash. I'd carried my sandals from the office to the bedroom and set them on the bed while I gathered enough nerve to slip over the ledge. I had every intention of putting my shoes back on again, but once the necessary adrenaline surged through my body, all I could think about was making it safely to the ground.

Irena had little patience. "I'm waiting for your answer, Mrs. Washburn."

"I must have forgot to wear them." It was, after all, the truth.

"Don't be ridiculous. I've a good idea what you've been up to."

"I seriously doubt that. But I swear, it had nothing to do with your husband. I have a hunk—I mean a husband—of my own. I'm happily married. See?" I waved my left hand.

At least a little luck was with me that morning, because the sun hit my engagement ring just right, and the minuscule stone appeared much more impressive than it usually does. At least it was enough to make Irena Papadopoulus back off a bit.

"Hmm. Well, I suggest you run along to Payless and pick up another pair of shoes. We wouldn't want you to hurt your feet."

"I didn't buy them at Payless," I snapped. "I bought them from Bob Ellis on King Street. They cost me over three hundred dollars."

With some effort, she arranged her thin dry lips into a smirk. "Just so you know, Nick and I won't be joining this little jaunt of yours this morning."

"Yes, we will." The man of few words emphasized each one.

There are those who might find it exciting to watch a married couple square off in public. I am not among their number—which is not to say that I didn't experience schadenfreude whenever Nick seemed to get the upper hand. He spoke softly and sparingly, but his steady gaze and calm spirit prevailed—although I had no doubt the two would exchange more words later. Just not equal numbers.

"I'll see y'all at ten o'clock then," I said, resurrecting my perky pageant voice. One of my best kept secrets is that I was once third runner-up in the Miss Kudzu contest of York County, South Carolina. I may not have been elected the Kudzu Queen, but I did bring home a trophy and the title of Miss Kudzu Personality.

Kudzu, for y'all who don't know, is a vine with

large leaves and sweet smelling flowers that grows faster than a teenage boy—up to sixty feet a year. It was first introduced in this country in 1876 by the Japanese in their garden display at the Centennial Exposition in Philadelphia. In the early part of the twentieth century it was touted both as forage for cattle and as an effective way to control erosion. It was commonly shipped to various parts of the Deep South by mail. Today it covers over seven million acres and advances farther north each year. Due to its explosive growth rate, landowners have to be constantly vigilant about its encroachment. The South may have lost the war, but its secret weapon, kudzu, will someday strangle unsuspecting folks north of the Line. One morning, in the not-too-distant-future, Yankees will wake up to find their houses and places of business smothered in green, and by then it will be too late to do anything about it. Don't say I didn't warn you.

It was already nine-thirty, so I decided to wait for Toy in my car. I also put on a spare pair of shoes. The veteran of numerous mishaps (please don't think I'm bragging), I never go anywhere without a complete change of clothes in my trunk. I have also found large plastic garbage bags, a shovel, a high-powered flashlight, and mixed nuts to be invaluable—although that is neither here nor there.

No sooner had I changed into my running shoes than the passenger door opened and Toy slid in. "Did you get it?" he demanded without preamble.

"What?"

"Mr. Webbfingers's Social Security number."

"Yes! Thank you, Toy. That was brilliant—you showing up at the door like that."

"I saw him drive up, sis. I couldn't abandon you."

"Did he fall for your sympathy bit?"

"It wasn't an act. Even though you'd told me he and his wife had been having troubles—well, you just know that on some level the guy had to be hurting."

"Even if he's the one who killed her?"

"No one is entirely evil, sis."

I leaned over to open the glove box.

"What is it you want, sis? I'll get it for you."

"There should be a plastic spoon in there somewhere. I'd like to gag myself with it."

He grinned. "I'm glad to see you haven't lost your spunk. Okay, I'll stop the moralizing. How about you show me that number?"

I turned over my wrist. "Voilà."

Toy groaned. "The last two digits are smeared, sis."

"What?" Sure enough, the two numbers on the

right were nothing more than blue streaks. All that work and risk had been for nothing—well, if I didn't count the naughty moment in Nick's arms.

"Sis—"

"I couldn't help it. The window ledge did it. But don't worry, I think I remember that this one was an eight—or was it a three? And that was definitely a five—unless it was a zero."

"What I was about to say, sis, is that I think we've got enough to go on. It will just take a little more time."

Poor Wynnell. This meant more time in the slammer for her. On the plus side, it gave Ed more time to revamp her shop. With any luck, absence would make both their hearts grow fonder, and they'd rediscover the vampish sides of each other. Just as long as Wynnell didn't leave a boyfriend named Bertha behind in the lockup.

"How much time?" I asked.

He shrugged. "You said you had a lawyer lined up for your friend. A Mr. White, was it?"

"Hammerhead. He's way up on King Street, almost to the Crosstown."

"Drop me off at the house, Abby, so I can pick up my car. I'll pay Hammerhead a visit—maybe he can help me run down these numbers. In the meantime, you take these folks on the outing you promised them."

"What about my shoes?"

"What about them?"

"I'm afraid these aren't the same ones I wore into the Webbfingerses' house. In my hurry to get out, I left my sandals behind."

Toy's frown was so brief it really didn't count. "Don't worry, how many men do you know who keep track of their wives' shoes? Chances are, he won't look at them twice."

"You've got a point, except for one small detail—how many women do you know with feet my size?"

"No offense intended, sis, but unless it involves food, sex, or sports, he's still not going to think anything about it. He'll just assume your sandals were left there by a niece, or a neighborhood kid—if he thinks about it at all. He certainly won't suspect that a four-foot-eight-inch, antique-dealing, detecting dynamo scaled the wall while he was out."

"I'm four-foot-*nine*. But thanks, Toy. I don't know what I'd have done without you."

"Hey, what are brothers for?"

I didn't answer the question, lest I stick my foot in my mouth. They may be minuscule feet, but so is my mouth. Literally, that is. Instead of unloading my litany of "Where were you when?"s, I managed to stick to small talk all the way back to my house.

Before Toy hopped out to get into his own car, he gave me a peck on the cheek. "Don't take risks, Abby."

I dutifully promised to behave—through gritted teeth, of course. But when I returned to La Parterre a few minutes later, I saw that I already had my hands full.

# 17

I am no prude, but Belinda Thomas's outfit was way off the charts for Charleston. Maybe in Calamari, California, one got away with sight-seeing in a halter top and spandex shorts, but not in the Holy City. Belinda bulged in all the right places, and a few of the wrong ones. If we were seen together, Mama's church lady friends were going to suffer sore tongues from all that wagging.

"Belinda," I said, ratcheting my perk factor up a few notches, "perhaps you'd be more comfortable in something else. The sun here is very strong, and I'd hate to see you get burned."

She flashed me her caps. "Thanks for your concern, but you can see that I'm quite tanned."

I could see that her spray-on tan was streaking even worse today. She looked a bit like a blond tiger, with unusually large breasts and pink claws, in a hootchie-mama outfit.

We took three cars, forming a miniature cara-van. The affable Zimmermans rode with me, the hunky Nick and his suspicious wife followed closely in their rental car with Irena at the wheel, while the Calamarians from Cambria lagged an inconvenient distance behind. They stopped at every yellow light, which, as every South Carolinian knows, is only optional. In fact, in parts of the Upstate there is a persistent rumor that *five* cars must go through a yellow light before it is allowed to turn red. As Charleston is not unknown for its curbside parking, the calm Californians raised my blood pressure fifty points by the time we reached the Cooper River bridges.

There are currently two bridges that span this busy port entrance, and a third in the making. All three structures are nosebleed high, and not a day passes that at least one acrophobiac refuses to cross the river at this juncture. To add to the general discomfort, the older of the two existing bridges, Grace Memorial, appears to be held together by nothing but a thick layer of rust. One gets the feeling that the backfire from a truck or a sudden gust of wind could reduce the bridge to nothing more than a pile of red dust. On this account, Greg even refuses to eat beans before crossing.

The Arthur Ravenel Bridge, as the new one will be known, will surely be one of the architectural wonders of the century. Purported to be the longest single-span suspension bridge in the country, it soars so high that a few of our more devout citizenry believe it an affront to the ultimate architect Himself and vow never to use it.

Most of us, however, look forward to using the new bridge. "Wow, just look at that," I said proudly. "Isn't it beautiful?"

Estelle Zimmerman, who was seated in the passenger seat beside me, wrinkled her nose. "I suppose they have to build it that high to allow big ships to pass under. But the bigger and grander it is, the more people will want to commit suicide here."

"I beg your pardon?"

"The Golden Gate Bridge in San Francisco is the number one spot in the world for suicides. The official count already exceeds one thousand, but some Coast Guard members have estimated the actual number may be ten times that. Some psychologists say that the spectacular setting is one of the reasons that bridge is so popular. If you're going to jump, why not there, instead of splitting your head open on some dirty sidewalk?"

"Why not, indeed?" What else was there for me to say?

"My Estee knows everything," Herman said. The pride in his voice was touching.

"Well, I'm sure the Charleston and Mount Pleasant police will figure out how to keep people from jumping off the Arthur Ravenel Bridge when it opens."

"Have they figured out how to extract the bodies from the old bridge?"

"Excuse me?"

"Well, in the 1940s a barge broke loose in a storm and hit a piling. A green sedan carrying six people plunged into the Cooper River, and of course they all drowned. Then when the bridge was being repaired, two workmen fell into the cement form of the new piling, and are said to remain there until this day."

"Ah, so you've been boning up on Lowcountry ghost stories."

In the rearview mirror I could see Herman lean forward and rap the back of his wife's seat with knuckles the size of walnuts. My guess was that he was trying to get her to shut up.

"Estee and me don't believe in ghosts."

I was about to comment on how curious it was that a woman from Wisconsin would know this bit of local lore when my rearview mirror revealed something quite disturbing. The Thomases' rental car, a dark green, was nowhere to be seen.

"Uh-oh, I can't see them."

"Who?" Herman's thick neck was almost as malleable as Linda Blair's in the *Exorcist*.

"John and Belinda."

"You're right. I just see them folks from New York."

I slurred over a minor cuss word. Now I had to

turn around as soon as I got across and hunt down the disobedient sightseers. What part of "keep up" didn't they understand?

Summer traffic in this part of the Palmetto state is about as bad as winter traffic in the Sunshine state. The chief difference between Florida's horde and ours is that our visitors tend to be a younger bunch with families, and many of them come from the inland areas of the Carolinas. They also tend to drive SUVs (or SAVs, as Greg calls them— Suburban Assault Vehicles), which make it impossible to see stoplights and street signs until the last second. Even a native can become disoriented when familiar landmarks are obscured by so-called recreational vehicles the size of elephants.

Okay, so I'm not a native of Mount Pleasant, and might have had trouble retracing my route anyway. But nonetheless, I couldn't find a spot in which to safely turn around until we got to Houston North-cut Boulevard, and by then I was in such a foul mood that I was no longer slurring my words. In the meantime, Irena Papadopoulus was leaning on the horn and mouthing the very same words.

Herman Zimmerman rapped on the back of my seat, barely missing my neck with his hairy knuckles. "My Estee is opposed to swearing," he said without a trace of jollity.

"Then perhaps one of you should drive," I snapped.

Of course, I immediately apologized. Not only was my rude behavior wrong, but if reported to the right ears (or wrong ones, depending on one's point of view), I might well be stripped of my Southern Bellehood. This happened to Mama's cousin Nattie Lee in Hattiesburg, Mississippi, when, in the middle of a shopping mall, she stepped in a wad of gum while wearing a brand new pair of shoes. That very evening a band of grim-faced ladies showed up at the door of her home and demanded her resignation from the National Association of Southern Belles.

In order to be reinstated in this organization, cousin Hattie Lee had to host a family from Michigan for two weeks, eat corn bread with sugar in it, drink unsweetened tea, and pronounce her state's name in just four syllables. In other words, live Wynnell's worst nightmare—until she landed in a Charleston clinker. At least in jail my buddy was served sweet tea. I'd be willing to bet my life on that.

"Well, see that you don't swear again," Herman said. Thanks to the review mirror, I could see that he was smiling. No doubt his crotchetiness had all been an act put on for the benefit of the "little lady."

I found the Thomases huddling inside their car just off the entrance ramp to Route 17. A black and white automobile with a revolving light was keeping them company. When I tried to pull over, the officer attempted to wave me away, but having finally found my lost charges, I wasn't about to lose them again. With one final blast of her horn, Irena Papadopoulus and her handsome, but henpecked, husband joined us.

Fortunately for everyone involved, it turned out that I knew both the officers that went with the squad car. Delbert Dittlebaum is Detective Bright's nephew, and his female partner is—let's just say I met her under unpleasant circumstances. With any luck, she wouldn't remember me.

Instead of waiting in my car like common sense dictated, I foolishly opened my door and started to climb out.

"Wait where you are," Officer Dittlebaum ordered.

"It's me, Abby Washburn. I'm a friend of your uncle—Detective Bright." Okay, so that was a gross exaggeration, but passing cars were beginning to slow, as their occupants stared goggle-eyed at us. Why is it that folks feel compelled to rubberneck? Don't they realize that it's not only dangerous, but accounts for most of the delay whenever there is an accident?

Officer Dittlebaum's partner stared as well. "It's you," she finally growled. It's not like she encounters four-foot-nine-inch adult women on a daily basis. Perhaps she thought I was a child who had stolen a car.

"Good morning, officer."

"Causing trouble again, are you?"

"No ma'am. I'm showing these visitors our beautiful city and some of our Lowcountry landmarks."

"I just bet you are."

"Honest. You can ask them."

"I did."

"And?"

"Did you know, Mrs. Washburn, that Mr. Thomas here is afraid to drive over the bridge?" She said it loud enough that poor John couldn't help but overhear.

"No ma'am. But that's not so unusual, is it? From what I understand, not a day goes by that someone doesn't need help getting over."

The contentious woman snorted. "If they're your guests, and if you had described your itinerary properly, you would have known one of them had agoraphobia."

"Acrophobia."

"What?"

"Acrophobia is the fear of heights. Agoraphobia is the fear of open spaces."

"Mrs. Washburn, at the very least I should issue you a ticket for improper parking, endangering the lives of fellow motorists, and—"

"I'm sorry. I promise it won't happen again."

She glared at me an interminable length of time. Meanwhile Officer Dittlebaum twiddled his thumbs. Were it not for the angry glint in the policewoman's eyes, I might have thought she was daydreaming. Or even sleeping. There are a few folks, I am told, who can nap while standing, and with their peepers open.

To pass the time I ran a couple of game plans through my mind. Bribes were out, but contributions to a widows' fund—now surely there was nothing wrong in suggesting that. And if that seemed too obvious, cheerful acceptance of my punishment, and a warm invitation to dinner, might induce her to tear up the ticket and issue a warning in its place. If that failed, and the fine was really high, I could sell my hair to Mr. Hammerhead in lieu of recompense, and he could plead my case in court. Oh, if only Toy were here. He could charm a snake out of its skin. How else could a pettifogger like him gain admittance to one of the South's most prestigious seminaries?

"Mrs. Washburn!" she barked, suddenly emerging from her daze.

I roused myself from a petite fog of my own. "Yes?"

"I'll drive these folks across myself, and Sergeant Dittlebaum will drive me back, but from then on you're responsible for them. I suggest that if they don't find someone else to drive them back over, you make sure they take I-526 around. Those bridges seem to be less intimidating."

"Yes, sir—I mean ma'am."

"Well, what are you standing there for? Get back in your car before you cause an accident."

I lit out of there like I was carrying a shovel full of coals.

Ever since Hurricane Floyd, when I spent eleven hours (I was one of the lucky ones) in a traffic jam on I-26, my philosophy of life has been "Pee whenever you can." After saying good-bye to the officers, I led our caravan directly to Fort Moultrie on Sullivan's Island. The fort, now a national monument, has free, if somewhat hot and stuffy, rest rooms attached to the Visitors' Center. It also has free parking.

We vied for a shady parking spot. After using the facilities, we revived ourselves with the air-conditioning inside the Visitors' Center, while enjoying the exhibits and browsing through a selection of historical books for sale. Herman Zimmerman wanted to watch the fifteen minute video (also free) but I vetoed his request. I had other things I wanted them to see.

I led them out the front door to the right, and just opposite Stella Maris Catholic Church, we turned left on a dirt lane that leads to the water. This easy-to-miss spot is one of Charleston

County's best kept secrets, and I pray that it remains so. Thus far it seems to be the haunt only of fishermen and a few summer renters who lounge in front of beach houses that have unparalleled views of Fort Sumter and passing ships.

It is here that the harbor opens to the ocean. The mix of waters, and the resulting currents, make this an unsafe place in which to swim, but very attractive to aquatic life. I am particularly fond of the dolphins that leap and dive for their dinners near the end of a rocky groin. Somehow these beautiful mammals manage to stay in approximately the same spot for long periods of time. I could stand and watch them all day.

Herman Zimmerman was enthralled as well. "Why, just look at them big fish."

"They're dolphins, not fish, dear," Estelle whispered, but the cool breeze blowing in from the ocean blew her words back to me. "They're air-breathing mammals, like you and I. They're supposed to be very intelligent. Maybe even more intelligent than chimpanzees."

"Just the same, I'd like to catch me one."

Belinda Thomas definitely heard that. "Hey, I love dolphins. *Flopper* was my favorite movie."

John put a protective arm around his wife. "That's 'Flipper,' dear."

A wise guide knows when it's time to change the subject. "Over there," I said, pointing to the east, "is Fort Sumter. That's where the Late Unpleasantness began. And just behind us, to the left, is Fort Moultrie. It was first constructed out of palmetto logs in 1776. The British attacked it, but since palm logs are fibrous, and not woody like real trees, they absorbed most of the impact from the cannon balls. The British fleet was defeated. That's why South Carolina is known as the Palmetto state."

Irena Papadopoulus swatted her arm. "Something just bit me."

I smiled reassuringly. "It was probably just a no-see-um."

"No-see-ums don't come out when it's this hot," she snapped.

I shrugged. She was certainly right about that; biting midges prefer the more moderate temperatures of spring and autumn. But the scourge of the Lowcountry, if there is one, has got to be our insect population. Where else does one find biting insects so small they can barely be seen, roaches as big as kittens (which we graciously refer to as palmetto bugs), and mosquitoes so swift a track star couldn't outrun them?

Although nobody else was attacked by microscopic vermin, Irena started to do the dance of misery. Footwork isn't important in this Lowcountry jig (unless one has stepped in a nest of fire ants), it's the flailing arms that count. If she entered a competition, I'd say the tourist from the Big Apple stood a fair chance of winning.

Even if she's not being paid, a good tour guide should always be mindful of her clients' comfort, so I got the show on the road as soon possible. We stopped briefly to view the triangular black and white lighthouse farther up the island, but remained in our vehicles when passing the two hurricane-proof "flying saucer" houses, and the World War II bunkers that had been converted to spacious homes.

The bunker houses are a favorite of mine. Through the glass entry of one these subterranean mansions, a magnificent chandelier can be observed, while on the roof, grass and shrubs grow happily. Even small trees.

After the lighthouse we didn't get out again until we reached Coconut Joe's on the Isle of Palms. This restaurant has the best ocean view east of the Cooper, and is the perfect place to have lunch on a hot summer day. Because the outdoor deck is high off the ground, and close to the sea, there is usually a breeze. However, just to be on the safe side, we unanimously voted to eat indoors. It was our hope that the air-conditioning would recharge our batteries.

While we feasted on coconut-breaded shrimp

and sipped margaritas (just half a one for me), we watched the swimmers and sunbathers take full advantage of their holiday on the beach. There was very little wave action at the time, but that didn't stop visitors from Ohio and Pennsylvania from trying to surf. Neither did extra poundage prevent the majority of people from wearing swimming garb, much of which was not to their advantage. One exceptionally large woman, who spilled out of her bikini like rising dough infused with too much yeast, was trying in vain to control a frisky little black dog on a leash. Finally the contrary canine broke loose and immediately started running frenzied figure eights across the supine bodies of sun-worshipers. Bedlam followed. A lot of bellowing as well.

"This certainly is entertaining," John said. He had an amused glint in his eye.

Belinda nodded. "Nothing like this happens back home."

"In Cambridge?" I asked, just to be wicked. It was the half a margarita's fault.

"That's Cambria," John said.

"Right."

Perhaps because she didn't have to drive, Estelle Zimmerman was well into her second drink. "What's the water temperature like there?" she asked.

Belinda tossed her naturally blond locks. "Nice and warm. I swim almost every day."

Estelle Zimmerman whipped her head around to look at me. It took another second for the bags under her eyes to catch up.

"This woman is not from California," she said.

# 18

John and Belinda exchanged glances. "Of course she is," he said.

Estelle's penciled brows disappeared into the creases on her forehead. "I don't think so, dear."

The handsome travel agent attempted to smile, but his blue eyes revealed his true feelings. "Are you calling us liars?" he asked softly.

The farmer's wife would not back down. "I read in the paper this morning that water in Charleston Harbor was eighty-five degrees Fahrenheit. Nowhere along the coast of California does the Pacific Ocean get that warm."

"Estee knows everything," Herman said proudly. He seemed oblivious to any ramifications of his wife's accusation.

John Thomas put a well-muscled arm around Belinda's shoulders. Then the couple rose to their feet in unison, as if they'd choreographed the action.

"Come on, darling, we don't need to listen to this." John's protective persona made me think of Greg.

"But you can't go yet," I said quickly. "How will you get back to Charleston?"

"We'll take the long way around, like the policewoman said."

"What if you get lost?"

"We'll take our chances."

It was time to be pragmatic. "But we haven't got the bill yet. We need to divide—"

He tossed a pair of twenties next to my plate. "Keep the change, Mrs. Washburn."

There was nothing I could do to stop them, had I wanted to. The funny thing was, now that I'd been reimbursed for lunch (Coconut Joe's is very reasonable), I didn't care if I ever saw them again. They were as fake as a four dollar bill, as phony as a photo of Tammy Faye without makeup. But my gut feeling was (and the tinier the gut, the more accurate, if you ask me) that the Thomases had nothing to do with the death of Marina Webbfingers. Stereotypes of blondes aside, they didn't seem to have the brain power. Besides, John's hair color wasn't even his own.

Yes, I know, there are a lot of stupid crooks out there. One might even go so far as to say that most crooks at least lack discernment, or they wouldn't put themselves in situations that involve such penalties as prison or, in some cases, capital punishment. But the Thomases came across as particularly inept. They were nice to look at, sure—if you like bulging biceps and straining bosoms—but let's face it, they couldn't find their way out of a paper bag if you gave them both scissors.

As Belinda's backside cleared the door, Irena Papadopoulus smiled smugly over the salted rim of her glass. "I didn't trust those two from the start."

"Really?" I didn't want to tip my hand, but I'd had my own doubts about the Calamari couple.

"They're fakes. Complete fakes. If you ask me, the police should be investigating them, instead of that crazy woman with just one eyebrow."

"Wynnell has two eyebrows—they're just closely spaced. And she isn't crazy."

"Whatever you say, Mrs. Washburn."

What I wanted to say next was that I didn't trust the Papadopouluses, either. No legitimate gem buyer would be ignorant of the four C's. And if the tall, dark, and usually silent man by her side was her husband, I'd eat my chapeau (I keep an easily digestible paper hat on hand for just such occasions). As for the Zimmermans . . .

A cell phone rang. Since mine had ended up in the drink, it took me a moment to remember that I had taken the backup phone from the car and slipped it into my bag before entering the restaurant. This is an older, somewhat unwieldy model, with an annoyingly loud ring. Normally I think it is very rude to have one's phone turned on in an enclosed space, particularly this phone, but my best friend's freedom was at stake. Maybe even her life.

I didn't recognize the number at first. "Hello?"

"Mrs. Washburn?" I didn't recognize the voice, either.

"Yes."

"This is Veronica Dillsworth. I'm—uh, Mr. Hammerhead's receptionist."

I knew now who she was; the bosomy, nearly bald woman, who was quite likely more than just the attorney's receptionist. If that was indeed the case, her job title suited her just fine. But it was not my place to judge.

"What trouble has my brother gotten into now?"

"He's not in any trouble that I know of—although he certainly is cute. Too bad he's a priest."

"He's only a priest-in-training. I'm sure the training he's had so far can be undone."

"I beg your pardon?"

"Never mind. What can I do for you?"

"I'm supposed to pass a message on to you, Mrs. Washburn. Mr. Hammerhead said you might find it important." She paused, presumably for dramatic effect.

"Don't keep me in suspenders, dear."

"Suspenders?"

"That was a joke. What is this important message?"

"The murder weapon has been located."

"The murder weapon?"

Five pairs of eyes locked on to me. Four, of course, belonged to my companions. The fifth, a remarkably large pair, were owned by our waitress, who had finally arrived with our bill.

"Mrs. Washburn, are you still there?"

"Yes. Please elaborate."

"It's says here—Mr. Hammerhead left a note—that a tourist spotted it at low tide. Just off the Battery. Thought it might be a valuable find."

"Just what exactly is *it*?" I tried to sound nonchalant, so as to disappoint the eavesdroppers.

"A statue of some kind—says here 'David.' Maybe that was the name of the guy who found it. Anyway, there were bloodstains on it."

"I see." The five sets of staring eyes didn't see, and they leaned closer.

"Oh, and Mr. Hammerhead said to tell you the arraignment was moved up. In fact, that's where he is right now."

"I see."

"That's all the note says, Mrs. Washburn."

"What else did the witness say?"

"Excuse me?"

It was my turn to pause. "Oh really? Did she describe the hair color?"

"Mrs. Washburn, I'm afraid you're not making any sense."

"Possibly a tourist, you say? From which state?"

"Yes, it was a tourist who found the statue, Mrs. Washburn, but it doesn't say anything here about where they're from."

"Well, I'm at Coconut Joe's right now, but as soon as we settle the bill, I'm heading straight for the Webbfingerses' place to deliver my passengers."

"Mrs. Washburn, is your brother as kooky as you?"

"Certainly. And yes, I am driving my own car. You've got all the information on that, right? Model, license plate number, etcetera."

"Mrs. Washburn, I really have to go." She hung up.

"Okay, I'll see you in a bit, Officer Bright." I turned my attention back to the ten twitching ears. "I'll take the check, this time."

Herman was quick to protest. "That's not necessary, little lady."

"But I insist. I have something to celebrate."

"What?" Our waitress pulled up a chair and sat next to Estee Zimmerman.

I scowled at the impudent youth. "I'm not free to discuss it, dear."

"That's no reason to be rude," Irena said.

How right she was. A properly reared Southern woman is charming at all times. When left with no choice but to reproof, she does so while smiling, always careful to add the phrase "bless your heart." Those three words, incidentally, can ameliorate even the foulest of insults, when said in just the right tone and in a Deep South accent.

"Darling," I said to the girl, whose name was Teena, "I do apologize for my behavior. I'm sure it isn't your fault you possess a paucity of manners, bless your heart."

She brightened. "Thank you, ma'am."

Having redeemed my reputation as a belle, I led my little flock back to Ocean Boulevard and cars that were five degrees hotter than Hades.

I led my diminished caravan across the Isle of Palms connector and back to Mount Pleasant. On the way, we crossed the Intracoastal Waterway and passed Goat Island, where a handful of adventurous souls live without the benefits of public utilities. Once we hit Highway 17 again, I aimed straight for the nosebleed high bridges and the Holy City. It was a half-hour trip, so we had plenty of time to talk, but it was the New Yorkers I wanted to grill, not the farmers from the dell.

Fate intervened when Estelle requested that I stop at a sweetgrass basket stand. The stands are nothing more than flimsy wooden lean-tos that dot the highway between the Cooper River and Awendaw like buttons on an expensive blazer, but they contain some of the finest handicrafts on the continent. Here, Gullah women, descendants of Western African slaves, weave intricate baskets out of sweetgrass and palm fronds, in the tradition of their ancestors. The baskets have become highly collectible, popular with both tourists and long-term residents, and prices can reflect that. Of course not all baskets are created equally, and quality does vary, but overall these keepsakes will appreciate in value. With every passing year sweetgrass becomes harder to find, and the older generation of women, those with the patient fingers, find themselves with fewer protégées.

While Herman and Estelle haggled over what was already a bargain, and the handsome Nick fondled a particularly attractive specimen, I edged the irritable Irena aside.

"Mrs. Papadopoulus," I said, "my wedding anniversary is coming up, and my husband wants to upgrade my diamond. But I've been thinking, and what I'd really want is to get a second ring—one for my right hand."

"One can never own too much jewelry."

"My thoughts exactly. And instead of a diamond in this ring, I'd like a nice big sparkling dolomite. Maybe a four carat stone. I realize you're on vacation, and I don't mean to bother you with business talk, but I was wondering if you could give me a ballpark figure."

She shrugged. "Yes, I am on vacation. Besides, I buy gems wholesale for retailers. I couldn't possibly give you a quote on a single stone. One that doesn't exist."

"Oh." That was disappointing. I thought sure I had her there, since dolomite is not a gem. It is, instead, a compact limestone, and in fact an entire mountain range of the mineral is to be found in northern Italy.

I must have sounded exceptionally pitiful, because that's what was reflected in her beady eyes. Fortunately the pity was served up with a nice dollop of scorn, which somehow made it more palatable.

"Well, you are talking about a hypothetical stone, aren't you?" she demanded.

My heart beat faster. "Yes, ma'am."

"All right then," she said brusquely. "If it's good quality dolomite—how does a thousand dollars a carat sound?"

"Fantastic."

"Is it a mar kiss?"

"Excuse me?"

"You know, shaped like this?" She shaped a classical marquise, elliptical but with pointed ends, on the back of her hand.

"No, ma'am. It's round."

"That's too bad, because mar kiss stones are the big thing now. Resale would be better."

"I don't plan to resell an anniversary ring."

She snorted. Whether it was diversion or a no-see-um up her nose, I didn't care. I had all the information I needed.

We were halfway across the first span of the Grace Memorial Bridge when it happened again. Just as we began the downward swoop over Drum Island, I happened to glance in the rearview mirror. Instead of the tanned and toned Nick, and the two-toned Irena, I found myself looking at a battered pickup being driven by a hygienically challenged man in faded blue overalls, and a head that wouldn't look out of place on Mount Rushmore.

"It's him," I gasped.

"Who?" Herman, who was riding shotgun, tried to turn, but his neck ruff became tangled in his shoulder strap, rendering him temporarily immobile.

Estelle didn't budge. "Abby, I don't mean to be a backseat driver, but you're awfully close to this side of the bridge."

Indeed I was. But in my defense, the Suburban Assault Vehicle to my left was well over the center line.

"There's someone tailgating us," I said through

clenched teeth. "He tried to run me off the road earlier. Can you try and get a description?"

Herman grunted as he ripped off a handful of hair in a valiant effort to cooperate. "The son of a gun just gave me the finger."

Estelle clucked disapprovingly at her husband's outburst. "Maybe you should speed up, Abby."

"I can't. The car in front of me is barely creeping along. We're boxed in."

"Then honk."

The woman was really getting on my nerves, but she had a point. Some folks, while not as nervous as the Thomases, creep across the failing structure, no doubt afraid that a faster speed will cause the rust to break apart and send them plunging to their deaths. Others plod along because their cars just don't have oomph for inclines that steep. Still others—and this is where honking is beneficial—meander through life, and traffic, in a perpetual fog. A sharp toot of the horn will sometimes startle them into momentary consciousness. With any luck, the driver in front of me would remain surprised and awake until we'd both made it across safely.

I honked. Two long blasts followed by three short ones. I attached no meaning to my beeps other than "get out of my way you slowpoke." But considering how things were going lately, I might consider learning Morse code. That way, when I was really frustrated, I could spell out something really naughty.

The driver in front of me responded with an immediate burst of speed. Then turning his head, he smiled and waved.

"Cheeky son of a gun," Herman muttered.

"B-But a handsome man," Estelle stuttered.

"That's no man," I sputtered. "That's my husband."

# 19

I can't blame Greg for pressing the pedal to the metal and making like a ghost; he simply disappeared. And while I gaped open-mouthed at the space left by my husband's car, the menacing pickup behind me did a vanishing act of its own. Perhaps the bridge really was haunted.

By the time I dropped off the Zimmermans and the Papadopouluses, Greg had showered and was sitting on the front steps with a salted margarita in each hand. If I hadn't been so furious, and thus capable of seeing only red, I might have noticed how much the white shorts and crisp blue shirt he'd changed into set off his tan. If I hadn't been so self-absorbed, I might have appreciated the fact that he was wearing cologne—something other than Eau du Poisson.

Greg extend the drink meant for me. "Here you go, hon. On a hot day like this, I think a little extra sodium is called for, don't you?"

"I don't want alcohol. I want answers."

"Okay, but you're not forgetting that I have to solve crossword puzzles in pencil first."

"Greg, I'm in no mood for jokes. What are you doing home this early?"

"The truth?"

"Of course."

"You're going to be pissed."

"It's too late now."

He sighed, and set my untouched drink next to the wrought-iron banister. "The truth is I love you too much. I couldn't bear it if something happened to you."

It was the truth, all right. I could see the love in his eyes. But I could *feel* his need to control me. And yes, I was pissed. I was an adult, for crying out loud. In a sense, Greg risked his life every day that he took the shrimp boat out. We both risked our lives whenever we drove anywhere—or, for that matter, walked. Especially during tourist season.

"Greg, you and Mama sicced Toy on me. Wasn't that enough?"

"No offense, hon, but your brother isn't the most responsible person in the world."

"That's not fair. For all you know, he's changed." Two days ago I would have bet a million dollars that those words would never pass my lips.

My darling husband was suddenly interested in

studying one of his brown kneecaps. "If he was responsible, he wouldn't have helped you climb a wall. That was a damn foolish thing to do, Abby. You could have broken your neck."

"But I didn't—Greg, you were *there*?"

"Someone had to keep an eye on you."

My legs felt weak, so I joined Greg on the steps—on the far side of the steps. "Did you follow me to Sullivan's Island?"

"Guilty."

"What did you do while we were eating lunch on the Isle of Palms?"

"I hung out on the beach behind an umbrella. I could see you the entire time."

"How did you end up in front of me on the bridge?"

"It was that sudden stop you made at the sweetgrass basket stand. I couldn't turn around fast enough. I thought I'd lost you—I thought sure you were on to me—so I decided to mosey on home. Wait for you here. I guess I moseyed too much."

One has to admire a man who can spend hours outside in our near tropical heat and not break a sweat. After admiring him briefly, one is then free to react in a more reasonable way.

"Gregory," I growled, "what you did is just plain unacceptable. I'm not going to take it sitting down." To emphasize my point, I jumped to my feet.

He lost interest in his kneecap. "What is that supposed to mean?"

"It means that until you can respect me as an equal, someone capable of making her own decisions—well, I'm just not going to put up with it."

His sapphire blue eyes locked on mine, but after a second or two seemed to fade in intensity. "Ah, I know what you mean. You're moving out, aren't you? More accurately, you're moving in with them."

"Them?"

"The Rob-Bobs. Every time we have a dispute, you either run back to your mama's or you move in with Rob Goldburg and Bob Steuben. Now that Mozella lives with us, it's narrowed your options, but you're just as eager to go. I'm telling you, Abby, just because they're gay—well, I still don't like to see you move in with two guys."

"You think I'd rather move in with them than stay here and work this thing out?"

"Don't you three have more in common?"

"Our work, yes. But you're my best friend."

He was quiet for a moment. "Sometimes it doesn't feel that way."

The trouble with having a handsome and charming husband is that it's hard to stay angry at him. There are times when I have to work to keep my hackles hiked. On the other hand, while a homely mate might make it easier to hold a grudge, the makeup sex might not be as good. Not that I'm speaking from personal experience, mind you, even though I was married to Buford "the timber snake" Timberlake. Back then it took at least half a bottle of wine—but I digress.

"Greg, I just need time to cool off. To sort things out." Already I was softening. But if, after two years of marriage, I couldn't get Greg to see how much I valued my independence, the road ahead was bound to be even rockier. It was my duty as a good wife to drive the point home now, while the potholes were still navigable.

The love of my life picked up my discarded drink. "Abby, you just need to calm down a bit."

"Calm down?"

"Just a notch, hon."

"That does it. I'm outta here for now. You see that Dmitri gets fed—and sift his litter for a change. Oh, and tell Mama where I am."

He looked at the margarita, which was sweating far more than he ever did, and then looked at me. "Let me know when you're done pouting, Abby."

"Damn you," I said.

He didn't even have the decency to wait until I'd turned away before downing the drink.

The Finer Things is arguably Charleston's finest antique store. While I carry a broad inventory, catering to a variety of tastes and pocketbooks, the Rob-Bobs deal only in museum-quality, one-of-a-kind pieces. Collectors come from as far away as New Orleans and San Francisco to do business with them.

I have sleigh bells on the back of my door to announce customers, but at The Finer Things, one has to be buzzed in. While my friends do not engage in racial, or economical, profiling, they do have a decided prejudice against fully expanded women in spandex. Shoppers deemed inappropriately dressed will be ignored.

Once inside, however, expect to be treated like a queen. A gold-plated samovar once owned by Nicholas and Alexandria is kept full of Russian tea. A solid silver salver, made by the revered Paul himself, spills over with petits fours and crustless sandwiches that somehow manage never to go stale. Should you open your mouth to speak, either Rob or Bob will pop up beside you, as if anticipating your comment or question. Guests—and that's what my friends prefer to call their clientele—leave with the impression that they were all that mattered during their visits.

Perhaps the Rob-Bobs had been tipped off to my impending arrival, because even though I leaned on the bell, neither even bothered to glance at the door. Finally, when by rights they should have been calling the police, Bob tripped over and pretended to do a double take.

"Oh my goodness," he said, pushing the door open with long slim fingers, like those of a pianist, "the buzzer must be broken."

"Bull."

"Abby," Bob did his best to whisper, "Greg called and he doesn't want us to enable you."

*"What?"*

He lowered his voice even further. Since Bob's normal register is bass, his deep rumbles echoed off the nearest pieces of furniture. It would have been easier to understand an elephant.

"I heard you better the first time, Bob. I want to know what he means by 'enable.' "

"I'm sorry, Abby, but he thinks you're being childish."

"Does this mean I can't stay with you?"

Bob's Adam's apple jerked violently, and I imagined a large fish—perhaps a bass—had just been snagged. "If it was up to me, Abby—oh the heck with it, it's my place, too. Of course you can stay."

"What about him?" I pointed with my chin to Rob's turned back.

"Forget about him. He's doing his alpha male thing, bonding with Greg. But he'll come around."

"You sure?"

"Positive. And who cares if he doesn't? You'll stay in my room—well, it's really the guest room, but you know what I mean. That's where I keep my vinyl collection. We'll have a great time, just the two of us. I have Judy Garland originals, Peggy Lee—hey, you like camel?"

"Cigarettes?"

"The meat."

"I beg your pardon?"

"Because if you do, you'll love alpaca. They say it's sweeter than camel. I'm serving a standing rib roast tonight, with yogurt and cumin sauce. I found the recipe in *Caravan Cuisine*. I had to adapt it, of course, seeing how alpacas come from South America, not Africa or Asia, but it smells good just marinating."

I must confess that for the next few minutes I found myself in a culinary quandary. I could refuse Bob's offer and have Greg think he'd won, or I could acquiesce and gag on alpaca. Because gourmets generally serve small, albeit attractively presented portions, I decided to risk gagging. And anyway, if I backed down now, I'd more than likely have to choke on my words, which didn't have the advantage of being served with yogurt and cumin sauce.

"Great," Bob said, when I agreed to his plan.

"Not so fast!" Maybe it's because Rob took two

years of ballet when he was boy, but that man can move as silently as a puma in slippers.

Bob crossed his rather spindly arms. "I'm not backing down. Abby's my guest."

"Correction—she's *our* guest." Rob stooped to kiss my cheek. "You okay with that, Abby?"

"Sure, but I thought—"

"That was just to throw him off track. Serve him right to worry even more."

Supper wasn't for a number of hours—alpaca roasts, even when well-marinated, are best cooked slowly to ensure tenderness—so there wasn't any point in my hanging around the shop. I tried calling Wooden Wonders several times to see if by chance Wynnell's husband, Ed, was there, but kept getting a busy number. Instead of adding to my frustration level, I decided to tool out there in person.

Compared to the old Cooper bridges, the Ashley River Memorial Bridge is sedate and dignified, almost European in appearance. Because the latter does not have to accommodate container ships, very few people who use it come down with high-altitude sickness. On a trip across the Ashley one invariably sees sailboats, and if headed into town, the Ashley Marina presents one of the prettiest sights on the Eastern seaboard.

When headed out of town, the first right turn puts

you on St. Andrew's Boulevard. By bearing left and staying on Route 61, the traveler finds him- or herself on Ashley River Road, downriver from some of America's finest antebellum-era plantations. Magnolia Gardens, Drayton Hall—this is the Old South about which Margaret Mitchell rhapsodized. It is still there—sans slaves, of course, and with ice cold beverages at one's fingertips, if one has the fortitude to make it past the strip malls and other dubious achievements of urban development.

Wynnell's shop is in one of these microshopping centers, sandwiched between a Subway and a coin-operated laundry. Her customer base tends to be drop-ins from the Laundromat, lower-income women who, unable to purchase washers and dryers of their own, are unlikely to buy "used furniture" at such fancy prices. An occasional well-heeled woman with a hankering for a low-fat sub will wander in out of curiosity. If it weren't for the munching matrons, Wooden Wonders would never have floated at all.

The front door was locked, but I could see Ed on the phone, his back to me. I rapped on the smudged glass with my knuckles until he turned around. He held a finger up as if to signal I should wait a minute, but then he hung up almost immediately.

"Abby," he said, struggling with the lock, "what a nice surprise."

"Ed, how was the arraignment? Were you there?"

"No. It happened too fast—but that was Wynnell on the phone just now. The arraignment was moved up. There was an opening on the docket, and so they were able to convene a grand jury this morning."

"And?"

"She"—his voice broke—"my Wynnell's been indicted for murder. In the first degree."

"Just like that? On what evidence?"

"Apparently there were several eyewitnesses who heard her threaten the deceased. And the so-called murder weapon was found."

"Yes, a statue. What about bail?"

"Denied. Too great a flight risk."

"Why? Because she once ran off to Japan with a group of tourists?" I immediately regretted my words. That episode occurred during a particularly low dip in their marriage—I wasn't aware of any equivalent high points—and undoubtedly brought back sad memories. Ed had to travel to Tokyo, where he made a public appeal to reclaim his bride of over thirty years. The Crawfords have all the luck of Saharan surfers, so it came as no surprise to me when Ed found himself on a Japanese television game show, encased to his neck in green tea-flavored gelatin, while a pair of trained seals vied to balance balls on his nose. Still, it had made sushi converts out of both Crawfords, and Ed now prefers sumo over baseball.

"Have you spoken with her lawyer?" I asked gently.

"Just got off the phone with him. He seems like a nice enough man. Said you brought in another helper."

"My brother, Toy. Ed, you mind if I have a seat?" Without waiting to be asked to sit, I wrestled a Victorian side chair out of a tangle of its littermates. The furniture hadn't been dusted in weeks.

"If Wynnell is going to make it in this business, she's going to need my help. From now on we're in this together. And Abby, thanks for offering to take us under your wing."

"My pleasure. Ed, the afternoon that Marina Webbfingers was killed—did Wynnell seem particularly upset?"

He jerked to attention. "Upset? What are you implying?"

"Nothing, dear. It's just that several witnesses claim to have overheard Wynnell and Mrs. Webbfingers fighting—well, at least arguing vociferously. They could be lying, of course."

Ed studied his knuckles. His lifestyle was such that he would never get all the grease from the creases.

"I suppose," he said, choosing his words carefully, "that you already know that the two of them didn't get along, on account of the bathrooms in the main house being off limits."

"When a gal's gotta go, a gal's gotta go. I don't blame Wynnell for finding it demeaning."

"You didn't."

"That's because I was remodeling the guest rooms, not working in the garden. There were facilities at my disposal all day long."

"But you're right, Abby, the day Mrs. Webbfingers was murdered—well, let's just say my Wynnell was fit to be tied."

"Tell me more about it."

"Well, you know she'd already done her job—been paid and everything—and then suddenly she gets this call saying a lot of the flowers were dying. So Wynnell closes up the shop early, goes over, and sure enough the flowers are wilted, but it's not her fault. Someone had turned off the drip hose."

"Drip hose?" What I know about gardening can be contained on the back of a seed packet.

"Like a garden hose, but with pinprick-size holes in it spaced at even intervals. It's left on all the time, but just enough water seeps out—and to just the right spots—so that nothing gets wasted. Farmers use them a lot."

"Hmm. Why would someone mess around with a hose that wasn't theirs?"

"Unless it was Mrs. Webbfingers. This may surprise you, Abby, but some folks get their kicks from being nasty."

That saddened me, but in no way was I surprised. Marriage to Buford had prepared me for anything—well, maybe not alpaca in yogurt and cumin sauce.

"What did Wynnell do, besides turn the hose back on?"

"Nothing—not to Mrs. Webbfingers. Yeah, they exchanged words, but I'm the one that caught the real heat when she got home. What's that old saying, you only love the ones you hurt?"

Again I thought of Buford. He must have loved me very much. He obviously still adores our children, since he never calls them—not even on birthdays or holidays.

"I know what you mean," I said. "But we both know Wynnell's bark is worse than her bite."

He settled on a chair opposite me. At least our backsides were good for dusting.

"Abby, what do you know about real estate law in South Carolina?"

"Virtually nothing—except that everyone needs a will. Daddy and Mama had good up-to-date wills, and when Daddy died, that made everything fairly easy for Mama. It's funny how intelligent, organized people freeze up when it comes to wills. Like talking about them is bad luck."

"Yeah, wills. Always a good thing. But what about property rights when there isn't a death but one of the parties is—uh, well, you know."

"Incarcerated?"

He looked away. "I mean, that could happen, right?"

"What could?"

"She could be found guilty, right? And if that happens, who gets the shop?"

"Whose name is it in now?"

"Hers, but I cosigned. Wynnell wasn't working then and . . ."

I tuned him out. Could it possibly be that this uninteresting man, who had only slightly more personality than a rutabaga, and was frankly less handsome, had framed his wife for murder? But why? The shop was failing, not making a dime—*unless*—no, there was no way he could count on a death sentence, so life insurance was out of the question.

This was nonsense thinking on my part, but just further proof that living with Buford is enough to make an incurable cynic out of the most trusting of maidens. Besides, there was another possible motive; perhaps Ed had been one of Marina's lovers. They were not from the same social set, to be certain, but maybe one day when he'd stopped by to pick Wynnell up from her gardening project—which he'd done upon occasion—the two locked eyes and in the words of Magdalena Yoder, engaged in the horizontal hootchy-kootchy. Absurd? Yes, but not out of the realm of possibility. Sex, especially when meant to punish a third party, often makes no sense.

So Wynnell found out about her husband's upscale lover, and confronted the woman. She then confronted Ed, who decided to capitalize on his wife's temper and have her locked away for good. Thereafter he would be free to lead the life of his dreams, the life he'd missed out on as a rug-weaving mill worker: fishing in the morning and shagging on shag carpets by night.

I tuned Ed back in. He was regarding me through hooded eyes, his lips slack, like he was in the process of dozing off in front of the TV. Thanksgiving afternoon football games came to mind. If indeed he was a killer, he wasn't a threat to me just then. Besides, unlike just about everyone else that day, he couldn't read my mind.

"Ed, darling," I said, as I stood and pushed my chair back, "I'll stay in touch. We've got to concentrate on clearing Wynnell, but then—and I promise—we'll do something about this shop."

He wasn't paying attention. Hadn't even bobbed his head when I stood up. How rude was that? Any Southern gentleman worthy of his sweet tea will automatically rise when a woman rises or enters a room. Even murderers (or so I suppose). This shocking turn of events could only mean one thing: the carpet maker had just exposed himself as a carpetbagger. Edward Eugene Crawford had Yankee blood coursing through his veins!

Suddenly I didn't know my best friend's husband at all. His strong Piedmont accent, his passion for the Panthers, his preference for vinegar-based barbecue sauce over tomato, were these just all affectations? A man capable of concealing Northern roots was capable of anything. How ironic that just a few weeks before, Wynnell had prattled on and on about the presence of Yankee spies among us. Was she trying tell me something then? Had I, in my enlightened arrogance, ignored a buddy's desperate cry for help?

Maybe Wynnell hadn't known then, maybe our conversation that day was merely coincidence. But there was no escaping the facts now. My friend was going to be heartbroken when she learned that the man to whom she'd pledged her troth, the man with whom she'd shared a bed all these years, was actually from "up the road a piece." Talk about the ultimate betrayal. At least there were no offspring from this unholy union.

Not being the least bit prejudiced myself, I didn't for a second think that a Yankee killer was any more diabolical than a Southern one. Good manners mean little when one is being murdered.

I gripped the Victorian side chair and pushed it between me and Ed. Let the S.O.B. from W.O.T.A. try and get me. I'd show him that we belles had balls—in a manner of speaking, that is. I mean, there wasn't a Yankee alive that could drink a Miss Kudzu contestant under the table.

One of the chair legs hit a knot in the pine floor, and when I jerked it past the rough spot, it hit the floor again with a thunk. It wasn't much of a jolt, but apparently it was enough to send the slack-jawed Ed sliding to the floor.

It took me a few seconds to scream.

# 20

Ed Crawford was either dead or in a coma. In either case, a phone call made a lot more sense than screaming. Still, a good scream has therapeutic value, so I held off summoning help until I was quite sure I'd exhausted all the benefits of vocalization. Then, as I was halfway across the room to use Wynnell's phone, it occurred to me that calling on my backup cellular, outside and in the bright sunshine, was the only way to go. Someone could have been hiding behind the heavy wooden stacks being peddled as furniture, or a dangerous substance might have been smeared on the receiver, which he had touched minutes before he died.

But outside in the glare reflected from parked automobiles, and the heat rising from the asphalt, death seemed far away. Still, just to be safe, I waited in the Subway, in the greasy Formica booth nearest the front door. The only other people in the shop were a pair of teenage employees, who were too busy popping toppings into each other's mouths to notice me. Lord only knows why they hadn't heard me scream.

The men in blue showed up almost immediately, which made me think I'd been followed. Before I could address the issue—like why the heck didn't *anyone* respond to my screams—Sergeant Scrubb walked in. My sigh of relief may have carried with it a few disobedient pheromones.

Sergeant Scrubb is a dead ringer for actor Ben Affleck, a man for whom he is constantly mistaken. The sergeant treats these cases of mistaken identity with good humor, as does his lucky wife, Aleena. The two give the impression of being happily married, which is good news for American women of all descriptions. Trust me, Aleena Scrubb looks nothing like Jennifer Lopez.

"Abby," he said "an ambulance is on its way." A second later it arrived. Sergeant Scrubb excused himself to confer with EMTs and watch them load Ed's body into the vehicle. When they left, sirens screaming, he immediately returned to me. "Okay, Abby, from the beginning."

I had many beginnings, because no sooner would I get started than one or another of the men in blue popped in to report to Sergeant Scrubb, or to ask him a question. I began to feel like the Pause button on a remote control. Finally the sergeant issued orders for us to be left alone.

"Sorry, Abby."

"No problemo. I'd kind of forgotten, but we mothers are used to that."

"One more time, if you will."

"You sure you don't want a sandwich first? This might take awhile."

"We prefer doughnuts, but what the heck. A roast beef with extra jalapenos sounds pretty good right now. How about you? Can I get you something?"

It seemed wrong for me to chow down while my best friend's husband was literally cooling his heels in the back of an ambulance. Besides, the kids hadn't been wearing disposable gloves during their food fun. On the other hand, the promise of an alpaca supper wasn't much to look forward to, and an empty stomach was only going to make me crabby and difficult to deal with later on that evening. Thinking only of others, I had the detective buy me a white chocolate and macadamia nut cookie, and a diet soda. Chocolate has been proven to contain medicinal properties, and the sugar-free beverage washes away any residual guilt.

While Sergeant Scrubb made short shrift of his spicy sandwich, I described what had transpired at Wooden Wonders. Uninterrupted, it took only a few minutes.

"So," I said, as I deftly licked a dainty finger,

"that was it. He just slumped to the floor. One minute he's alive and well, and the next minute he's dead."

"How do you know he's dead?"

"Well, I don't. Isn't he?"

His eyes answered my question, without committing him to an answer. "Abby, I realize there is no point in demanding that you back off this case"—he paused—"is there?"

"None. Wynnell is my best friend—after Greg, of course."

"That's what I thought. But we can agree that you want her cleared and Marina Webbfingers's real killer caught."

"Of course. That would be Ed's killer, too, right?"

I couldn't tell if he winced or winked. "Trust me, Abby, we will find this person—or persons. And as much as we appreciate your willingness to help, it's our job, not yours."

"Yes, but—"

"You could help us out a lot, Abby, if you concentrated on your area of expertise."

"Oh?" Flattery will get anyone just about anywhere with me. That's how I ended up with the surname Timberlake.

"You're an authority on antiques, am I right?"

"Well, I wouldn't say that—although there are those who would."

"Abby, what I'm about to say is confidential."
He let his gaze linger on me until I broke eye contact. Another couple of seconds and I would have
offered to raise his child by another woman.

"I won't breathe a word," I gasped softly.

"Something was found in the harbor this morning—a little statue of some kind. It has what appears to be a bloodstain, and it was recovered only
a short ways from double 0 Legare Street. The lab
is checking it now to see if there is a tissue match."

I nodded. Knowledge is power, but silence is the
most powerful tool of all. As far as I was concerned, there was no need for the agreeable
Scrubb to know just how much—or little—I already knew about the case.

"How can I be of help?"

"I want you take a look at a Polaroid of that
statue. See if it rings a bell." He extracted a photo
from his shirt pocket and handed it across the
table. The picture was still warm from his chest. If
I'd been by myself, I might have given it a quick
sniff.

Instead, I pretended to examine it closely. "Yes,
I've seen that statue before."

"Where?"

"Everywhere. It's a copy of Michelangelo's
David. They're as common as garden gnomes.
More so even, because a lot of people decorate in-
doors with them. Can you believe that? I mean,

not that I'm being snobbish or anything—but you know what I mean."

He gave me no sign that he did. "Is it possible you've seen this very one?"

I shrugged. "There was one in the Webbfingerses' garden, but like I said, they're ubiquitous. And they all look alike."

Sergeant Scrubb was far more skilled than I when it came to the silence game. He sat entirely motionless, like one of the statues in Madame Tussaud's Wax Museum in New York City the last time I was there. The figures are eerily realistic; even the vein patterns in the eyes have been duplicated, and each hair is reportedly applied by hand. Some of Madame Tussaud's statutes seemed more likely to move than the detective did just then.

"Well, it's the truth," I wailed. I practically flung the picture back at him.

He sprang to life. "Abby, please keep the photo. Study it. There might be an important clue in there."

"Right." I thrust the photo in my purse. "But if it's clues you want, then I suggest you interrogate that bunch of so-called guests staying at La Parterre."

The artists at the wax museum could have applied a new hairline to their Scrubb version in the time it took him to respond. "Would you like to tell me more?"

"I'm sure there is no need to. You probably have bulging files on every one of them."

"Let's say I did. What would be in them?"

"Well, the Papadopouluses aren't who they pretend to be, for one thing. Irena is not a gem buyer—unless it's baubles for herself—and I doubt if that studmuffin sidekick is her husband. If the Thomases are really travel agents, I'll eat my—alpaca without complaining. As for the Zimmermans—"

A sharp rap on the window from one of the men in blue made me spill the dregs left in my soda cup. Sergeant Scrubb scowled at the intrusion and tried to wave the young officer away, but the man was insistent.

"What the hell?" Sergeant Scrubb mouthed behind cupped hands. He was obviously unaware of his reflection in the glass.

The young man on the other side also cupped his hands to his mouth. "Phone!" he yelled, his face just inches away from the window.

"You idiot," Sergeant Scrubb yelled back. He strode outside and carried on a conversation that grew more animated by the second. Finally he turned to the window, his face all smiles.

I waited patiently until he came back inside. "What gives?" I asked.

"Abby, you're not going to believe this."

"Try me."

"Officer Ditzski was just on the phone with one of the EMTS—anyway, it seems that Mr. Crawford has a pulse—"

"*What?*"

"Did you know he was a diabetic?"

"No! And Wynnell has been my best friend for years." Frankly, I felt betrayed.

"Well, he should have been wearing a medical alert tag. They save lives, you know."

I was about to open my mouth, to tell him he was preaching to the choir, when a Channel 2 news truck pulled up. Sergeant Scrubb excused himself yet again.

Being four-foot-nine does have its advantages. I slipped out of the Subway unnoticed by anyone. Certainly not by the teenagers, who had progressed from food popping to tongue swapping. I thought I heard someone call my name just as I was closing my car door, but I knew better than to turn around. They say there is no such thing as bad publicity, and while that may hold true for people in the arts, such as film stars, musicians, and even writers, those of us in the retail sector know that even a little bad press can shut your business down overnight. Especially when murder is involved.

Sure, a few ghouls might stop by the Den of Antiquity to get a gander at the woman whom death and disease seem to follow like a pack of snarling hyenas, but discerning folks who have a choice where to shop are more likely to choose a store with a prestigious reputation. Another mug shot of me in the *Post and Courier* was the last thing I wanted.

I drove quickly, but not recklessly, to the Rob-Bobs' mansion south of Broad. My wealthy friends do not even pretend not to be pretentious. They purposely picked the house with the grandest columns, the finest ironwork, and the lushest garden they could find for under five million. Then they sprang for a million dollars in "home improvements." Maison de Robert has been the backdrop for three movies of which I am aware, and has been featured in eight magazines.

What was once the carriage house now serves as a three-car garage, which in this part of town is as rare as hoarfrost. The two stalls on either side were taken, so I parked in the middle. I must confess, it usually gives me a thrill not to have to park on the street, along with the tourists and those of lesser means. Tonight, however, I was numb.

Bob saw me through the kitchen window and rapped on it, motioning for me to take the side entrance. "Hey," he said, pressing his six o'clock shadow to my cheek. "You're just in time to help with the salad."

"Great. Let us begin." It wasn't meant to be

funny; I needed to keep my hands busy, if not my mind.

"Oh no lettuce, Abby. We start with a layer of baby endive, then a scoop of Albanian albino artichoke aspic, sprinkle a few sun-dried tomatoes over that, and top it off with a drizzle of basil-infused olive oil."

"Albanian albino artichokes?" I was beginning to feel like Alice in Wonderland.

Rob laughed as he entered the kitchen from the dining room. He bussed my cheek briefly.

"I thought I heard you in here."

"Just arrived." I turned back to Bob. "What kind of artichokes did you say?"

"You heard him right," Rob said. "Guess where he got them?"

I shrugged.

"Go on, guess."

"You had them shipped in from California?"

"No, I picked them up from a specialty shop in Mount Pleasant, but they were grown in Albania. You see, it's a very labor intensive process, because although they're not really albino, they're shaded from the sun as soon as they start to form flower heads."

"Sounds delicious," I said, without the least bit of sarcasm.

The younger partner nodded vigorously. "They're the perfect accompaniment for alpaca."

Rob made a face. "I say that we hog-tie Bob, throw this mess into the harbor, and then make a beeline for McCrady's."

"Do that," Bob said, "and after I gnaw myself free, I'll make a fleet of paper boats from your collection of Broadway Playbills. See which one floats furthest out into the harbor. I bet *Cabaret* makes it halfway to Fort Sumter."

Normally I would have joined in the good-natured banter, but I had just witnessed my best friend's husband slip into a diabetic coma. The jokes, the alpaca sizzling away in the oven—it all seemed so trivial. I gripped the edge of the island table with both hands.

"Guys, I've got something to tell you."

Rob clasped his hands in mock joy. "We're going to be uncles again!"

Bob pushed a ladder-back chair to my derriere. "Sit," he ordered. "And here I was about to put the mother of our nephew to work."

I kicked the chair away. "Stop that! I've got something important to tell you."

Rob winked at Bob. "Ah, it's a niece, not a nephew. Well, we can handle that, can't we? At last, a legitimate excuse to shop at Victoria's Secret."

"I suppose she'll start out as a baby," Bob said. "Maybe we should begin by shopping at baby stores."

"Right. But I hear they grow up fast. We'll have

to start planning for her coming-out party right away."

"We don't know yet if she's going to be a lesbian," Bob said. "Or were you referring to a debutante ball?"

I toppled the chair. "Shut up, please!"

That got their attention.

"And keep it shut until I finish—please."

The two clowns were now the picture of concern. They nodded silently.

I set the chair upright and hoisted myself to the seat. "It's about Ed Crawford. He almost died this afternoon."

They stared, open-mouthed, while I related the afternoon's events. Neither of them had known Ed very well, and neither had they been particularly fond of him, but tragedy seems to have a way of drawing folks together. When I was through with my narration, they made sympathetic sounds, asked a few relevant questions, but then seemed eager to get on with the evening.

"Holy smokes!" Bob said. "The alpaca! I forgot to set the timer."

Rob nudged me. "Maybe McCrady's isn't out of the picture after all. I'll call and see if they have a cancellation."

"Over my dead body," Bob growled. He clapped a hand over his mouth. "Sorry, Abby. It's just that I can't stand to see good food go to waste."

"Neither can I," Rob said. "That's why I want to call McCrady's."

I found my friends' preoccupation with themselves strangely comforting. That's what the living should do—live. How they reacted to an acquaintance's brush with death had no bearing on my life. Just because I felt unsettled didn't mean they had to. Besides, if we didn't consume the camel's cousin now, it would show up later under another guise. Perhaps as alpaca pâté.

"Guys," I said, "let's stick to the original plan. But first I need to show you something." I fished the Polaroid of the stupid statue from my purse. "Believe it or not, *this* is what the police think was used to bludgeon Marina Webbfingers."

Bob tapped the picture with the business end of a wooden spoon. Thank heavens it was a clean utensil.

"Well, I'll definitely have to remove your name from my list of suspects, Abby. That monstrosity has got to weigh at least twenty pounds."

Instead of contributing his own wisecrack, Rob snatched the picture from my hand and held it closer to the overhead hanging light. In the process the spoon was sent flying across the room, where it smacked against a Baccarat crystal vase filled with summer roses. The vase didn't shatter outright, but from the sound of the collision, I knew it was cracked.

But Rob was oblivious to the damage he'd done. "Somebody get me a magnifying glass," he shouted.

"Rob," I said patiently, "I may not have seen as many as you, but trust me, when you've seen one, you've seen them all."

"I'm not talking about a plaster putz, Abby. This statue could be worth a fortune."

# 21

"**S**ay what?" I snatched back the photo. Nothing had changed.

Rob's arms are twice as long as mine, and he has the agility of a basketball player. "Look," he said, holding the photo so that both Bob and I could see.

"We're looking," Bob said. "But we don't see anything—except a middle-class cliché."

"Look at the scale."

Wynnell, the horticultural expert, often complained about scale. Spider mites and aphids as well. I had always associated those pests with plants, not with inanimate garden ornaments.

"Maybe we need the magnifying glass after all," I said. "Still, I don't see why a little bit of scale should make an otherwise piece of junk worth a fortune."

Rob's forehead assumed more folds than a Japanese fan. Then he burst into laughter.

"Not that kind of scale. Scale as in 'proportions.'"

Bob hates it when Rob's superior knowledge of the trade shows him up. "So, this statue is a little head-heavy. So what?"

"It *is*?" I tried in vain to reclaim the snapshot from the hotshot.

Rob was still laughing. "Abby, did you actually see this with your own eyes?"

"I used Bob's," I said.

"Good one. And where did you see it?"

"In Marina's garden, of course."

"There's no 'of course' about this, Abby. Unless I'm mistaken—and I seldom am about this kind of thing—what's in this picture is not a statue at all, but a maquette."

"Why didn't you say so to begin with? Rob—sorry, dear, but I haven't the vaguest idea what you're talking about."

"I do," Bob said, and his Adam's apple bobbed twice, like a cork on the line from which the fish got away.

"Then please explain it to me."

He looked to Rob for approval, and getting it, cleared his throat. "They're called maquettes. They're scale models—most often smaller, but made from a variety of materials—of major statues. The purpose is to give the sculptor a chance to see the finished product in miniature, before committing a large, expensive block of marble to the chisel. Sometimes the models survive along with the important pieces, but often they weren't considered valuable enough to save. Never mind that the practice pieces *are* the originals."

I was glad I'd decided to sit. "Are you saying this could be Michelangelo's original statue of David?"

Rob stroked the photo with a patrician finger. "I'm saying that it could be. Right now it's just a gut feeling."

"I still don't get it. How can you tell by looking at one photo? And no offense to the photographer, but it's not even a good one. If that was a picture of Mama, I wouldn't hang it on the refrigerator. It would be a waste of magnet space."

Bob sighed. "I hate to say this, Abby—because I don't want Rob's head to get any bigger than it is—but the man's got incredibly sharp instincts. When he gets a gut feeling, he's almost always right."

"Except about food," Rob said generously.

"My alpaca!" Bob lunged for the stove.

While our cook fussed and stewed over a leathery roast, Rob located a jeweler's loupe and we examined the photo more carefully. My silver-haired friend was right about one thing—this was not your run-of-the-mill David knockoff. As Bob had pointed out, the head on this one seemed a little larger than normal.

"Allowed them to fit in more detail," Rob said.

"The student sculptors just had to remember to use two scales when transposing the work to a larger piece. And, of course, in sculpting, one can always take away, but never put back."

I shook my head. "But what if this one was made in some concrete factory outside Gatlinburg, Tennessee? Maybe the so-called artist just couldn't get the hang of sculpting. Maybe this David was intended to be bought by a tourist from Ohio, because it would look cute between Snow White and St. Francis of Assisi."

"Abby," Rob said quietly, "you saw the statue close up. What was it made of?"

"Well, it wasn't concrete. I would have noticed that."

"Plaster? Some of them can look pretty good when finished properly."

"I remember thinking that it was compressed marble—at best. More likely resin."

"Could it have been solid marble?"

"I never considered the possibility. Good golly, Miss Molly, what if it was?"

"Then I'd say the chances of it being something really special are pretty good." He tapped his head with a corner of the photo. "Incredibly sharp instincts, remember?"

"If your head gets any bigger, you'll have to ride with your sun roof open. Think how your hair will look then."

"As long as it's all there, who cares? Abby, you have got to let me see this statue."

"It's being held as evidence, Rob. It's the alleged murder weapon."

"Okay, so maybe I won't be allowed to see it, but you can. Take copious notes. Write down anything and everything you observe. Are there any marks on it that could possibly be a signature? Are the edges polished or crude? What the heck is it made of—and oh, try to guess its weight."

"Rob, why do you think I'd be allowed to see it?"

He appeared to be baffled by my question. "Because you're a woman, Abby."

I slid off my chair. Unfortunately that didn't make me any taller.

"Are you suggesting that I sleep my way into seeing it again?"

"Sergeant Scrubb is awfully sexy," Bob said, pausing briefly in his efforts to scrape excess carbon from the roast.

I gave him the evil eye. "You guys better be kidding about this, or I'm out of here."

They exchanged glances. "Yeah, we're only kidding," Rob said. "But you still have an advantage."

"What exactly would that be?"

"You're petite, pert, and pretty. That's a winning combo."

"Ha, that's what you think. Studies have proven that taller people are treated better."

Bob went back to his roast while Rob did his best to rescue me from a slow burn. "There are always exceptions to the rule, Abby, and you're one of them. People like you. They connect with you."

"Go on."

"You're a quick thinker, too. You have the ability to talk yourself into, or out of, just about any situation."

"It didn't work with the alpaca," I whispered.

"Touché."

"Hey, I heard that!" Bob waved a meat fork in our direction.

I sighed. "I'll see what I can do, but I don't want you to get all bent out of shape if my report isn't exactly what you wanted. I obviously don't have your eye for beauty."

"I heard that, too," Bob said, but he was smiling.

It startled me to see the table set for five. I knew we weren't going to eat in the kitchen, because the Rob-Bobs make an occasion out of every meal, but they generally restrict entertaining to the weekends. Tonight's table sagged under the weight of their best Limoges porcelain (reputedly made for the Queen of England), heavy ornate St. Christopher's pattern silverware, a bewildering assortment of glasses and goblets, and a floral arrangement that looked like it had been swiped from a funeral home. Perhaps it had, because both men know better than to create a centerpiece that interfered with one's line of vision. Unless they planned for me to peek under it, while they peered over.

"Is that a pyre for the entrée?" I wasn't being mean, because Bob couldn't hear me. He was still in the kitchen fretting over the albino artichoke aspic, which seemed to have a mind of its own.

Rob chuckled. "Well, actually, they *are* from a funeral home."

"You're kidding!"

"It was Bob's idea. We have a friend who does makeup there, and she's always bringing discarded arrangements home. Anyway, Bob thought it would be a clever way to divide the table, in case you and one of our other guests didn't get along. I can remove them if you like."

I racked my brain, which took all of three seconds. There are few people I truly don't get along with, and none at all that I know of on the Rob-Bobs' roster of friends. Okay—so I don't particularly care for Randy Dewlap. But for the record, it has nothing to do with his split tongue, and everything to do with his split personality, both halves of which are acerbic to the point of being abusive.

"Keep the flowers right where they are. Last time I watched Randy eat, I had nightmares when I went to bed."

"It isn't Randy."

"Oh. Well, that mystery writer friend of yours with the frizzy blond hair isn't so bad, once you get to know her. But I doubt if she wants to look at me. She once called me an illiterate pipsqueak."

"That's because you criticized one of her books. Writers think of their books as their children. They never forgive slights. Besides, it isn't her, either."

I gulped. "Not Mr. Mansour!"

"Abby, in all fairness, it was you who said he'd attract less attention by wearing one of his Persian carpets than with that hideous comb-over he has now."

"But I said it to you, not him. You weren't supposed to pass that along."

"So I had too much to drink that night. We all did. I'm sure Manny doesn't remember a thing."

"Then who is it?" I shrieked.

"Did y'all want something?" Bob called from the kitchen.

We ignored him.

"It's C.J. and your brother, Toy," Rob said. His arms were out, as if to block me from running.

"Get out of town! You've never even met Toy."

"Still haven't. Mozella came in earlier this afternoon and spilled the beans. Bob and I thought we'd take advantage of your distracted mind and meet the brother-from-hell. We weren't ever going to get a chance otherwise. Fortunately, he and C.J. were flexible about their plans."

"I'm surprised you didn't invite Mama and Greg."

"We did invite Mozella, but *The Amazing Race* is on tonight. She says she never misses an episode. But you can forget about your studmuffin. As long as you're sore at him, he's in our doghouse as well."

That's what friends are for! What a lucky woman I was to count these two dear, sweet men among my budding list of buddies. I felt the same way about them. I might not be willing to lay down my life for the Rob-Bobs, but I would definitely give the cold shoulder to any exes they wanted snubbed. Just as long as my friends didn't snub each other.

Still, it wasn't fair of them to invite my baby brother without first checking with me. They'd heard all my Toy horror stories, but they had no way to know that Toy and I had forged a temporary truce. Perhaps the Rob-Bobs were hoping for a spat of sibling incivility to serve as the evening's entertainment. I was about to give them what was left of my mind when the doorbell rang.

# 22

I must admit that Toy and C.J. make a handsome couple. Both of them are tall, blond, and robust. They definitely look more like brother and sister than Toy and I do. If their relationship ever became serious, it would behoove me to question Mama about any trips to Shelby she might have taken when I was a little girl.

At any rate, C.J. had changed into a white cotton eyelet dress, and looked cool and comfortable. On the other hand, not only was Toy still wearing his apprentice priest clothes, but he'd added a baseball cap to his ensemble.

"What gives?" I asked.

"Don't tell me you're not a Braves fan."

"It looks silly, Toy. Take it off."

"Can't."

"Come on." I reached for it, but he jerked away.

"You've been away from the South for a long time, bro. Maybe in L.A. they wear hats indoors, but not here."

"Toy's a grown-up," C.J. said. "You can't tell him what to do. Besides, I think it's cute."

I glared at the big galoot. "He's my brother. I can tell him what I want. And anyway, C.J., this isn't your business."

"Leave her alone, sis," he hissed.

"Fine. Just take it off."

Toy whipped it off. It was the most surreal experience I'd had since my wedding night. Not that I was little Miss Innocent back then, mind you; it's just that I'd never seen a naked one eye-to-eye—so to speak. At any rate, my baby brother was now as bald as Dr. Phil McGraw—that is to say, he had some hair. However, unlike the pop psychologist, Toy Wiggins's locks had been reduced to scattered patches of fuzz located hither, thither, and yon. And a lot more yon than anyplace else.

"Toy!" I gasped. "What happened to you?"

"Take a guess, Abby."

"Not Mr. Hammerhead!"

He nodded ruefully. "But I got the info you wanted, sis. Fisher Webbfingers is loaded—at least by my standards. I don't think he was after insurance money."

My peepers brimmed with tears. What a loving thing for my little brother to do on my behalf. I reached up to give him a kiss, probably the first since he'd been out of diapers.

"Thanks, Toy. I'm really grateful."

"It's okay, sis. It had to be done."

Meanwhile, Rob was staring at us dumbfounded. His only sister is a pillar of society up in Charlotte, North Carolina. It was a safe bet that Rob would never let a lawyer cut his hair, no matter what was at stake. It was an even safer bet that Rob's sister would never put him in that position.

"Toy had the most beautiful blond hair," I tried to explain. "Like Doris Day, but even thicker. Mama used to say that if he'd been born a girl, she would have named him Rapunzel. She's going to freak when she sees this."

"Que sera sera," Toy said bravely.

"Well I like it the way it is," C.J. said.

Toy blushed. "Can I put the cap back on now?"

I attempted a warm smile. "By all means, dear. But at this point wouldn't it make more sense to just shave your head altogether?"

"That's easy for you to say; it isn't your noggin."

"I have the prefect razor for the job," Rob said. "We can be through by the time Bob gets dinner on the table."

"I don't know—"

"Ooh, ooh," C.J. cooed. "Shaved heads are sexy."

Pseudosister or not, C.J., bless her overgrown heart, was the perfect addition to this last minute dinner party. "This is the best albino Albanian artichoke aspic I've ever eaten," she said, taking a third helping. "It reminds me of Granny Ledbetter's pink Portuguese parsnip pudding—except for the color, of course. And that just comes from adding a few strawberries."

Bob beamed. "Thanks, I'm glad you like the aspic."

"And the alpaca was superb. Most people undercook it, you know."

"Really?"

She nodded her lioness head vigorously. "Really. A lot of folks these days think that food has to be undercooked for it to taste good or be nutritious. Restaurants especially. They wave their veggies over steam for a few seconds before they serve it. The truth is that many canned and frozen foods actually retain more vitamins than their fresh counterparts, because they are picked at the height of ripeness and processed immediately, whereas the vegetables you buy at produce markets are generally picked green and shipped long distances. Besides, you don't have to worry about lizard heads blinking at you."

Bob blanched. "I beg your pardon?"

"C.J. found a lizard head staring at her from her steamed broccoli once," I said, hoping to cut the story short.

"It wasn't just staring at me, Abby; it was winking."

I sneaked a peak at Toy. Perhaps the two of them were meant for each other. Between her tall tales and his flat-out lies, they would never find themselves wanting for entertainment.

"Dead reptiles don't flirt," I said gently.

"This one did."

Three of us rolled our eyes, while the fourth licked his lips in anticipation. My brother had to be in seventh heaven. Without even trying, he'd found a Carolina girl as kooky as any in California. And if he played his cards right and married her, she would, no doubt, continue to work and put him through seminary. What's more, Calamity Jane has what the folks up in Shelby call "breeding hips." In a few years my late blooming brother could be the patriarch of a swarm of wee Wigginses—as numerous as locusts, but without any of their good qualities. Yesiree, from Dumpster digging to dynasty building, things were finally looking up for Mama's baby boy.

But in the meantime I had an investigation to conduct. "C.J., darling, why don't you tell Bob about that new recipe your Granny Ledbetter sent you?"

"The one for rhubarb and possum pie?"

"That's the one."

C.J. was happy to oblige me. "The trick," she said to Bob, "is to start with a really tender possum, preferably one under a year old . . ."

I leaned across the table and poked my day-dreaming brother with my fork. "I've got some bad news. Wynnell's husband, Ed, is in the hospital."

"What happened?"

"Diabetic coma. It happened in Wynnell's shop. I was there. We were talking, and suddenly he just slid out of his chair."

"How are you dealing with it, Abby?"

I shrugged. "This was the first time I've actually seen someone come so close to dying. It still doesn't seem real. When it sinks in—"

"You'll call me, right?" Rob's eyes shone with devotion.

"Right."

"And me," Toy said. Perhaps I'm an optimist, but he sounded jealous.

"I'll call you both. I promise."

"Because your little brother is here for you, Abby. I mean it."

"Thanks."

Rob opened his mouth to say something, but I cut him off. "Toy, did you hear about the statue?"

"Yeah. I was—uh, being shorn when he got the call. Abby, did you see it when you were remodel-ing?"

I would have hung my head in shame had not my nostrils already been too close to my plate. "Yes, I saw it. But Toy, there are so many cheap knockoffs of David—I just assumed it wasn't real."

"Real?"

Rob sat straighter. "Abby showed me a Polaroid. It looks to me like a maquette, possibly a model for the real David."

Toy whistled, drawing Bob and C.J.'s attention as well. "This is getting interesting. What's a thing like that worth?"

"That all depends on whether or not it can be authenticated. If it can be, then theoretically it's priceless. But as most of you already know," Rob said, looking pointedly at Toy, "in this business there is always a price."

"Not being in the biz," Toy said, "I haven't a clue. Can you give me a ballpark figure?"

"Whatever the market will bear. A lot of it depends on whether or not there is a prior claim on the piece."

"He means 'stolen,'" I explained. "It's one thing to pay a fortune for a status symbol; but it takes a special customer to shell out money for something that only they will ever see. Not that I have any personal experience along these lines."

Toy winked. "Of course not, sis. Who are these special customers?"

I turned to Rob. "This is your area of expertise," I said wickedly.

"Thanks a lot, Abby," my friend said. "Like I knowingly deal with thieves on a regular basis."

"Then tell Toy what you unwittingly do from time to time."

"Well, it used to be that wealthy Japanese businessmen and Saudi Arabian potentates were happy to spend megabucks on private collections—things viewed only by them—just for the joy of having something unique. But the bottom pretty much fell out of the Japanese market when their economy took a nosedive following nine eleven. The Saudis have been cutting back on collecting items that are distinctly Western, or have non-Muslim religious themes. That pretty much leaves Europe, where collectors have traditionally been more frugal."

"What about America?"

"Anything's possible, but we Americans like our possessions to be noticed. If it's not going to show up in a glossy magazine, with our names attached, then why bother?"

"Aren't you generalizing?"

Although Rob's forehead barely puckered, I could tell he was annoyed. "Of course I'm generalizing. I'm just trying to convey a sense of what black-market antiquing is like."

"You still haven't named a price."

Rob's puckers became furrows. "Because it's not

that simple. But okay, if a number is what you want—let's say a million dollars."

"A million?"

"That's just an example—the first number that popped into my mind. It could be worth ten million. A lot depends on what precedents have been set. To my knowledge, this would be the first known maquette of David—if indeed that's what it is."

"So now you're suddenly not sure?"

"I never said I was sure."

"You sounded pretty sure to me. You even named a price."

"Because you pressured me to."

Perhaps I'm more wicked than I thought, because it amused me to see my flesh-and-blood brother and my brother-in-absentia posturing like a pair of stags in autumn over a doe that neither of them could claim. What a waste of energy. Toy would always be my kin, and Rob would always be my friend. Nothing was going to change that.

I cleared my throat. "Boys, may I have your attention?"

"It's about time, Abby," Bob boomed.

C.J. clapped hands the size of Virginia hams. "Give them heck, Abby!"

I cleared my throat again. "If you please, no interruptions from the peanut gallery. Now, first thing tomorrow morning, I'm going to call Detective Scrubb to see if we can't get a look at that thing—*whatever* it is. In the meantime, can we just enjoy our dinner?"

Bob brightened. "So you like my dinner."

"Like it? It's absolutely remarkable."

"Sounds like dubious praise," Rob whispered.

Perhaps because his ears stick out from his head at right angles, but Bob is capable of hearing a frog fart at forty paces. "And what exactly is that supposed to mean?"

I started to applaud. "Kudos to the chef!" I yelled.

C.J. clapped twice, but stopped abruptly. "Granny Ledbetter knows the best recipe for kudu."

"I said kudos, dear, not kudus."

"Oh, I know, Abby. A kudu is a species of large African antelope. Granny got some kudu meat as a gift once. The way she fixed it was so good, my tongue wanted to slap my head silly."

Bob bounced in his chair with excitement. "I know where to get kudu meat! I just got this catalogue of exotic meats from a game farm in Texas . . ."

I had to tune them out in order to finish my meal.

*    *    *

I slept in the Rob-Bobs' guest room. Their Queen Anne bed is said to have belonged to the grand dame herself. The silk damask bed-curtains purportedly provided the royal body privacy, but thank heavens the guys have changed the bedclothes since then. Nothing beats a four-hundred-thread-count sheet from Linens-n-Things.

I'll blame it on the food, but that night I had the weirdest dreams. I dreamed I was the other Queen Anne, the one who lost her head in the tower of London. Already headless, I was wandering around the halls of a dank, dark castle, searching urgently for a replacement. Alas, there were no new noggins to be found, but in one spidery corner I spied a giant Albanian albino artichoke. Desperate, I tried it on for size. To my amazement, it fit perfectly.

"Abby," a male voice called from just behind me.

I whirled, but the leathery leaves prevented me from seeing anything.

"Abby, can you hear me?"

"Yes, I can hear you." But the artichoke didn't have a mouth and I knew my muffled words weren't being heard in return.

I started to run, but managed to take only steps before my assailant tackled me and I fell flat on my vegetable face.

# 23

"**A**bby, it's me—Rob!"

I tore at my artichoke head.

"Hey, hey, take it easy, Abby. No one's going to hurt you; I'm only trying to help. You're all tangled in that sheet."

Dream and consciousness duked it out until the latter won. I was indeed wrapped in a sheet—that delicious four-hundred-thread-count creation—but I was also, thank heavens, swaddled in one of Rob's T-shirts. I may as well have been wearing a floor-length nightgown.

"Uh—sorry. I was having a nightmare."

"Bob's cooking will do that."

I sat and wedged two large fluffy pillows behind me. "Thanks for letting me stay over."

"Any time. Look, Abby, it's almost nine. I've got to run. Bob's already left to open up our shop. I just wanted to touch base before I split."

"Nine? In the *morning*?"

"I certainly hope so, or else I really overslept.

And speaking of sleep, you got a full twelve hours sleep. You should be raring to go."

I groaned. "I feel like something Dmitri dragged in through his pet door."

"Stress will do that." He picked up a tumbler from the bedside table. "Here, I brought you a magic potion."

I made no move to take it from him. "What is it?"

Rob laughed. "It's an elixir Bob made. It's supposed to get you from zero to sixty in the blink of an eye."

"Zero to sixty what?"

"Who cares? I wouldn't drink it if I were you."

"I don't plan to. But what's in it?"

"Let's see—it's got vodka, soybean milk, castor oil, carrot juice, balsamic vinegar, and a dash of cayenne pepper. Oh, and a raw egg. Bob calls it his Wake the Devil Morning Special."

"Yuck!"

"How about if I dump this crap out and start with a fresh glass. I just squeezed a pitcher of orange juice. I'd be happy to add a splash of vodka to make it qualify as medicinal."

"OJ straight up is fine. Thanks—and I mean for everything."

"My pleasure." But instead of fetching the liquid gold, Rob sat on the bed.

"I thought you were in a hurry."

"I am. But I've been thinking. If the statue in

that Polaroid really is the maquette for Michelangelo's *David*, and therefore worth a fortune, why the heck did he throw it in the harbor?"

"How do you know it was a he?"

"Don't give me a hard time, Abby. The question has been bugging me all night."

It was time for me to at least pretend to think. Some detective I was; this simple, but valid, question hadn't denied me a moment of beauty rest.

"I'll take that orange juice now—and some coffee if you have it."

"Coming right up." He was back in the shake of an alpaca's tail, but it was clear that he wasn't in a big hurry after all. Besides the juice, the tray he brought bore a sterling silver coffee service, a plate stacked high with buttered toast, and a carnival glass compote dish filled with English marmalade.

He sat beside me on the bed. For the umpteenth time I was aware of how lucky I was to have gay friends. There was no sexual tension between Rob and me to get in the way of being buddies, and certainly no competition.

"So did you give it some thought, Abby?"

"You were only gone a few seconds. But you're absolutely right. If the maquette was worth killing for, then why didn't Marina's killer take it with him?"

"Don't you mean 'her'?"

I stuck my tongue out at him. "Whatever."

Rob poured his coffee first, into a bone china cup, and set it aside. He then dribbled some coffee into a standard mug, dumped in five heaping teaspoons of brown sugar and enough heavy cream to clog a gorilla's arteries, stirred vigorously, and handed the customized concoction to me. Sweet coffee-scented cream is my brew of choice. It always has been, but Greg would never have gotten the proportions right.

"Maybe the murder was not premeditated. The theft, either. Maybe the killer wasn't prepared to lug around a three-foot statue, and the harbor was the best place to hide it. Temporarily, of course. Until he or she could return for it."

"That would mean the killer was on foot, right? I mean if not, why not just stick it in their car and be done with it?"

Rob took a sip of his coffee, which he drinks black and bitter. "Or maybe the killer was unaware of the statue's value."

"Like I was?"

He grinned. "My point is that the theft may have been totally inadvertent. The murderer—let's say it's a guy—whacks Mrs. Webbfingers over the head with the maquette. Why, doesn't matter just yet. So now he's got a bloody statue to dispose of. The question now is, where? If he stashes it in his car and gets stopped by the police for whatever

reason—and things somehow get out of hand—
he's got a lot of explaining to do.

"On the other hand, the harbor is just a block
away. If tourists spot him carrying a statue, it's really no big deal. They're likely to assume that authentic Charlestonians lug statues around all the
time. He only has to be careful that he is not observed throwing the dang thing out to sea, because visitors from the square states would jump
in after it like lemmings. And not only does the
harbor make a good hiding place, it's also full of
fish and other slimy things that, given enough
time, will eat the evidence. What the killer doesn't
anticipate is that the statue will be discovered so
soon."

I licked a glob of marmalade off my index finger. "I'll buy that. Now if only I can talk Detective
Scrubb into letting us have a peek at the thing."

"Abby, you could talk a clam out of its shell,"
Rob said, and thrust the bedside phone into my
hand.

I called the hospital first for an update on Ed. The
good news was that he was feeling fit as a fiddle.
The bad news was that he was raring to get back to
work on the new and improved Wooden Wonders.

I told Ed that if he didn't listen to his doctors, I'd
get Sergeant Scrubb to issue him a speeding ticket

whenever he as much as took his car out of the driveway. I was only half-kidding. Then I called the sergeant and asked if Rob and I could peek at the statue.

"Sorry, Abby, no can do."

"But my friend is an expert, and he has a gut feeling that this is an extremely valuable piece of art. It's called a maquette. You see, sculptors sometimes make scale models—"

"I know what a maquette is, Abby, and this isn't one."

It's a good thing I'd set my mug down. "You do? I mean, it's not? I mean, how do you know?"

"What did he say?" Rob demanded in my left ear.

"Shhh! That's wasn't meant for you, Sergeant," I added quickly.

"I take it your expert friend is eavesdropping."

I pushed Rob's head away with my free hand. "Not anymore. Detective Scrubb, if you would please, tell me what makes you think this statue is not a maquette—with all due respect, sir."

"Because this one is made from poured concrete."

"Get out of town!"

Rob's head bounced back like a punching bag clown. "What did he say?"

"It also has a logo stamped on the bottom," Detective Scrubb said.

I pushed harder at Rob. "A logo? What does it say?"

" 'Made in Pollywood.' "

"Did you say *Pollywood*?"

I gave Rob my best effort. He staggered backward, but fortunately, through an irreproducible sequence of acrobatics, managed to not spill a single drop of coffee. Then I had to sheepishly ask the detective to repeat what he'd said.

"We ran a fix on that," he said, sounding more tired than annoyed. "It's a garden ornament manufacturer just outside Dollywood, Tennessee. They sell to the entire eastern half of the country. Anyway, the David statues come in all sizes. It's $49.95 for the three-footers. Add ten bucks if you want it fitted for a lamp—indoor use only. Twenty extra if you want the concrete bowl that goes on top to turn it into a birdbath. That's how come it has an extra large head."

"It does?" I tried to sound surprised.

"Abby, you were right. It wasn't worth stealing."

I squelched my impulse to say "I told you so."
"Thank you, Detective."

"Anytime. Say Abby, I thought you might like to know that—well—you were right about something else."

"I was?" I didn't have to fake my emotions that time.

"None of the guests at La Parterre are who they say they are."

"Do tell!"

"I've already said too much. I just didn't want you to think that—uh, that I think that you're—uh—"

"A total idiot?"

"I've got to go, Abby."

"Not yet! Give me something—a crumb! Anything!"

"It's been nice talking to you, Abby." He hung up without further ado.

I set the phone back in its cradle and looked up at Rob. I fully expected him to be as mad as a rooster in an empty henhouse. Instead he cocked his head while holding one hand under his chin and regarded me with eyes that were both amused and accusing.

"Why Abigail Louise Wiggins Timberlake Washburn, I do declare. You've got the hots for that man."

"I most certainly do not!"

"You can't con a carny, darling."

"When did you ever work for a carnival?"

"You know what I mean. I've been there—where you are now. The tax accountant we used last year was to die for. I thought of every excuse in the book to visit his office. Just seeing him made my heart race—made me feel guilty as heck, too. It wasn't that I was unhappy with Bob, you understand; it was the thrill—the high—you get when you start a new romance. Not that I got that far. Thank God I came to my senses in time and realized I was playing with fire. Then I had to come up with an excuse to change accountants before anyone got hurt. But it could have been an all-around disaster."

"Bob never found out?"

"And he won't, either. Just like Greg won't find out about your crush on Inspector Clouseau."

"Ben Affleck!"

"Whatever. Are we on the same page now?"

My face burned with shame. "I love Greg with all my heart, Rob. You believe me, don't you?"

He sat on the bed again and I let him put his arm around me. "Of course I believe you. And I have every confidence that we're never going to have this conversation again. Right?"

"Right."

"Good. Want some more of what you call coffee before I go?"

"Yes, please. But put an extra sugar in it."

"You're going to rot your teeth," he said, before adding an additional three packets. "But before they fall out and you lose your ability to enunciate, fill me in on the statue."

"It's a fake—poured concrete. Can you imagine that?"

Rob recoiled in genuine horror. "Whoa, Abby. You're slipping, girl. You said you thought it was composite."

"I could swear it was. I must be losing my mind. Mama's daddy had dementia—"

"You're too young to lose your mind, Abby. It doesn't happen until you start to lose your waist-line—nature planned it that way so that you won't care quite as much. But neither of us are anywhere near that point, so it must be the stress. You're probably just remembering wrong."

"Thanks." But I didn't feel comforted. It was like going to bed in a brick house and waking in a stucco house. At a cursory glance one might con-fuse marble with one of its imitators, but marble and concrete aren't anywhere close in texture.

Rob stood and stretched. "Well, I really do have to go, so promise me you won't."

"Won't what?"

"Whatever it is that will bring the wrath of Greg down upon my head because I didn't stop you."

I slid out of bed. "I'm not staying here all day, I can tell you that."

"Abby, *please.*"

"I'm a big girl—well, you know what I mean. I can take care of myself."

"Abby, please get back in bed."

"I most certainly will not. I've got things to do, and time and tide wait for no man—or woman, either.

"Get back in bed just for a second."

"What?"

"Humor me."

I sighed. "Okay, but you've got to give me a boost. Rob, you really should keep a step stool beside the bed. I know, it won't have been stepped on by Her Majesty's royal tootsies, but a gal could break her neck getting in and out of this thing."

Rob boosted me. He also insisted that I crawl back under the covers and that he tuck them around my neck. He even made me close my eyes. But the second I did, he bolted from the room like a coon with a pack of beagles on its trail.

I must be only demi-dimwitted, because the reason for his quick exit eventually dawned on me. The last time Rob Goldburg had seen the little troublemaker, she was tucked safe and sound in his Queen Anne guest bed, and apparently sound asleep. How could he possibly get in trouble for that?

Let me count the ways.

# 24

I would have showered at the Rob-Bobs', but I needed a change of clothes. After briefly considering wearing one of Rob's shirts as a dress, with a silk tie as a belt, I abandoned the idea in favor of a pit stop at home. First, however, I needed to get Mama out of the way. Greg, too, if he still happened to be home.

"Wigginses' residence," she said when she picked up the phone.

"Shouldn't that be *Washburn* residence?"

"I live here, too—Abigail Louise, how dare you treat my darling son-in-law that way?"

"Mama, this is between Greg and me."

"Well, I am fit to be tied. In my day a good wife—"

"Wore pearls to vacuum in and said 'yes dear' whenever her husband asked her a question?"

"There is nothing wrong with wearing pearls when you clean, just as long as you're wearing a dress. Of course that goes without saying. Still, only last week I saw a woman at the mall wearing pearls with blue jeans. Can you imagine that?"

"I am shocked, Mama."

"You're making fun of me, aren't you?"

"Sorry, Mama. Is Greg there?"

"Gracious no. He's at work like a good husband should be."

"How about Toy?"

"He is supposed to be at work, too—I mean with you, dear."

"He's not. Maybe he spent the night at C.J.'s."

Mama's pearls clacked against the phone, which meant she was fingering them in agitation. "He slept here last night."

"Are you sure?"

"Of course I'm sure. I fed him breakfast. And not just the bowl of cereal you would have fed him, either. Did you know that he still likes me to make a happy face in his grits and fill it in with melted butter?"

"Mama, you have too much time on your hands. How would you like to have a job?"

"Abby, you know I haven't worked since before you were born. While I may have managed to keep my looks, dear, my secretarial skills are undoubtedly a bit rusty. Besides, I don't know anything about computers, and every job these days seems to require one."

"Not this job. C.J. will do all the computer work,

if that's how you want it. All you have to do is be charming to the customers."

Mama gasped so hard, I swear I felt my ear being sucked into the receiver. "Are you offering me a job, darling? At the shop?"

"A temporary job, Mama. Just until we get this whole Wynnell mess straightened out. Or," I added softly, "until you make it impossible for me not to fire you."

"You'd fire your own mother?"

"It's within the realm of possibility. You and C.J. together are a bit like Laurel and Hardy. I can't promise that I won't. So think about it, but let me know as soon as possible what you decide. Otherwise I need to put an ad in the paper."

"Would I get to dust?"

"Get to? Mama, it's a requirement. Everything in the Den of Antiquity needs to be dusted—at least once a day. And the rest room has to be cleaned twice. And while I wouldn't dream of imposing on you, I've been thinking about serving some kind of refreshments—maybe homemade cookies and fresh-squeezed lemonade."

I could hear Mama count softly; she got as far as three. "When do you want me to start?"

"Right now. As soon as you can hustle your bustle over there."

She hung up.

I called C.J., who, much to my relief, was delighted to take on an assistant. Especially one who would dust. The big gal and my minimadre are pals, but they're both as hard-headed as coconuts, and as predictable as hurricanes. Either they would make an awesome selling team or provide me with the wherewithal for making some world-class macaroons.

"Abby, when is Mozella going to start?"

"Now. In fact, expect her any minute."

"And I get to tell her what to do?"

"You know better than that. Bossing Mama around would be like trying to play fetch with a cat."

"So what are you saying, Abby?"

My young friend isn't owned by a feline. Perhaps she was really clueless.

"Cats don't take directions, C.J. They do whatever they want, whenever they want. That's why they're not the ideal pet for just anyone."

"Oh, but you're wrong, Abby. Great-Uncle Mortimer Ledbetter had a cat that used to help him run his moonshine still, in hills west of Shelby. Great-Uncle Mortimer would make the corn mash, but it was his cat, Snerd, that kept the fire fed by adding wood one stick at a time. 'Fetch me another stick,' Uncle Mortimer would say, 'one about two feet long,' and Snerd would dash into the woods and bring a stick that was just the right size. Great-Uncle Mortimer was just as proud of

this cat as could be, and even named his hootch after him. 'Catatonic,' is what he called it. Then one
day he ran a bad batch and some of his customers
were sort of paralyzed—not their bodies so much
as their minds. Up until then—"

"C.J., mental illness is not a joking matter."

"But I'm not joking, Abby. Look up the word
'catatonic' in the dictionary. There was no such
word until 1904, the year before Great-Uncle Mortimer's white lightning struck down some of his
best customers."

"Whatever, C.J." There was no point in telling
her that Mortimer Snerd was the name of one of
Edgar Bergen's dummies. Sure as shooting she'd
have an explanation for that, and our conversation
would segue into one about wry wooden people
and their ventriloquists. She might even tell me
that Pinocchio was her brother, and worse yet, I
might believe her.

"I know you're just saying that to humor me,
Abby, but it's true. If you don't believe me, go to
the College of Charleston and look in one of their
old yearbooks. Try the twenties. You'll see a picture of Mortimer Junior who was my uncle. Uncle
Morty, we called him. He looked just like his
daddy, Great-Uncle Mortimer, but he looked like
me, too. Anyway, Mortimer Junior was very popular on campus, on account of he always brought
some of his daddy's recipe with him, even though

Catatonic was no longer being sold, just made for private consumption. They say that for years Uncle Morty's classmates made sure they attended every reunion, so as not to miss out on the booze. Fortunately there were no bad batches since that one, but with moonshine you can never tell."

C.J. was right about one thing: homemade whiskey, sometimes known as rotgut, can be extremely dangerous and can, in fact, cause paralysis of the extremities. Even blindness. But I wasn't going to waste a minute of time looking up her bogus uncle in old yearbooks. If I was going to look up anyone it would be Fisher and Marina Webbfingers, if only to get a better understanding of what they saw in each other when they were young. Heck, I'd look up their guests, too, on the off chance one of them was a College of Charleston alumnus. Take Irena Papadopoulus, for instance . . .

"Abby, are you still there?"

"No I'm not, C.J.!" And I wasn't.

Founded in 1770, the College of Charleston is the thirteenth oldest college in America. Smack dab in the heart of the city, the historic campus embraces a variety of architectures, with the older buildings being by far the most interesting. To me the most intriguing one is the Martindale Bell house, now home to the mathematics department. In 1844 it was acquired by Sally Johnson, a free woman of African descent who owned four slaves. This contradiction characterizes the campus and, indeed, the city itself.

Located as it is in the middle of the peninsula, the college is at times devoid of breezes, but offers generous shade in the form of massive oaks and lush, subtropical plantings. When I arrived at the library, I was damp with dew, but being a true Southern woman, I most certainly was not sweating. I took a moment to dab the moisture from my forehead before approaching the reference desk.

"Excuse me, miss, where would I find back issues of College of Charleston yearbooks?"

"They can't be accessed now."

"What does that mean?"

She shrugged before turning back to her task of attaching orange slips of paper to small piles of books. Her insolence made me want to snap her with one of the rubber bands. They were, after all, very thin and capable of producing only a light sting.

"Ambrosia," I said, grateful that I'd bothered to read her badge, "what a beautiful name."

"I hate it," she mumbled.

"I'm not too fond of my name, either."

She cocked her head. "What's *your* name?"

"Abigail. My friends call me Abby, but when I was growing up the kids at school would call me Dear Abby."

That got her full attention. "I'd never do that to a kid of mine. I'd name her something regular like Caitlin, or Ashley."

I tried to keep a straight face. "Yes, but there are a million Caitlins and Ashleys out there. Having a name like Ambrosia makes you special. Do you know what it means?"

Her nose crinkled. "Some kind of gooey dessert. I hate it, too."

"Yes, but originally ambrosia was the food that Greek and Roman gods ate. It became synonymous with any food that was extremely pleasing."

"Yeah?"

I nodded. "And it suits you. You have the prettiest hair."

Ambrosia smiled. "Thanks." She started to turn away again, but stopped. "Hey, about the yearbooks. The reason I can't let you see them is because some of them were vandalized."

"Excuse me?"

She leaned over the counter. "I'm probably not supposed to be telling you this, but some old lady tore out a bunch of pages and stuffed them in her purse."

"You're kidding! When this did happen?"

"Monday—I think. Yeah, Monday. I was working the afternoon shift."

"You saw it happen?"

"Nah, but I wish I did. It would have been fun to bust her. All I know is that she asked to see them and was looking at them at that table over there. One of my jobs is to put away reference books you're not allowed to check out, and when I collected those—man, you wouldn't think an old lady like that would trash something, would you?"

"What happened next? What did you do?"

"Well, I told Mr. Muffet—that's my supervisor—on account I didn't want to get blamed, but he said there was nothing he could do to the old lady, because I didn't actually see her do it. I'm just supposed to keep an eye out for her, that's all."

I tried to imagine one of Mama's cronies ripping pages out of a library book. Perhaps if there were obscene pictures involved, ones in need of a better home. But why would anyone, young or old, tear pages out of a yearbook? Unless their photo was in the volume, and the picture had been taken on a particularly bad-hair day. *Or*, someone was trying to cover up the fact that they had once attended the College of Charleston.

"How old was this woman?"

"I don't know. Your age—maybe older."

One of the few perks of being so small and perky is that I can generally pass myself off as being ten years younger than I am. Never, ever, has anyone referred to me as an "old lady"—except for my daughter, Susan. And that was when she was a teenager and, at times, very irritated with me.

"I'm forty-seven," I said stiffly.

"Yeah? So's my mom. But this woman was even older. She had one of them dye jobs that don't look natural—just makes you look even older. My mom calls it the 'shoe polish look.' "

"Her hair was jet black, almost blue?"

"You know her?"

"Were the bags under her eyes so big she could pack—" I slapped my own mouth. "Never mind, that was mean-spirited of me."

Ambrosia giggled. "But it's true. Hey, I guess I could let you see them yearbooks, but you gotta do it fast. Mr. Muffet's in a meeting, and I don't know how long it will last."

"That would be wonderful."

While Ambrosia hightailed it to the storage room, I pretended to be engrossed in a world weather almanac lying on the counter in front of me. Who would have guessed that the highest temperature ever recorded in the shade was 136 degrees Fahrenheit in Aziza, Libya? I would have sworn that Columbia, South Carolina, which critics claim was built over Hell, held that record. I had just learned that Johannesburg, South Africa, occasionally sees winter frost, when Ambrosia returned. She held out two books, her fingers marking the place in each.

"This one has two pages missing," she said, handing me the one on my right first. "Only one from here." She handed me the second volume.

Pushing the almanac aside, I laid the books side by side on the counter. The missing pages had not been ripped from the book, as I had been led to understand, but sliced out, possibly with a razor blade. The annual with two pages missing was dated 1960–61, the other 1967–68. Both books appeared to be minus one of their S pages, with at least part of T on the flip side. The first volume, however, was missing most of the K's as well.

I jotted this information down on the back of a Piggly Wiggly receipt I fished from the bottom of my purse. "Thank you, Ambrosia. I really appreciate this."

"No problem."

A door behind her, presumably one leading to a conference room, opened. Ambrosia had the reflexes of a cat, and before I could react at all, she had scooped the annuals down the front of her shirt and was leaning on them.

"Yes, ma'am, I sure will," she said, far louder than was necessary.

I caught a glimpse of a man as I turned. If that was Mr. Muffet, I had best get my tuffet out of there pronto. I forced myself to walk to the door.

# 25

Toy picked up after the first ring. "Wiggins."

"Where are you?"

"Abby! I was just about to call you. I'm at Hammerhead, White, and Sand. Mr. Hammerhead let me use of some of his contacts. You'll never guess what I just learned."

"That Estelle Zimmerman attended the College of Charleston?"

I savored his stunned silence.

"I'm right, aren't I?"

My baby brother coughed a couple of times before finding his voice. "How the heck did you know?"

"She knows too much about the city to just be a tourist. Besides, I had a hunch. You know, sort of like the way Mama smells trouble."

"Our mother, bless her heart, couldn't smell dinner if it was burning. Guess what else I learned."

"That the Papadopouluses aren't really a couple, that Irena is not a gem buyer, and that both of them attended the C of C as well?"

"Abby, that's incredible! How did you come up with that?"

I told him about Ambrosia and our escapade with the yearbooks. "I'm guessing that they are brother and sister," I said, "and that their last name starts with the letter K. But I could be way off base, even though a hunch from a woman is worth two facts from a man."

Toy chuckled. "You're not wrong at all. Their family name is Keating. And the Zimmermans are really the Hansons. Estelle Hanson, Irena Keating, and Fisher Webbfingers were classmates. Nick is Irena's younger brother—seven years younger, in fact. The Hansons really do own a dairy farm in Wisconsin. Irena is a Manhattan housewife, and Nick just sort of kicks around— from what I can tell by his Social Security withholdings."

"Ah, the black sheep."

"Baaaaaa."

"Sorry Toy, I couldn't resist. What about Estelle? What was her maiden name?"

"Simonson. Except for speeding and parking violations, none of them have been in trouble with the police."

It practically scares the zip out of me when I

pause to consider how much information is available to the public in this, the computer age. But if I had to scale a wall to steal Fisher's Social Security number, how did Toy manage to get so much information, in such a short time, with no numbers for the rest of the gang? Computer age or not, it seemed suspicious to me. Of course I asked him.

"That was an easy one, sis. I called the car rental agencies. They're not supposed to give out customer information, but they usually crack, if you trot out the right story."

"The right story? Toy, where did you learn to be a such a con man—never mind, I don't want to know. Please, continue."

"Well, to make a long story short, the third agency I called had a rental in the name of Hanson who was staying at La Parterre. The same for Keating. If you have an address, and sweet talk whomever answers the phone, the rest is easy as taking candy from a baby."

"You obviously haven't tried taking candy from a baby, but I get the picture. What about the Thomases?"

"Funny you should ask. John and Belinda Thomas are their real names, but they're from New Jersey, not California. Well, at least according to their photo IDs."

"How interesting! Toy, you're a miracle worker."

"Nah, just His disciple. Okay sis, what do you want me to do now?"

"This morning I gave Mama a job at Den of Antiquity—"

"You *what*?"

"I had to get her out of my hair. Anyway, could you pop in there in, say, half an hour to see if she and C.J. are still both alive. I mean, they're really good friends and all, but—oh my gosh! What was I thinking?"

Toy, who had nothing to lose by my business blunders, had his laugh of the day. The important thing is that he promised to check on my petite progenitor and my gal Friday. Almost as important was the fact that he didn't ask me what I planned to do next. I wouldn't have told him anyway.

There were three rental cars parked along the street in front of La Parterre, but Fisher's car was missing from the garage, and there was no sign of Harriet's car. Despite the heat, the tourists were out in full force, and it was obvious most of them had yet to learn the three cardinal laws of walking in Charleston during the summer: wear wrinkled linen, walk slowly, and keep to the shade. By and large, they were large. They were also pink, puffing, and dripping with sweat. A kid with a lemonade stand could have cleaned up.

I parked along the seawall again and hoofed it over the hot pavement. The Webbfingerses' garden was empty, save for one tourist, who was too busy jotting notes in a spiral notebook to notice me. Even the crunch of gravel under my feet didn't give me away.

"Can I help you?" I asked as I sneaked up to her right elbow.

Pen and notebook fell on the walkway as the tourist staggered forward in surprise. But by the time she turned to face me, she'd regained her composure and then some.

"Who are you?" she demanded.

A tourist wandering around in Fisher Webbfingers's garden was really none of my business—although, come to think of it, the man had asked me to play the role of hostess, and even a middling hostess knows who her guests are. The truth is, it irked me that she was trespassing. I periodically find smudges on my front windowpanes, left there by folks with more bucks than breeding. Once, someone even tried to take a picture of me standing *inside* my living room, just minutes after I'd exited the shower. Thank heavens I'd thought to put on a robe.

"I was just about to ask who you were," I said curtly. "This is private property, you know.

The way she snorted and tossed her head suggested that in a previous life she had been one of the horses that spend their days plodding around the historic district. "The sign there says it's is a bed and breakfast," she neighed. "Maybe I'm a potential customer."

Having just used up my rudeness quota for the month, and having nothing to gain, or lose, by her actions, I nodded and started to walk in the direction of the main house. The wayward tourist caught up with me in a couple of giant strides, all but forcing me off the path and into the hedge.

"My name is Ramat Sreym," she said.

I looked at her blankly. The name didn't ring a bell. There was something shifty about her eyes, suggesting that she might be a politician, or a used-car salesperson. She certainly was not one of the many movie stars that headquarter in the Holy City while on location.

"I'm a novelist," she added when I made no response.

I think I was supposed to be impressed. The truth is that not only was the Charleston area crawling with writers, but it's home to a plethora of published authors. It's gotten to the point that one can't enter a bookstore without having to pass a table with a seated author hawking his, or her, product. Sometimes I wish those busybodies would stay home, and let me browse the racks in peace.

"That's nice," I said. "I'm Abigail Timberlake. I'm an antique dealer. I own the Den of Antiquity, on King Street. Just past the intersection with Queen. I also own a sister shop up in Charlotte, if you ever get up that way. Here, let me give you a card."

The tourist-cum-novelist had the temerity to hand me a bookmark in exchange. The colorful strip listed her titles, some of which, I'm reluctant to admit, were quite clever.

"My books are available at bookstores everywhere," she said, trumping me. "And of course you can buy them on the Net."

I glanced at her notebook. "Are you writing now?"

"In a manner of speaking. I'm taking notes."

"Good. I think an author owes it to her readers to get the facts right. It always stops me cold when I find mistakes in a book."

She shook her head, but suppressed the snort. "Yes, but some of my fans have too much time on their hands. Some women—and it's always women—circle typos and then send photocopies of them to me. Little do they seem to realize that I'm not the last person to see the manuscript. It's not like I set the book in print."

She had a valid point. "How do you respond?"

"I send them thank-you notes and pass the notes to my publisher so they can be corrected in the next printing." She smiled, displaying a bite worthy of a Morgan. "Although perhaps I should send them lists of available men."

I was beginning to like this woman. "This," I said, waving my arm to include most of the garden, "is going to be the setting for your next novel?"

"At least one scene. I walked all over the peninsula, and these are the prettiest grounds." She pointed to the flower garden in back. "It's all so tasteful."

"My friend, Wynnell, is responsible for that."

"Really? Tell her she did a great job."

I motioned to a wrought-iron bench set in a recess of the parterre. She took my hint and sat. The Canary Island date palm loomed directly in front of us, providing shade from the morning sun, its trunk partially obscuring us from the curious stares of tourists.

"So," I said, having warmed up to her considerably, "what's your new book about?"

She reared back as if she'd seen a rattlesnake. "Ms. Timberlake, a writer doesn't reveal her current plot."

"Sorry. I didn't know."

"But I can tell you this. It involves three loud and obnoxious middle-age sisters—from up the road a piece—who go to Paris to look for a diamond necklace their father stole and hid under a bridge on the Seine. They figure it's been so long, that even if they are caught smuggling it back to the States—and they're positive they won't be—that they won't get into serious trouble. The oldest one, Miranda, even tempts fate by wearing the jewels on the plane—oh," she said, clamping a hoof-size palm over her mouth, "I've said too much already. We writers are like that; when we're not writing, we're talking."

"That's all right. I'm sure I'll have forgotten by the time it comes out. So what happened? Did they get caught?"

"That was their first big mistake—they thought they were so clever, but what they didn't know is that there is no such thing as a statute of limitations on stolen property—oh, I've done it again!"

The wheels in my head were grinding so loudly that I could barely hear her. "Did you say there is no such thing as a statute of limitations on stolen property?"

"Yes, ma'am. So the sisters are arrested, but that happens only halfway through the book. Miranda has an affair with the prison chaplain, who turns out to be—" She jumped to her feet. "Mrs. Timber-lake, are you sure you're not a writer? If you are, promise me you won't use this in your own book."

"I can't write a check without losing my concentration."

"I hope you're telling the truth. If you're not—well, you should know that this has all been written down in a synopsis that I sent to my editor, signed, dated, and everything."

"I understand. But please, tell me the name of the book, so I can look for it when it comes out."

"'An Embarrassment of Bitches,'" she said, before holding the notebook up to her face like a shield. But that didn't stop her from talking. "It's scheduled to be released next April, and you can buy it at any bookstore . . ."

I honestly didn't hear her after that.

It was too early for lunch, but it's never too early for chocolate. I'm convinced that Eve gave Adam the apple because she had a candy bar stashed away in her fig leaf purse. At any rate, I keep a Three Musketeers bar and a Reese's Peanut Butter Cup in my purse for emergencies. Because I'm afraid that these provisions, like my hurricane supplies, might go stale if not rotated on a regular basis, I have taken on the discipline of renewing them on a weekly basis. Friday is my day of choice, but I have nothing against Wednesdays.

Of course a person of my height has to be especially conscientious about not putting on the pounds, so I usually perform my solemn duty while walking. And while I may not walk as much as Ramat Sreym, the blabbermouth writer, I do a fair amount. At any rate, I had a lot of thinking to do, so it looked like it might be both a bar and a cup day, so I followed Murray Boulevard from White Pointe Gardens toward the Coast Guard station. The mansions along this stretch enjoy an unobstructed view of the water, and I would trade in my house at 7 Squiggle Lane in a heartbeat to live in any one of these grand houses.

So, I mused, there is no such thing as a statute of limitations on stolen property. *If* the statue of David that I'd seen in the Webbfingerses' garden was an authentic maquette for the famous one in Florence, it could have been stolen anytime in the last five hundred years. But maybe it wasn't stolen at all. Or maybe it was stolen so long ago that its origins were forgotten. It could have been in the Webbfingers family for umpteen generations, its significance entirely forgotten by now. There are, after all, countless tales of real finds showing up at garage sales. At least that scenario explained how a priceless work of art ended up in a bed of begonias.

On the other hand, if the maquette had gone

missing more recently—say, within the last one hundred years—it was possible that the family was biding its time, waiting for a magical date to pass, after which the stolen property would legally become theirs. I took a bite out of Reeses's new dark chocolate peanut butter cup, and then popped the rest of it in my mouth. This sudden infusion of sugar and caffeine gave my tired brain a much needed boost.

"Let's say," I said aloud to myself, "that the statue was stolen during World War Two. Lots of Europe's treasures were either confiscated by the Nazis or went missing during the chaos. And looters—every war has looters. I know of plenty of cases where American servicemen returned, sometimes unwittingly, with priceless works of art.

"Let's say that Fisher Webbfingers's daddy—or Marina's daddy, for that matter—served overseas during the war. They would have been about the right age. Let's pretend for a minute that they stole the statue from a museum—or maybe just a private collection—and one of them brought it home to Charleston, but decided to wait until—"

"Mrs. Washburn," someone behind me said, taking me totally by surprise. As I spun to see who it was, the candy wrapper sailed from my hand into the street.

# 26

"**M**rs. Spanky!"

I was practically nose to breast-bone with the Webbfingerses' maid. Who knows how long she'd been following me, if indeed she was, but she had to think I was nuts. This was the second time she'd caught me talking aloud to myself.

"Ma'am, you gotta minute to spare?"

"Sure thing, Mrs. Spanky."

"Please call me Harriet, ma'am, remember? I don't stand on no formalities."

I glanced around. Few tourists make it down this far on foot, and most of them who do stick to the residential side of Murray Boulevard. There wasn't anyone else within thirty yards of us. The woman must have been hiding behind the trunk of a palm tree. And why the heck wasn't she at work?

"Yes, Harriet, I remember. And you must call me Abby."

297

"Yes ma'am."

"There's a bench over there, would you like to sit down?"

"No ma'am, this will just take a minute."

I edged closer to the seawall to take advantage of the breeze. "Sure, I've got a minute."

"In case you're wondering, ma'am, I ain't at work because I've been helping Mr. Fisher pick out a coffin. The police say the body—I mean Mrs. Fisher—will be released this afternoon. I know, it should be the family helping out at a time like this, but there ain't nobody left in Charleston but a cousin over in Mount Pleasant, and she's teched in the head. Not that it's my place to say so. Anyway, we was coming back and I seen you out walking. Thought I'd run you down and speak my piece."

I leaned against the seawall for support, in case Harriet's piece was particularly upsetting. "Go ahead, Harriet."

Harriet planted her feet farther apart, as if she, too, was bracing. "It's about them shoes you left behind in the missus's bedroom."

I could feel the color draining from my face. "I beg your pardon?"

"Ma'am, it ain't no use pretending with me. I knowed them little things was yours right off. Ain't no one got feet that small, except for a child, and them ain't children's shoes."

"Uh, well, I don't know what to say." Truer words were never spoken.

"That's all right, ma'am, I ain't judging. I'm a Christian woman myself, and ain't about to commit adultery, but I also ain't one to throw the first rock."

"Excuse me?"

"Like in the Bible, when they stoned them adulteresses. Anyway, what you and Mr. Webbfingers done is between you and the Almighty. The Bible says 'do unto others,' and the Lord knows Mrs. Webbfingers did unto others many a time, so I don't blame the mister none."

I took a deep breath, but the warm moist sea air seemed to contain very little oxygen. "Harriet, I assure you that Mr. Webbfingers and I are not having an affair."

The look in her eyes was one of pure disbelief. "Like I said, I ain't judging. And it ain't my business, excepting you being a newcomer to town, I thought you might like to know the way things is."

"How are things?" I asked, with what seemed to me like remarkable calmness.

"Folks around here talk, ma'am."

"You mean gossip, right?"

"Yes, ma'am. Stories have a way of getting around and blowed all out of shape."

I tried to think of a reason why Harriet would be concerned about my reputation. Perhaps it was because I treated her with respect, and had even asked her to call me by my given name—not that she had, of course. Or maybe she wanted to borrow money, or even come work for me now that Marina was dead.

"It ain't got nothing to do with you, ma'am," she said, yet another person to read my mind. Perhaps I should consider growing bangs.

"Then whose reputation are you trying to preserve?"

"It's Mr. Webbfingers I'm thinking of. The Lord knows that woman put him through enough. I don't want to see him suffer no more, that's all."

I'd had enough. "We are *not* having an affair. I am a happily married woman, and even if I wasn't, I assure you that Mr. Webbfingers would not even be on my radar screen."

Harriet blinked. "You and the mister really ain't—" She blinked several more times before switching tracks. "What about them shoes, then?"

It's been said that every good lie should contain a kernel of truth, and I am quite capable of supplying a plate full of corn. "You were right about the shoes. They are mine. And believe me, they're not so easy to come by in that size anymore. It seems that feet have gotten bigger along with waistlines.

"Now where was I? Oh yes, like I said, the shoes are mine—but I certainly didn't leave them there because I was having an affair. You see, I stepped

in some gum the last time I was at La Parterre—
you know how hard that can be to remove, 'spe-
cially from the tread—and Mrs. Webbfingers said
she was about to go to the cobbler's anyway, and
she'd dropped them off to have them professionally cleaned. Obviously she got them back, but
hadn't gotten around to calling me."

It was a mite far-fetched, but not an implausible
story. Although cobblers are a dying breed, they
do exist, and a lot of their business does come
from repairing shoes that are too valuable to
throw away when in need of mending. Old money
never likes to throw anything away, especially not
thousand-dollar loafers.

Harriet took her sweet time considering my explanation. "You got gum on both shoes?"

I nodded vigorously. "Don't you just hate that
when that happens? I mean, how hard can it be to
find a trash can, or stick it behind your ear or
someplace until you locate one? Why just look at
the sidewalks in our beautiful city—they look terrible. You wouldn't find gum blobs all over the
place in Singapore. Or cigarette butts for that
matter."

"Ma'am?" I was starting to lose her.

"Of course our mayor, bless his heart, would
never support an ordinance that required litter-
bugs to be caned. What a shame. But the courts
wouldn't stand for it, either, I'm afraid. Can you

imagine the number of suits that would be filed if such a law were to be enforced?"

"Mrs. Washburn, there's something else I'd like to talk to you about, but my dogs are killing me. You mind if we sit?"

"Not at all, dear."

I led the way to the nearest bench. Harriet moved sprightly for someone her age, until I remembered that she wasn't nearly as old as she looked. From then on her slowness irritated me, but I held my tongue. When we were both settled, facing the harbor, she sighed dramatically.

"You ain't fooling me none, Mrs. Washburn. I know who you really are."

If I hadn't been holding onto the wrought-iron handrail, I might have toppled from my perch. "I beg your pardon!"

"You're with the police, ain't you?"

"I most certainly am not!"

"Are you sure?"

"Quite sure. What on earth would make you think such a thing?"

"Well, you ain't no decorator, that's for sure. Them rooms you did don't look like no motel I ever stayed in."

"I'll take that as a compliment."

"But if you ain't the mister's honey, there's got to be some other reason you got the job." We stared at each other for a few seconds before her face turned as white as Confederate jasmine. "Lord have mercy! It's you and the missus that was having the affair."

"What? Absolutely not! I don't swing that way, never have, never will—not that anything's wrong with it."

"Oh there's plenty wrong with it. Just read your Bible."

I smiled. "Harriet, is that maid's uniform you're wearing made of polyester?"

She looked baffled, but pleased that I'd changed the subject. "It's one of them blends. Polyester don't breathe good enough, and I ain't about to iron cotton every morning—not with all the other work I have to do."

"I understand. I just thought you might like to know that the Bible says you're not allowed to wear clothing made out of more than one kind of material."

"*My* Bible?"

"I'll bet it does. Try reading Leviticus, chapter nineteen, verse nineteen," I said, grateful that the Rob-Bobs had drilled that bit of biblical trivia into me. I slid to my feet. "Well, I really need to be going."

To my great surprise she grabbed my right arm and pulled me back, slamming my buttocks against the hard slats of the bench. "I ain't through yet, Mrs. Washburn."

"Really, Harriet, I am not interested in arguing theology."

"I ain't, either, Mrs. Washburn. It's them guests I want to talk about."

I ignored my throbbing coccyx. "What about the guests?"

"Some of them ain't who they says they is."

Resuming my perch, I gave her an encouraging smile. "Please, tell me everything."

She reached into a battered black purse she'd placed between us. "Do you mind if I smoke?"

I considered the ramifications of an honest answer. "Go ahead."

Her leathery hands performed a rite they were obviously used to. Her first inhalation lasted several seconds, like she was sucking life from the cigarette, and not the other way around. When she finally exhaled through her nostrils, the harbor breeze pushed the smoke air into twin puffs, conjuring up a dragon in my mind.

"That woman who calls herself Estelle Zimmerman—you know, the one who's trying to look young but ain't—I knowed her when she was just a kid."

"You're kidding!"

"No ma'am, she and Mr. Webbfingers was sweet on each other. Only back then folks called her Mary Estelle. Simonson was her family name—don't that sound foreign to you?"

"Not really."

"Just between you and me, Mrs. Washburn, all them foreigners should go back to where they came from, and leave this country to us real Americans."

"My friend Alma Cornwater shares those sentiments."

Harriet frowned. "Don't know anybody by that name. Anyway, like I was saying, Fisher Junior and Mary Estelle was students together up at the college. Hung around here all the time. Word was they was fixing to get married—though I didn't never see a ring or nothing. Their families was close, too. There was always a bunch of folks at the house, and just me to do all the waiting." She took another long drag.

"Don't stop there! What happened to the romance?"

She waited until the second pair of puffs dissipated. "Mary Estelle found herself another boyfriend, is what happened. Some Yankee tourist she met at the beach. Mrs. Webbfingers—Fisher Junior's mama—was fit to be tied. Took to her sickbed for weeks." She gripped my arm again. "Guess who had to take care of her, waiting on her hand and foot twenty-six hours a day?"

I resisted my impulse to inform her that even

Charleston days are not that long. I did, however, gently peel her fingers from my arm.

"My guess would be you."

"As if I didn't have my hands full enough. Harriet, be a doll and do this. Harriet, darling, would you bring me a fresh glass? This one has a ring around it." She gulped another lungful of smoke. "I wanted to ring her neck, that's for sure. But I needed me this job. Had me a little boy to support. And back then jobs was hard to get if you didn't have no kind of education. There wasn't all them fast-food restaurants and the like, where you could get a job real fast. I thought of maybe working for another family, but what I heard from my friends, them rich families is all alike. Besides, I had me a place to stay—in one of them rooms you fixed up—and I always found me a way to sneak food from the kitchen."

"How fascinating."

She dropped her cigarette and mashed it into the pavement. "It was due me. It wasn't like I was stealing. Stealing is a sin in both our Bibles."

"I wasn't judging. Please, tell me more."

"There ain't much more to tell, except that I nearly dropped my teeth when I seen this woman who calls herself Estelle Zimmerman prance into the place, acting like she never been there before. Then when I seen her and Mr. Webbfingers meeting like they was strangers—shoot, you could have knocked me over with a feather. I knowed right then there was trouble brewing—of course I had no idea it would be the death of the missus."

"What was the expression on Estelle Zimmerman's face when she saw you?"

She made me wait for her answer while she lit a new cigarette. "Ha! She paid me no-never-mind. Looked right through me, like I wasn't even there."

We sat in silence for a moment, while she puffed and she pondered. So I was right. There was a connection between the Webbfingerses and at least one of the bed and breakfast guests. But since Mary Estelle—assuming that was really her name—and Fisher Webbfingers had once been an item, they obviously weren't siblings, as was the fictional case in Ramat Sreym's cheesy-sounding mystery. That sort of thing doesn't happen in the South nearly as much as stand-up comedians would have you believe—okay, so maybe excepting certain parts of Arkansas.

I broke the silence. "What about the other guests. Do you recognize them?"

Harriet squashed her second cigarette. "Not them folks from California. But them other foreigners—Mrs. Washburn, I may have been wrong about them."

"How so?"

She fished yet another cancer stick from her faux leather bag. "Well, ma'am, the more I think about it, the more I recollect seeing her face. Of course it was a lot different back then, it being forty years ago and all. Now that good-looking young fellow that's supposed to be her husband, I seen him before, too, only he hasn't changed a bit. But that don't make any sense, does it?"

I would like to say that at the moment of my epiphany, trumpets sounded, the breeze turned cool, and a handsome young man in a sarong handed me a margarita. Instead, I got bitten by a sweat bee. I slapped my arm so hard a welt appeared, but the critter got away.

"Harriet, is it possible that Nick Papadopoulus is the son of the man you knew so many years ago?"

"No offense, Mrs. Washburn, but that is the silliest"—she paused to light her Marlboro—"you know, maybe it ain't so silly after all."

# 27

"So you recognize Nick?"

"Didn't say I did. But that thing on his chin, the other man had one just like it."

"What thing?"

"Clef, I think it's called."

Treble or bass, I wondered, before my heat-drained brain was able to make sense of the word. "Cleft! Just like Kirk Douglas."

"That's what I said. Anyway, Mr. Keating had him one of those."

"Keating!"

"I just said that, too. Anyway, Fisher Webbfingers Senior and Mr. Keating were like two ticks in a dog's ear. The boy, he was just a little thing. Cute as a button, but you ain't never seen a kid that shy. His big sister—that would be the one that calls herself Irena—she had enough brass to make up for him. Never liked her as a young woman, don't like her now."

I caught myself nodding and stopped. "Harriet, can you think of any reason any of these people would be here under assumed names?"

She cocked her head, perhaps the better to think. "It's the end times," she finally said.

"I beg your pardon?"

"The Bible warns us that there will be strange happenings."

"That's it? That's the only explanation you can think of?"

"Ain't that enough? Mrs. Washburn, I suggest you get right with the"—she jumped up—"Lord have mercy, I didn't realize how late it's getting. I'm supposed to be over at the church right now seeing to the eats. Although the Webbfingerses don't have no family to speak of, they have plenty of high society friends."

"You don't say."

"You may not know this, Mrs. Washburn, but them blue bloods is mighty picky eaters.

"When is the funeral?"

"Day after tomorrow, eleven o'clock. But I ain't been to this fancy church before, so I gotta check out the kitchen."

I stood as well. "Thanks for your time."

"No problem. Just remember what I said. Judgment Day is coming, and them that ain't ready . . ."

I let the rest of her sermon go in one ear and out

the other. Nodding my head and murmuring "Yes" every few seconds seemed to speed things along. I have no idea what I might have agreed to, but when Harriet finally left, she appeared quite pleased with herself.

Obviously, it had been a productive encounter for me as well. I started to call Toy on my cell phone with my big news, but changed my mind before pressing the Send button. This was going to be too much fun to share.

Fisher Webbfingers's car was in the garage when I returned, and all three rentals cars were parked along the street. I headed straight for the Hansons' a.k.a. Zimmermans' suite.

"We're busy," Estelle called out in answer to my knock. I paid close attention to her accent. One thing was for sure, whoever she really was, either she had not been raised in the South or had one heck of a voice coach. Her R could have cut through three-inch plywood.

"It's me, Abigail. Your tour guide for the day."

There followed a period of mumbling and rumbling, after which Herman came to the door. But he did not open it.

"We've decided not to go out today, little lady. Estee, here, isn't feeling so good."

"No problemo," I said, with true tour guide vivacity. "May I come in for a minute?"

"That wouldn't be such a good idea, ma'am, seeing as how it might be catchy."

"Don't worry about me, dear, I've had all my shots."

"Well, I was hoping not to have to say this—you being a lady and all—but I'm not dressed."

"I don't mind. Besides, you've seen one, you've seen them all." It had to be the chocolate speaking.

There was more mumbling than rumbling this time. Although I couldn't hear what she said, it was clear that my flip comment had rubbed Estelle's fur the wrong way.

"Ma'am," Herman said, while his wife's gums were still flapping, "maybe you better leave."

"Not until I've spoken to at least one of you. This isn't about sightseeing—it's about a vandalized yearbook at the College of Charleston."

The door opened immediately. "Come in," Herman said.

He was fully dressed, by the way, except he wasn't wearing shoes or socks. Estelle was wearing a pale pink linen shift and pink Gucci leather shoes. A matching handbag lay on the freshly made bed.

I entered saying a silent prayer of thanksgiving for the man who invented air-conditioning. Without this invention the South would never have attracted the economic growth for which it is now known.

Herman motioned to an overstuffed chair that I had had re-covered in Brunschwig & Fils fabric. The vibrant fruit colors gave a touch of pizzazz to an otherwise muted decor. It was one of my favorite pieces, and one I had yet to enjoy.

"Thank you very much," I said, but getting seated was no easy task. When it was time for me to leave, I would have to use a rope and rappel down.

Estelle sat on the bed beside her purse, as if to guard it, and Herman chose the desk chair, a rather frail Biedermeier. I was about to suggest that we switch, but Estelle spoke up.

"I had every right to take that picture, Mrs. Washburn. If you let me explain, I'm sure you'll understand."

"That's why I'm here. Explain away!"

She glanced at her husband and then back at me. "Perhaps I didn't mention that I attended the College of Charleston." She waited for my reaction, but I wisely refrained from making any sarcastic remarks. "Well," she said, when it was clear I wasn't there to play games, "I had a terrible case of acne when I was growing up. Persisted far too long, into college even. Makeup wasn't enough to cover it. In fact, it just made things worse. You should have heard the names the kids called me throughout high school. Pizza Face, Hamburger Girl—anyway, the day they took the yearbook pictures, I planned to be absent, but my roommate told the dorm representative, and—well, to make a long story short, I got pressured into having it taken."

"My Estee's got a smooth face now," Herman felt compelled to interject. "Dermabrasion, it's called. See? Her face is as smooth as custard. Cost me a pretty penny, but it was worth it."

I tried not to stare. Her skin was actually fairly smooth. Maybe only the slightest hint of scars. Just why the plastic surgeon hadn't touched the bags beneath her eyes was a whole other story.

"You look very nice," I said.

"Oh, but I didn't then. Believe me. For years I regretted having that picture taken. Nobody forced me, of course, I just wasn't strong enough to resist pressure. Then there comes a point in life when you say 'screw it'—pardon my French, Mrs. Washburn, but I'm sure you know what I mean."

I did. Last year I gave up panty hose for Lent. My legs aren't perfect, but neither are they hideous. Why should I feel obligated to encase them in plastic, as if they were giant hot dogs? But still, this newfound freedom to express myself did not extend to the destruction of someone else's property.

"But Mrs. Zimmerman, the yearbooks don't belong to you."

"My likeness does. So, what are you going to do, Mrs. Washburn, turn me in?"

Herman lurched to his feet, knocking over the Biedermeier. "Little lady, I can't let you do anything that's going to get my Estee in trouble."

I was pretty sure that the big guy was too much of a gentleman to do me any physical harm. Besides, if that was his intent, he could have turned me into pâté in the length of time it took me to get out of the chair. My best defensive move was to snuggle back into the down-filled cushions, making myself even more inconspicuous than ever.

"I'm not going to turn her in—not if she can tell me why she cut out pictures other than her own."

Herman froze. With one arm extended and one foot just leaving the ground, he reminded me of the game "statues" that we used to play when we were children. Estelle had gone rigid as well. Had it not been for the bags beneath her eyes, one might have surmised she'd been the recent recipient of beaucoup Botox injections. C.J. refers to this as the Lot's Wife Syndrome. She also, bless her heart, believes that Shelby and Gastonia, North Carolina, are the Sodom and Gomorrah mentioned in the Bible. But that's a whole different story as well.

At any rate, Estelle sprang to life first. "Okay, so maybe I cut an extra page or two out of that dang book. I fail to see what this has to do with you. Are you just a nosy woman with too much time on her hands? Is that it, Mrs. Washburn? Come up to Wisconsin and we'll show you how real American women spend their days."

It was the moment of truth. It was not, however, my place to confront the suspects, no matter how convincing the evidence. Besides, I had only one piece of what was undoubtedly a very complex puzzle. One wrong word out of me and Herman would undoubtedly whack me over the head with the Biedermeier and throw both me and the chair into the harbor. What a waste of a perfectly fine piece of furniture.

Alas, there are times when I just can't hold my tongue. "It's my business because Wynnell Crawford is my best friend. I'm not about to let her take the rap for you."

Herman's body thawed enough to let him pick up the fallen chair, which he did, but he did not sit. "Let me get this straight, little lady. You think we killed Mrs. Webbfingers?"

"Did you? Oh, and just so you know—I'm wired."

Estelle blinked rapidly, the Botox phase well behind her. "We didn't kill anyone, Mrs. Washburn. And it was never part of our plan."

Herman cringed. "Estee—"

"No, Herman, it's time we came clean. We can't

be indicted for a crime we never got the chance to commit."

Herman's mouth opened and closed a couple of times but no sound came out. Finally he turned to me. His eyes said everything.

"She's right," I said. "If you didn't commit a crime, and haven't been covering up for one, there really is no reason to worry. Now the year-books—that's another story. I'm afraid that's between you and the College of Charleston. But you're going to have to tell them what you did. Is that understood?"

They nodded.

"So," I said, waving my hand like a grand poobah on her overstuffed throne, "who would like to go first?"

"It's mostly my story," Estee said. "I should be the one to tell it."

I made a show of looking down the front of my sundress, supposedly at a microphone. What I saw was a pair of rather nice but otherwise unremarkable breasts, and a very pretty bra from Victoria's Secret.

"Speak nice and loud," I said. "And take it from the beginning."

# 28

"I was born and raised right here in Charleston. My parents owned a candy store across from the Market—actually a whole string of gourmet chocolate shops up and down the East Coast. Rosenkrantz and Sons, they were called—even though there was no son, and our family name was Simonson. Did you ever hear of these chocolate stores?"

I shook my head. "Sorry."

"But don't think for a minute that we were part of the working class. My papa was the grandson of Danish immigrants—farmers, to be sure—but my mother's mother was a Danish baroness. *The* Baroness Christina Rosenkrantz."

"Some kind of cousin to the Queen," Herman said proudly.

"A distant cousin through Christian IV. Anyway, although we couldn't claim three hundred years of local history, my mother's lineage was good enough for Charleston, and we moved in the best social circles—for a while at least. I grew up knowing Fisher Webbfingers. Was in this very house often as a guest."

"They even got engaged," Herman said, still sounding proud.

"Then one day while I was in college—I went to school right here, so my mother could keep an eye on me—I met a fellow student at the beach. He hadn't put on any tanning lotion, and he was as red as a Maine lobster."

Herman grinned. "I still burn pretty bad."

"I offered to put Noxzema on his back, and then we got to talking, and the next thing I knew, I found myself breaking up with Fisher and marrying Herman."

"You should have seen the look on her parents' face when I met them. Kind of like my cows, if you leave the milk pump on too long."

I pushed that image out of my mind. "Funny, Mr. Zimmerman, but your wife doesn't have a trace of a Southern accent."

"She did when I met her. But all those years living up North finally got her talking regular most of the time."

Estelle nodded. "It comes back when I get excited. Or when I dream."

"This is all very interesting, Mrs. Zimmerman, but what does any of this have to do with Marina Webbfingers's murder?"

"You said to start at the beginning."

I tried to smile. "Please restart where it's relevant."

"But you see, it's all relevant. I would have never known Fisher and the others if my mother hadn't had such an enviable pedigree, and if Fisher and I had married, then I most probably would have known the statue's location all along."

Now we were cooking with gas. "What statue?"

The pair of them gave me a pitying look. "Honestly, Mrs. Washburn," Estelle said, "you're the one who's wasting time now."

"The maquette of *David*," I mumbled. "I wasn't sure you knew about it."

"Yes, the maquette. The one my father and the others stole from the wine cellar of a villa outside Florence."

I gasped with excitement. "The diamond necklace!"

Estelle gave me a peeved look. "It's not a necklace, it's a prototype for a statue."

"I know what it is. You said your father and the others stole it?"

"The villa was abandoned. It's not like they had to hurt anyone to do it."

It was no time to give her a lecture on morality. "Did they know what they'd found? I mean its value? It is a maquette of *the David* statue, isn't it?"

Estelle's eyes gleamed. Not only did their unexpected fire make her look years younger, but she was suddenly almost attractive.

"Nick and Irena's father—they're brother and sister, as you undoubtedly know by now—taught art history at Columbia University in New York City. Professor Keating knew more about art than my daddy knew about candy. So the answer is yes, they had a pretty good idea of what it was they'd found."

"How did they get it back to the States?"

Herman laughed. "This is the good part. Tell her, Estee."

"Daddy covered it with chocolate."

"Get out of town!"

"It was only a thin layer, of course, but the guys saved up their rations and managed to barter until they had just enough. First Daddy covered the maquette in white wax—candles they'd borrowed from different churches—so that the chocolate wouldn't stain the marble. Then the chocolate. He had to mix some wax in that to make it stick, but it had a nice chocolate aroma. It nearly drove them crazy, they used to say."

My cell phone rang. Suddenly the gleam left Estelle's eyes and she looked as jumpy as a monkey on a barbed-wire fence. Herman bit his lower lip.

"It's my cell," I said calmly, willing the machine to self-destruct. But it wouldn't stop. "What is it?" I demanded on the fourth ring.

"Abby, it's me, Greg."

"Yes, officer. Everything is fine."

"Abby, what's going on?"

"So you have no problem hearing everything we say?"

"Huh? Abby, are you in some kind of a jam?"

"Absolutely not. They're being very cooperative."

I swear I could feel Greg's sigh. "Okay, I give up. Do what you have to do. Just be careful."

"Got that. Anything else, officer?"

"Yes. I just called to say that I hate fighting, and I'm sorry for all the crap I gave you."

"Same here."

"And I love you, hon."

"Ditto."

I turned the phone off and did my best to present a grave face to the Zimmermans. "Now where were we? Oh yes, the chocolate-covered maquette. How did they get it through customs?"

"Daddy, Fisher Webbfingers Senior, and Professor Keating called themselves the Three Musketeers. Anyway, it was the war, and they were GIs. The Three Musketeers had no trouble boarding their return ship. Stateside, they were questioned by immigration, but they had a story already concocted. Something about it being a cheap souvenir they'd picked up, sort of as a mascot. Turned out smuggling it into the country really was no problem at all.

"The question was, what to do with it now that it was here? There was a lot of discussion—maybe even a few arguments—but in the end they decided that the best thing to do was to do nothing. They made a pact that they would wait fifty years, or until the statute of limitations on stolen property ran out. Then they, or their heirs, would sell it. 'The big secret,' they called it."

"But there is no such thing as a statute of limitations on theft," I said, and then immediately wished I'd stuffed one of the Brunschwig & Fils–covered cushions down my gullet before speaking.

I needn't have worried. "Of course there is," Estelle snapped. "They were all bright men. They wouldn't have made such a silly mistake."

"My Estee knows everything," Herman opined from the peanut gallery.

"Then it's my mistake," I said, grateful for the second chance. "Please, go on."

Estelle flashed me a triumphant smile. "So anyway, the big secret became sort of a rite of passage. When I turned eighteen, Daddy told me about the statue and where to find it, should something happen to him before the fifty years were over. Fisher's daddy did the same thing for Fisher Junior, and Professor Keating told both his kids on their eighteenth birthdays."

"And it was a good thing they did," Herman said, "because all three men died before the fifty years were over."

"But you kids—I mean the younger generation—knew its whereabouts, right?"

"Not that it did any good in the end," Estelle said, sounding a tad less victorious.

"I beg your pardon?"

"The Three Musketeers hid the statue in a hammock in Copahee Sound. Do you know what a hammock is, Mrs. Washburn?"

"Yes. It's higher ground, sort of like an island, that sticks out of the marshes. Hammocks usually have permanent trees on them—oaks, palms, whatever."

"You get a gold star, Mrs. Washburn. And as you probably know, there are hundreds of channels that cut through the marshes and dozens of hammocks to choose from. This particular hammock was exceptionally high, and like you said, a real island. In fact, a lot of fishermen referred to it as Doubloon Island, because a Spanish doubloon was said to have been found on it." She shook her head, but her faux black locks, which had been heavily lacquered, remained in place. "But it didn't stay that way. Hurricane Hugo did a heck of a job of reconfiguring the marshes. New channels were cut, old ones obliterated, and the hammocks—well, none of them looked the same after that."

"So the statue was lost?"

"That's the sixty thousand dollar question, isn't it? But one thing for sure—the hammock was gone. At least it was unrecognizable after the storm. The Three Musketeers—all old men by then—combed the marshes around Copahee Sound. They followed every channel, slogged over every hammock, braving alligators, snakes, and clouds of mosquitoes. But no maquette. Finally they were forced to give up, but not before things had gone sour."

"Do tell."

"They started accusing each other of having stolen the statue at some point before Hurricane Hugo."

"No honor among thieves," I whispered.

Apparently Estelle had the hearing of a fox. "My daddy was no thief."

"But you just admitted that the three of them stole the maquette from an Italian villa."

"That was different. Besides, Daddy would have never stolen from the others. Professor Keating, either. It had to be Fisher Senior."

"Why is that?"

"He was the only one who stayed in the area. Shortly after I married Herman, my parents retired to Florida. And the Keatings, who were originally from New York, moved back home when the professor got a job offer from Columbia University. So you see, it was Fisher Senior who had the time and opportunity to remove the statue from Doubloon Island and hide it somewhere else—or maybe it was Fisher Junior. Either way, the Webbfingerses stole it from the rest of us. Then along came the hurricane, presenting the perfect opportunity for them to claim that the maquette of David was lost."

"Where do you think he hid it?"

Herman's guffaws might have put the cows off milking all the way up in Wisconsin.

Estelle and I waited patiently for a lull. "He *didn't* hide it," she said, her words as staccato as gunshots. "It was right there in the middle of a flower bed when we drove up."

I breathed a huge sigh of relief. "Well, at least I can tell concrete from marble."

Her eyes narrowed. "Are you trying to be funny, Mrs. Washburn?"

"No, not at all. As you know, I decorated this room. I remember seeing the statue and thinking it was compressed marble. I certainly didn't think it was concrete—which the police report says it is." Oops, perhaps I'd gone too far.

"No, it was real, and just like Daddy described. Fisher claims it just showed one morning, out of the clear blue. He says he called me first, and then the Keatings. He asked us to come down to Charleston, but under assumed last names. He said he and Marina had just built a B and B, and we could stay here until we figured out what was going on. But then no sooner do we get here than Marina gets killed and the statue goes missing."

"Why the assumed names?"

"He said Marina had just registered their first guests, a very suspicious couple—walk-ins from the street. Fisher had a hunch they were undercover cops working for the Italians."

"You mean John and Belinda from Calamari?"

"Fisher always did have a good imagination. He was a lot of fun to play with as a child."

"Just one thing escapes me," I said. "Why did the Webbfingerses open a B and B in the first place? It's not like they needed the money—or did they?"

"Let me answer that," Herman Hanson, a.k.a. Zimmerman, said with zeal.

"Please. Be my guest."

"The woman was a slut—sorry, little lady, but that's the best way I can put it. The whole thing was her idea. Thought it would give her extra opportunities to fool around."

Estelle frowned. "That's what Fisher says, dear. We don't know that for sure. Maybe he was lonely and felt the need for company." She turned to me. "Besides, there is a difference between needing money and wanting more. That's the thing about money—everyone wants more."

I couldn't argue with that. The more one has, the more one spends. Money, like water, has the ability to insinuate itself into every void and crack it encounters, creating new desires, which in turn become new needs. Some people wonder how the fabulously rich can suddenly find themselves in dire financial straits. I think it's a miracle that even more of them don't declare bankruptcy.

"Okay, officer," I said, speaking to my bosoms one last time, "I think that covers it. Are there any questions you want me to ask them?"

The Zimmermans waited anxiously for a moment, until Herman used his brain. Alas, it was something I'd forgotten to do.

"Hey little lady, you're not even wired."

"Of course I am."

"The heck you say. You're pretending to wait for an answer, but you're not wearing an earpiece."

"Yes, I am. It's very tiny."

Estelle stood and approached me, while I tried to be absorbed by my overstuffed chair. She towered over me.

"Get out" she said, in a tone that one of her royal ancestors might have used to banish a subject who'd fallen from grace.

It was time to go anyway, now that I knew who had killed Marina Webbfingers.

# 29

"Abby, at least wait until I get there."

"I'll be fine, Toy. Harriet Spanky let me in, and I'd be willing to bet my shop—even the one up in Charlotte—that the so-called Zimmermans were watching me through their window."

"Where's the creep now?"

"He's taking a call in the den. I'm in the living room, which, by the way, is absolutely stunning. You didn't tell me the walls were covered with silk damask. That shade of peach is just what I've been looking for. I wonder if Fisher remembers who did the work and where they got the material."

"Sis, you're there to tie up a few loose ends, not to engage in a fashion powwow."

"But that's my plan of attack. I'll ask a few casual questions and then—I've got to go. He's coming back."

I barely had time to slip my oversize phone back

into my purse. In fact I was fumbling with the zipper when Fisher Junior strode into the room.

"Sorry about that, Mrs. Washburn. That was my rector who called. Apparently his secretary lost the list of hymns I'd requested for Marina's service. He needed them now, or it would be too late to include them in the service leaflet. I chose 'Be Still My Soul' and 'Amazing Grace.'"

"They're beautiful hymns," I said. But I felt like a first-class heel. What if I was wrong about Fisher? What if Fisher wasn't guilty of his wife's murder? One thing for sure, I was going to skip the silly decorating questions.

"I'm glad you like the hymns. They were Marina's favorites." He glanced at the French ormolu clock on the white painted mantel. "I don't have a lot of time, Mrs. Washburn. How can I help you?"

"By telling me the truth. Were you and the woman who calls herself Estelle Zimmerman childhood sweethearts?"

I'll give the man credit for having remarkable composure. Other then fixing his colorless eyes on mine, I could detect no reaction.

"Yes, it's true."

"It is?"

He gestured to a Louis XV fauteuil. The chair was upholstered in a floral needlepoint, which contained small touches of peach that tied it to the walls beautifully. I was grateful for the chance to sit. My knees were knocking like the pistons of my very first car, one that leaked oil so badly our neighbors complained to the city that I was ruining their street.

"Mrs. Washburn," my host said calmly, "I was hoping you'd have that conversation with the Simonsons."

"You *were*?"

"I thought it would save me time. Plus, I thought it might be useful to get your take on them. Have you spoken with the Keatings as well?"

"You were involved with Irena, too?"

"Involved? Certainly not romantically. But I did know her. Whenever the Three Musketeers met—and it was usually here—they brought their families. The Thomases, by the way, are legitimate guests and have nothing to do with the Three Musketeers. If they seem a little odd to you, it's because they're having an affair. He's from Chicago and she's from St. Louis. He was quite up front about it to me—wanted to know if I would be discreet. I told him it wasn't any of my business. Anyway, you do know about the Three Musketeers, don't you?"

"Yes." With the wind taken out of my sails, I was with nothing but a bunch of sagging cloth. It seemed to have wrapped around my tongue.

"Do they think I'm guilty of my wife's murder?"

I yanked my lingua loose enough to form some simple words. "I haven't spoken to the Keatings about it, just the Simonsons. They didn't accuse you, but I don't think they've eliminated you from their list of suspects."

"Is that what you have, Mrs. Washburn? A list of suspects?"

"Well, I know my friend, Wynnell Crawford, didn't do it. Therefore, it had to be someone else."

"And I'm at the top of your list, am I? Allow me to try and guess why. Let's see"—he rested his chin on a closed fist and pretended to think—"ah, yes, my motive would have been the ultimate payback to a cheating wife. How's that? Do I pass detecting class?"

"I can do without your sarcasm, Mr. Fisher. And yes, I can see how a philandering wife could provoke someone into committing murder."

"But don't you think murder is going too far? If I really wanted to punish her, I would have drugged her and had someone tattoo a scarlet A on her forehead. Think how that would go over in Charleston."

I had to admit that a scarlet A would take the prize. Death is a onetime thing, then it's over, but even with the advent of lasers, some tattoos are almost impossible to obliterate. At the very least, the experience can be painful.

"And what about the statue?" he said, not giving me time to answer. "It goes missing for sixteen years, and then suddenly shows up in our garden. Do you think I would have risked drawing attention to myself by committing murder? Not to mention the fact that it happened the very day I had guests coming into town."

"Why *did* you call others? If the maquette just showed up, like you claim, why didn't you and Marina keep mum about it?"

He smiled, and I found myself both surprised and relieved. "You have a good head on your shoulders, Mrs. Washburn. I like that. But you see, the statue wasn't put in my wife's flower bed by fairies. Someone put it there, and we didn't know who. It seemed like the wise thing to do was to call for backup. More importantly, the maquette belongs to all of us—the descendants of the Three Musketeers."

"But that's where you're wrong; it belongs to whomever your fathers stole it from. For your information, Mr. Webbfingers, there is no such thing as a statute of limitations on stolen property."

The watery eyes seemed to freeze into glittering disks. "Says who?"

"Call your lawyer if you don't believe me. Better yet, call one of those legal hotlines that answer questions from anonymous callers."

"Like I said, I have things to do. Please see yourself out, Mrs. Washburn."

He turned and walked from the room. A moment later I heard the side door slam and then the engine of his car. The squeal of tires confirmed the fact that Fisher Webbfingers was in a hurry to go somewhere.

I settled back into the fauteuil. What if I'd been way off base and a man with something to hide wouldn't have left a proven snoop alone in the house? Unless it was a trap. But how obvious was that? At least as obvious as leaving a petite pair of shoes—

"Mrs. Washburn," a voice said, breaking through my reverie.

I sat bolt straight. "Harriet?"

The elderly maid was standing in the pillared doorway of the living room. In her gnarled hand the ugly black barrel of a handgun bobbed menacingly.

Once, in my single days, I took a self-defense class. The instructor said that the single most important lesson we could learn was never, *ever*, get into a car with your assailant. If you do, he said, you surrender all control. He also stressed the fact that handguns are frequently inaccurate, and that a moving target is difficult even for an expert marksman to hit.

He made us chant the word "run" like a mantra. That was all well and good from a theoretical standpoint. But when faced with a real gun, I found that my legs had apparently not been paying attention during class. Try as I might, I couldn't get them to move until Harriet pressed the muzzle against my left temple and threatened to blow my copulating brains out.

My Judas legs betrayed me by obeying her command to walk beside her into the kitchen. There they gave out. I guess I can't blame them, because the rest of me almost fainted when I saw the enormous man wielding a crowbar just inside the back door.

The giant, who was dressed in faded bib overalls, was both barefoot and shirtless. Sweat streamed over rolls of blubber, disappearing into crevices and then appearing again, all while creating ribbons of white against a dirt gray background. He had no noticeable neck, but his head made up for this flaw by being twice as wide as it should have been. His bloated cheeks resembled a pair of volleyballs, and it took me a second to notice that he was smiling. From what I could see, he had exactly three teeth.

"This is my baby boy Nolan," Harriet said, just as proud as if she was introducing the Prince of Wales.

"Pleased to meet you, ma'am," Nolan said, and thumped the crowbar against the callused palm of his hand.

I had nothing to say,

"Mama, I don't think she likes me."

"She likes you just fine, son." The gun pressed harder against my skull. "Don't you, Mrs. Washburn?"

"Yes ma'am," I heard my Benedict Arnold mouth say. "Pleased to meet you, Nolan."

"That's better. You see, Mrs. Washburn, my Nolan here has taken quite a shine to you over the last couple of days."

Nolan revealed a fourth tooth.

"I don't see how," I said. "We've never met."

"I seen you, ma'am. I says to myself, 'Nolan, you gotta admire a woman who can drive fast like that and not get rattled.'"

"So that was you driving the blue pickup!"

His grin widened—there were no more teeth—as he balanced on the outer sides of his feet. A twelve-year-old schoolboy with a crush is what came to mind.

"She ain't a pretty sight, Mrs. Washburn, but she got her a whole lot of power. Just you wait and see."

"What is that supposed to mean?"

"He means that you'll be taking a little ride," Harriet said.

"If it's all the same, I'd rather not. I get motion sickness when I'm that high off the ground. That's one of the reasons why I don't own an SUV."

Harriet cackled like a hen who'd just laid her first egg. "If you get motion sickness, then you ain't gonna like what we've got planned for you."

"And what would that be?"

Nolan's massive face looked about to dissolve, like the head of a snowman in a winter rain. "Mama. Do we hafta?"

"Have to what?" I demanded.

"Kill you," Harriet said. "And the answer is yes."

# 30

There were two of them and a gun, versus me and my mouth. They won. While Nolan, who may have been crying as much as sweating, held me in his viselike grip, Harriet bound my wrists and ankles with duct tape. Mercifully, they didn't tape my mouth. Perhaps they decided that I was too entertaining to mute. Either that or Nolan was hopeful that he and I would exchange sweet nothings during my last minutes on earth.

When they were through trussing me like a turkey, Harriet slipped a cloth sack over my head. Then without as much as a grunt, Nolan swung me over his should like bag of laundry and carried me to his truck, where I was propped up in the middle of the seat. Mother and son took their places on either side.

"What happens if we get stopped by the police?" I asked as we sped along at what I guessed to be twice the speed limit.

"Ain't none of your concern," Harriet snapped.

"You know that some of the guests must have seen me being carried out."

"What they seen was a bag of laundry."

"You'll never get with away with it."

"Shut up, Mrs. Washburn."

"I'm afraid I can't. It's not in my nature."

"Mama," Nolan wheezed, "ain't she just the spunkiest thing?"

Harriet snorted. "Baby Boy, I warned you not to get attached to her. You start thinking about all them things we're gonna buy with the statue money."

*Baby Boy?* Baby Huey was more like it. But one thing was becoming rapidly clear: there would be no use in trying to pit mother against son. Experts say that kidnapping victims stand a better chance if they can humanize themselves in the eyes of their captors. It appeared that I had a good start with Nolan.

I wiggled closer to the big guy, snuggling up against the wet rolls of fat. Although Nolan's body odor was so strong I thought I might retch, I made sure that the length of my thigh pressed into his.

"Do you like to travel, Nolan?"

"Don't know. Ain't never been nowhere—excepting for Florence."

"Florence, Italy?"

"They got one of them over there, too?"

"So you mean Florence, South Carolina. That's a lovely city as well. You know, Nolan, I was thinking—"

Harriet yanked me in her direction. The woman was remarkably strong for her age, I'll give her that.

"I thought I told you to shut up."

"I was just making polite conversation."

"You ain't fooling me, Mrs. Washburn. I know what you're up to, and it ain't gonna work. Nolan don't even breathe without I say so."

For a nanosecond I thought about pressing the flesh with Harriet. But it was my tongue that had gotten me into this jam, so it would be my tongue that got me out again.

"That isn't a real statue, Harriet. It's just a model."

"I'm not stupid, Mrs. Washburn. I already know that."

"You do?"

"It's what they call a maquette. Mrs. Webbfingers told me all about it."

I gasped, sucking in a mouthful of filthy sack, which I promptly spit out. "Then you must know about the Three Musketeers."

"Yes, ma'am, I sure do. I told you I been working for this family a long time, didn't I? Knowed them guests, too, the ones who changed their names. Funny, but I don't think they recognized me." She chortled. "But it ain't no surprise, me being just the maid. Rich folks can look at you all day, but they don't see you."

"That's because they're snobs."

"Don't you be agreeing with me none, Mrs. Timberlake. Baby Boy might fall for your games, but not me."

The truck halted at a stoplight. It occurred to me to hop up and down as much as I could, or at least wiggle like a worm about to be impaled on a hook. There aren't too many laundry bags that can do that on their own. Surely someone would spot me and report the strange phenomenon to the police. In the end it was the pressure of the gun barrel, this time against my gut, that stopped me.

"I'm sorry, Harriet. I won't do that again. But since it's obvious that I'm not going to come out of this alive, you may as well tell me the whole story. I'm sure it's very interesting."

"Mama," Nolan bawled, "you didn't say nothing about killing her."

"Hush, Baby Boy. Your mama knows best. Ain't I always done the right thing by you?"

"Yes, Mama." He started to sniff, and I was

pretty sure it wasn't because sweat had gotten into his nose.

"So Harriet, how about filling me in? How long have you known about the maquette?"

She was silent for a while, but I was just a bag of laundry, not long for this world, and she had some powerful secrets to share. Triumph is far less fun when kept to oneself, and Nolan wasn't exactly the perfect listener.

"Since right after the war."

"World War Two, right?"

"Yeah, back when the world was normal. Not like it is today, with all them preverts and the like trying to take over things. Anyways, one Sunday— and this was way before Hurricane Hugo—Baby Boy's daddy and I was out crabbing. Sunday is my day off, you see. Has been ever since I started working for them Webbfingers, when I weren't but fifteen years old. Anyways, I don't let nothing stop me from attending the house of the Lord. So we was out crabbing, like I said, and we seen this boat with three men in it poking about them marsh channels like they was up to something fishy. I seen it first, so I tell Baby Boy's daddy—his name was Bubba Boy—to get down—not like that would do much good—and then I get down, and we sort of spied on them."

"Tell her who you seen in the boat, Mama."

"I am about to, son." At first I thought she was pausing for dramatic effect. Then I heard Nolan whimper. "Stop your whining, Baby Boy."

"Yes, Mama."

The barrel pushed against my abdomen. "Now where was I?"

"Three men in a tub," I said quickly. "Rub-a-dub-dub."

"You're plum local, Mrs. Washburn, so I'll ignore that. And yeah, it was three men, but you'd never guess who they was."

"Fisher Webbfingers Senior, his friend Mr. Simonson, and Professor Keating."

She swatted me, knocking me into Baby Boy's shoulder. I bounced back to my upright position as easily as if he'd been a trampoline.

"That ain't fair, Mrs. Washburn, knowing all them answers ahead of time. Where's the fun of it for me?" Mercifully, she didn't wait for an answer. "Anyways, what they was doing was trying to hide this statue on one of them bitty islands that ain't hardly an island. Took them awhile to find just the right one, but they did. Soon as they left for good, me and Bubba Boy goes and finds that statue and puts it in our boat."

"Dang, but that thing is heavy," Nolan said. "Even for me."

"Now didn't I tell you to shush?"

"Sorry, Mama."

"I told Mrs. Webbfingers Senior what we'd seen, only I don't tell her what we'd done—that we'd already taken the dang thing. She says the statue is just a piece of junk, and that if I had a mind to, I should hide it under this big old camellia that Mr. Webbfingers Senior hated, on account of she got it from one of her beaus as a wedding present. Kinda like a joke, she said. So I done just that, and then I plumb forgot about it. But you see, the whole time she must have knowed it was worth a lot, but she didn't care, on account of there was about as much loving going on between them old Webbfingers as there was between the young ones. Anyways, she had her own money.

"Well them years just go ticking by, and Baby Boy here is born, and Bubba Boy dies, and so does Mr. Webbfingers Senior and his missus, and then finally along comes Hurricane Hugo. Well, who woulda thought it possible, but that Hugo messes everything up, even that itty-bitty island. So Mr. Webbfingers Junior gets it in his head to see how his daddy's statue is faring—he has him a little map drawed and everything—but there ain't nothing there for him to admire."

"Then what?" My excitement was genuine.

"Mr. Webbfingers Junior 'bout went crazy, that's what. Combed them marshes like he was looking for nits. Them other kids of the Musketeers come back to help him look, but of course they don't find nothing. And all the time I'm laughing behind the back of my hand, on account of them society folks is so bent out of shape over nothing. Finally, the Musketeers give up—I mean, what else they gonna do? Then you come along, Mrs. Washburn—"

"*Moi?*"

"And that dang statue suddenly appears in the flower bed. Mr. Webbfingers was fit to be tied. Called his buddies right away. But when them kids of the Musketeers showed up and they all got to talking, I kept my ears open, that's what I did. Learned that that hunk of stone is worth a million dollars. Maybe more. And it lying there under that camellia the entire time!"

"It's probably worth even more than a million." She grunted. "You see, Baby Boy?"

"But I didn't mean to kill her, Mama."

"I know you didn't, baby." She jabbed me again with the gun barrel. "You see what you done? If you and that friend of yours hadn't showed up, this would never have happened."

"But you knew about the statue all along!"

"Only I didn't know what it was worth. A million dollars might not mean much to you, Mrs. Timberlake, but me and my son can't even dream about that much money. Now where was I?"

"About to describe the dastardly deed itself?"

"T'weren't bastardly. Wasn't nothing like that supposed to happen—it just kinda did. I tell Baby Boy to get the statue in the middle of the night and switch it with this cheap one we find at one of them junk stores. You see, he was supposed to do it when everyone was asleep. But that afternoon he has himself a few beers, and reckons he'll get the job over with early. So he comes over to the house, gets him the statue, and puts it in the truck. Then he remembers he's supposed to put the cheap one in the flower bed, so he goes back to the house with it, but before he can even put the dang thing down, Mrs. Webbfingers sees him and starts hollering. That's when Baby Boy panicked and did what he done."

"I didn't mean to hit her so hard, Mama."

"I knowed you didn't." I could feel her reaching around me, presumably to pat him on the arm.

"So let me get this straight," I said, after I'd waited long enough, "Baby Boy—I mean, Nolan—panicked again and tossed the bloody replica into the harbor."

"That's right. And now that you know the whole thing, just you hush, too, on account of all this talk is upsetting my son."

At last I was happy to be quiet. And for the time to think.

\* \* \*

We drove for at least half an hour. When we got to our destination, some obscure dirt put-in on a marsh channel, Harriet mumbled something as she slipped off the laundry bag. The sunlight blinded me to distraction, and I asked her to repeat what she'd said.

"I said, it ain't right that you go to Glory and don't see how you get there."

"This is it? You're going to kill me now."

She cackled again. "We ain't gonna kill you, Mrs. Timberlake; that would be against the Bible. We're gonna let the crabs do you in."

"Excuse me?"

"Baby Boy here's been working hard on this extra big crab pot. When them critters get done with you, won't be nothing left but bones. Who knows, maybe they eat bones, too. Ain't never tried to feed them any."

"That's still murder. And killing Mrs. Webbfingers was murder as well."

"Mama, make her stop saying that."

"You see what you done?" Harriet demanded. She didn't wait for an answer. Instead she whacked me on the left side of the head with the butt of her gun.

I didn't see stars, perhaps because it was broad daylight. I did, however, taste blood. It took a minute for the world to stop swirling.

"You'll never get away with this, Harriet. Someone's bound to see us."

"Not here they ain't. Not until duck hunting season. Besides, it's high tide now."

I watched in fascinated horror as mother and son unloaded a small boat and what looked like a giant lobster trap. The only thing left in the bed of the trunk was an aluminum anchor attached to about six feet of chain. Maybe it went with the boat, or maybe they were going to use it to tether the crab pot to one place. It didn't matter, though, because a better use popped into my head.

"Harriet, dear, do I at least get to pray first?"

"What?"

"You assumed I'm going to Glory, but the truth is, I'm just a lapsed Episcopalian. Don't you think I should make things right with the Lord first?"

She sighed heavily. "It's not like you didn't have plenty of time on the ride over."

"Yes, but we Episcopalians kneel when we pray. Surely, you don't have anything against kneeling."

"Hmm. Then kneel. It don't bother me none."

"Thanks. But somehow it doesn't seem right to pray with my feet tied together. My hands, I understand, but my feet—I don't think that's respectful."

"I don't see how it ain't."

"Nolan, you understand, don't you? Have you ever prayed with your feet tied?"

"No ma'am." He turned to his mother like an oversized cuckoo bird chick begging to be fed. "Mama, just her feet, okay?"

Harriet turned the gun and brought it up to eye level. "Okay, but if you try anything, I'll shoot. Then I'll most likely be really mad, on account you caused me to sin, so I'll shoot you again."

"I understand."

Nolan did the honors. His touch was tender, causing me to doubt that he would have used the crowbar back at the house, unless unusually provoked. Harriet was another matter. I was convinced that she would happily blow my head to smithereens, and repent of it later.

I had only a second in which to react. As the last bit of tape ripped loose, I brought one knee forward, where it connected solidly with Baby Boy's nose. He stumbled, and while he struggled in vain to regain his footing, I leaped as high as I could, throwing myself against the lowered tailgate of the truck. With hands still tied, but outstretched, I managed to grab a few inches of the anchor rope.

"Drop it now!" Harriet screamed.

I had no option but to follow through. The anchor didn't exactly sail off the end of the truck; it dropped. But as luck would have it, Baby Boy now lay facedown in the dirt, and the sharp tines came to rest in his gluteus maximus. I have only twice before in my life heard such anguished cries, and both times I was giving birth.

Harriet may have been willing to kill me, but she was still a mother. As she tended to her son, I slipped away into the tall marsh grass. Three deep gashes and a hundred bug bites later, I was rescued by a pair of retirees who had taken a wrong turn in their bass boat.

# 31

"**H**ere's to our Abby," Mama said, raising her tea glass as high as her tailored dress allowed.

"Here, here!" everyone shouted. The taller folks at our table clinked glasses, much to the amusement of the other customers gathered for lunch at Slightly North of Broad.

Wynnell and Ed, who was now on an insulin pump and feeling as fine as frog's hair, were among my most vocal supporters. I was both surprised, and glad, to see them sitting so close together. While not exhibiting the behavior of lovebirds, neither were they glowering at each other like a pair of disgruntled vultures. And Wynnell, much to my great relief, professed to being pleased at the prospect of Ed joining her in the business.

The Rob-Bobs, bless their hearts, weren't quite as content. Bob had planned to cook the lunch himself—octopus à l'orange, or something like

355

that—but I'd begged Rob to talk him out of it, on the grounds that having almost become crab food, I wasn't up to devouring marine life anytime soon. Needless to say, my buddy with the bass voice was pouting.

Toy, however, was in high spirits. Although it had been four days since my ordeal, he was still in town. I was beginning to suspect that his deacon's collar was a rental, and that I would be stuck having him as a house guest until he qualified for Medicare.

"To my brave sister!" he said, rising to his feet. "May she have as many lives as a sack full of cats."

"Please, no sack references," I said.

Greg squeezed my knee under the table. He'd been nothing but affectionate lately. I knew how hard it was for him to bite his tongue. You had to give the man credit for trying to keep an open mind.

C.J. stood beside Toy. "So Abby, how much is that statue worth?"

"According to the rightful heir—a Senor Giovanni Gastelli—about thirteen million. That's the highest offer he's gotten since the news broke."

"Ooh Abby, is it true you're going to be in *Time* magazine, just like my cousin, Horatio Ledbetter?"

"Our Abby is going to be in a lot of magazines," Mama said proudly, "but it's you and Toy who have the really big news, isn't it, dear?"

The big gal grinned.

# Welcome to the
# Den of Antiquity

*Home to rare antiques, priceless artwork—
and murder!*

Celebrated author Tamar Myers invites you to enjoy
her hilarious mystery series featuring Charleston's
favorite shopkeeper-turned-detective,
**Abigail Timberlake.**

"A very funny mystery series . . . a hilarious hero-
ine."

*Charleston Post & Courier*

"Professionally plotted and developed, and fun
to read."

*San Francisco Valley Times*

"Rollicking!"

*The Washington Post*

"Who do you read after Sue Grafton or Margaret
Moron or Patricia Cornwell? . . . Tamar Myers!"
*Greensboro News & Record*

Step into the world of Tamar Myers, and see what
mysteries the Den of Antiquity has in
store for you . . .

TELL THE WORLD THIS BOOK WAS

| GOOD | BAD | SO-SO |
|------|-----|-------|
|      |     |       |

# Larceny and Old Lace
*For whom the bell pull tolls . . .*

As owner of the Den of Antiquity, recently divorced (but *never* bitter!) Abigail Timberlake is accustomed to delving into the past, searching for lost treasures, and navigating the cutthroat world of rival dealers at flea markets and auctions. Still, she never thought she'd be putting her expertise in mayhem and detection to other use—until a crotchety "junque" dealer, Abby's aunt Eulonia Wiggins, was found murdered!

Although Abigail is puzzled by the instrument of death—an exquisite antique bell pull that Aunt Eulonia *never* would have had the taste to acquire—she's willing to let the authorities find the culprit. But now, Auntie's prized lace collection is missing, and sombody's threatened Abby's most priceless possession: her son, Charlie. It's up to Abby to put the murderer "on the block."

## Gilt by Association
*A closetful of corpse . . .*

Abigail Timberlake parlayed her savvy about exquisite
old things into a thriving antiques enterprise: the Den
of Antiquity. Now she's a force to be reckoned with in
Charlotte's close-knit world of mavens and eccentrics.
But a superb, gilt-edged eighteenth-century French armoire she purchased for a song at an estate auction has
just arrived along with something she didn't pay for: a
dead body.

Suddenly her shop is a crime scene—and closed to the
public during the busiest shopping season of the
year—so Abigail is determined to speed the lumbering
police investigation along. But amateur sleuthing is
evading the feisty antiques expert into a murderous
mess of dysfunctional family secrets. And the next ca-
daver found stuffed into fine old furniture could wind
up being Abigail's own.

# The Ming and I
*Rattling old family skeletons . . .*

North Carolina native Abigail Timberlake is quick to dismiss the seller of a hideous old vase—until the poor lady comes hurtling back through the shop window minutes later, the victim of a fatal hit-and-run. Tall, dark, and handsome homicide investigator Greg Washburn—who just happens to be Abby's boyfriend—is frustrated by conflicting accounts from eyewitnesses. And he's just short of furious when he learns that the vase was a valuable Ming, and Abby let it vanish from the crime scene. Abby decides she had better find out for herself what happened to the treasure—and to the lady who was dying to get rid of it.

As it turns out, the victim had a lineage that would make a Daughter of the Confederacy green with envy, and her connection with the historic old Roselawn Plantation makes that a good place to start sleuthing. Thanks to her own mama's impeccable Southern credentials, Abby is granted an appointment with the board members—but no one gives her the right to snoop. And digging into the long-festering secrets of a proud family of the Old South turns out to be a breach of good manners that could land Abby six feet under in the family plot.

# So Faux, So Good

*Every shroud has a silver lining . . .*

Abigail Timberlake has never been happier. She is about to marry the man of her dreams AND has just outbid all other Charlotte antique dealers for an exquisite English tea service. But an early wedding present rains on Abby's parade. The one-of-a-kind tea service Abby paid big bucks for has a twin. A frazzled Abby finds more trouble on her doorstep—literally—when a local auctioneer mysteriously collapses outside her shop and a press clipping of her engagement announcement turns up in the wallet of a dead man. (Obviously she won't be getting a wedding present from him.)

Tracing the deceased to a small town in the Pennsylvania Dutch country, Abby heads above the Mason-Dixon Line to search for clues. Accompanied by a trio of eccentric dealers and her beloved but stressed-out cat, she longs for her Southern homeland as she confronts a menagerie of dubious characters. Digging for answers, Abby realizes that she might just be digging her own grave in—horrors!—Yankeeland.

## Baroque and Desperate
*Good help is hard to keep—alive . . .*

Unflappable and resourceful, Abigail Timberlake relies on her knowledge and savvy to authenticate the facts from the fakes when it comes to either curios *or* people. Her expertise makes Abby invaluable to exceptionally handsome Tradd Maxwell Burton, wealthy scion of the renowned Latham family. He needs her to determine the most priceless item in the Latham mansion. A treasure hunt in an antique-filled manor? All Abby can say is "Let the games begin!"

But when Abby, accompanied by her best friend C.J., arrives at the estate she receives a less than warm welcome from the Latham clan. Trying to fulfill Tradd's request, Abby finds she could cut the household tension with a knife. Only someone has beaten her to it by stabbing a maid to death with an ancient kris. Suddenly all eyes are on C.J., whose fingerprints just happen to be all over the murder weapon. Now Abby must use her knack for detecting forgeries to expose the fake alibi of the genuine killer.

## Estate of Mind

*A faux Van Gogh that's to die for . . .*

When Abigail Timberlake makes a bid of $150.99 on a truly awful copy of van Gogh's *Starry Night*, she's just trying to support the church auction. Hopefully she'll make her money back on the beautiful gold antique frame. Little does she expect she's bought herself a fortune . . . and a ton of trouble.

Hidden behind the faux van Gogh canvas is a multi-million-dollar lost art treasure. Suddenly she's a popular lady in her old hometown, and her first visit is from Gilbert Sweeny, her schoolyard sweetie who claims the family's painting was donated by mistake. But social calls quickly turn from nice to nasty as it's revealed that the mysterious masterpiece conceals a dark and deadly past and some modern-day misconduct that threatens to rock the Rock Hill social structure to its core. Someone apparently thinks the art is worth killing for, and Abby knows she better get to the bottom of the secret scandal and multiple murders before she ends up buried six feet under a starry night.

# A Penny Urned
*Pickled, then potted . . .*

All that remains of Lula Mae Wiggins—who drowned in a bathtub of cheap champagne on New Year's Eve—now sits in an alleged Etruscan urn in Savanna, Georgia. Farther north, in Charleston, South Carolina, Abigail Timberlake is astonished to learn that she is the sole inheritor of the Wiggins estate. Late Aunt Lula was, after all, as distant a relative as kin can get.

Arriving in Savannah, Abby makes a couple of startling discoveries. First, that Lula Mae's final resting place is more American cheap than Italian antique. And second, that there was a very valuable 1793 one-cent piece taped to the inside lid. Perhaps a coin collection worth millions is hidden among the deceased's worldly possessions—making Lula's passing more suspicious than originally surmised. With the strange appearance of a voodoo priestess coupled with the disturbing disappearance of a loved one—and with nasty family skeletons tumbling from the trees like acorns—Abby needs to find her penny auntie's killer or she'll be up to her ashes in serious trouble.

# Nightmare in Shining Armor
*The corpse is in the mail . . .*

Abigail Timberlake's Halloween costume party is a roaring success—until an unexpected fire sends the panicked guests fleeing from Abby's emporium. One exiting reveler she is only too happy to see the back of is Tweetie "Little Bo Peep" Timberlake—unfaithful wife of Abby's faithless ex, Buford. But not long after the fire is brought under control, the former Mrs. T discovers an unfamiliar suit of armor in her house. And stuffed inside is the heavily siliconed, no-longer-living body of the current Mrs. T.

Certainly some enraged collector of medieval chain mail has sent Abby this deadly delivery. But diving into their eccentric ranks could prove a lethal proposition for the plucky antiques dealer turned amateur sleuth. And even a metal suit may not be enough to protect Abby from the vicious and vindictive attention of a crazed killer.

# Splendor in the Glass

*Murder is a glass act . . .*

Antiques dealer Abby Timberlake is thrilled when *the* Ms. Amelia Shadbark—doyenne of Charleston society—invites her to broker a pricey collection of Lalique glass sculpture. These treasures will certainly boost business at the Den of Antiquity, and maybe hoist Abby into the upper crust—which would please her class-conscious mom, Mozella, to no end. Alas, Abby's fragile dream is soon shattered when Mrs. Shadbark meets a foul, untimely end. And as the last known visitor to the victim's palatial abode, Abby's being pegged by the local law as suspect Numer Uno.

Of course, there are other possible killers—including several dysfunctional offspring and a handyman who may have been doing more for the late Mrs. S than fixing her leaky faucets. But Abby's the one who'll have to piece the shards of this deadly puzzle together—or else face a fate far worse than a mere seven years of bad luck!

# Tiles and Tribulations

*Supernatural born killer . . .*

Abigail Timberlake would rather be anywhere else on a muggy Charleston summer evening—even putting in extra hours at her antiques shop—than at a séance. But her best friend, "Calamity Jane," thinks a spirit—or "Apparition American," as ectoplasmically correct Abby puts it—lurks in the eighteenth-century Georgian mansion, complete with priceless, seventeenth-century Portuguese kitchen tiles, that C.J. just bought as a fixer-upper. Luckily, Abby's mama located a psychic in the yellow pages—a certain Madame Woo-Woo—and, together with a motley group of feisty retirees know as the "Heavenly Hustlers," they all get down to give an unwanted spook the heave-ho.

But, for all her extrasensory abilities, the Madame didn't foresee that she, herself, would be forced over to the other side prematurely. Suddenly Abby fears there's more than a specter haunting C.J. And they'd better exorcise a flesh-and-blood killer fast before the recently departed Woo-Woo gets company.

## Statue of Limitations
*Death by David . . .*

Abigail Timberlake, petite but feisty proprietor of Charleston's Den of Antiquity antiques shop, stopped speaking to best friend and temporary decorating partner Wynnell Crawford a month ago—after questioning her choice of a cheap, three-foot-high replica of Michelangelo's David to adorn the garden of a local bed-and-breakfast. But now Wynnell has broken the silence with one phone call . . . *from prison!*

It seems the B and B owner has been fatally beaten—allegedly by the same tacky statue—and Wynell's been fingered by the cops for the bashing. But Abby suspects there's more to this well-sculpted slaying than initially meets the eye, and she wants to take a closer look at the not-so-bereaved widower and the two very odd couples presently guesting at the hostelry. Because if bad taste was a capital crime, Wynnell would be guilty as sin—but she's certainly no killer!

And don't miss the next
Den of Antiquity mystery
coming in Spring 2005

## Monet Talks

*Birds of a feather die together . . .*

Abigail Timberlake is thrilled to purchase an elaborate Victorian birdcage that is a miniature replica of the Taj Mahal. However she's less excited by the cage's surprise occupant—a loud, talkative myna bird named Monet. But Monet soon becomes a favorite with Abby's customers—until one day he goes mysteriously missing. In his place is a stuffed bird and a ransom note demanding the real Monet painting in exchange for Abby's pet. "What Monet painting?" is Abby's only response.

Abby tries to put the bird-snatching out of her mind, dismissing it as a cruel joke—until Abby's mama, Mozella, is taken too. This time the kidnapper threatens to kill Mozella unless Abby produces the painting.

What do a talking bird, Mozella, and a painting hidden for hundreds of years have in common? Abby must figure it all out soon before the could-be killer flies the coop for good.

# TAMAR MYERS'

# M

"A_____
sai_____
"W_____
again?"

Please don't misunderstand. I love my
mother dearly, but she makes Ozzy Osbourne
and his family seem like boring, middle-class,
everyday people.

"I'm not in trouble, Mama. Wynnell is."

"That's the same thing, dear. You two are
practically joined at the hip. Well, at least you
used to be. Before your silly little tiff. Besides,
you know I can smell trouble, and that's
exactly what I smell now."

Mama was serious. She claims she can
detect danger with her nostrils. I respectfully
dismiss the notion that she has the ability, and
suggest that this delusion is a result of all the
hair spray she uses.

"All I did," I said, "was speak to a lawyer
on her behalf."

"But that's not all you're going to do," she
replied. "Is it, dear?"

*Other Den of Antiquity Mysteries by*
**Tamar Myers**